THE
AFFAIRS
OF THE
FALCÓNS

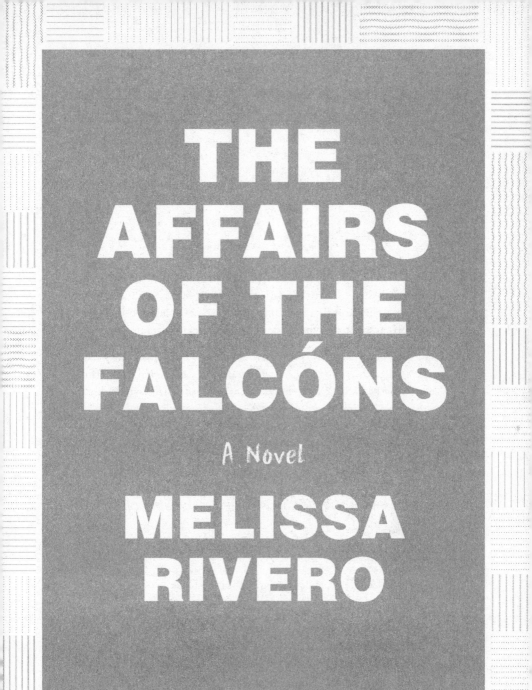

THE
AFFAIRS
OF THE
FALCÓNS

A Novel

MELISSA
RIVERO

An Imprint of HarperCollinsPublishers

THE AFFAIRS OF THE FALCÓNS. Copyright © 2019 by Melissa Rivero. All rights reserved. Printed in the United States of America. No part of this book may be used or reproduced in any manner whatsoever without written permission except in the case of brief quotations embodied in critical articles and reviews. For information, address HarperCollins Publishers, 195 Broadway, New York, NY 10007.

HarperCollins books may be purchased for educational, business, or sales promotional use. For information, please e-mail the Special Markets Department at SPsales@harpercollins.com.

FIRST EDITION

Designed by Renata De Oliveira

Library of Congress Cataloging-in-Publication Data

Names: Rivero, Melissa, author.
Title: The affairs of the falcóns : a novel / by Melissa Rivero.
Description: First edition. | New York, NY : HarperCollins Publishers, [2019]
Identifiers: LCCN 2018022068 (print) | LCCN 2018023847 (ebook) |
  ISBN 9780062872371 ( ) | ISBN 9780062872357 | ISBN
  9780062872364
Classification: LCC PS3618.I854 (ebook) | LCC PS3618.I854 A68
  2019 (print) | DDC 813/.6—dc23
LC record available at https://lccn.loc.gov/2018022068

19 20 21 22 23 LSC 10 9 8 7 6 5 4 3 2 1

Para Pury y Juan

THE
AFFAIRS
OF THE
FALCÓNS

1

ANA LUCÍA CÁRDENAS RÍOS CELEBRATED HER TWELFTH BIRTHDAY ON the day she killed her first chicken. Months before her cumpleaños, she woke to the cackle of a rooster pulling the sun over Santa Clara, her small town on the edges of the Peruvian rainforest, and to a bedsheet tinged in her blood. The spot made her cower at the top of her bed, as if the thing might rise up on tentacles and nip at her terracotta skin. She hid her stained underwear beneath her thick straw mattress, convinced she was pregnant. But the blood stopped after a couple of days, and the baby never came. She wondered if perhaps this was La Virgencita's way of warning her for being fresca, sucia. El Señor would work through her mother and punish her if she didn't change her ways. And so she stopped kissing Betty, her ten-year-old neighbor with the birth-marked lip and drowsy gaze, who always seemed ready for a kiss. She even stopped kissing Pepito, though she was certain she was in love with him. Instead, she made sure she woke early to make her mother and uncle breakfast, and even lit a candle at her mother's altar for her dead relatives. She knelt each night beside her bed and prayed for the blood to stay away. But weeks later, another stain was on her sheet, and she feared more than just a beating. What if God had a worse punishment for her? She decided to be truthful and told her mother.

Only Ana didn't get hit. Instead, Doña Sara—determined to teach her only daughter how to survive now that she was a woman—told her to pick a chick from one of the nests in their coop. A clutch had hatched, and the hen was no longer guarding her chicks as feverishly as she once had.

And so Ana chose one. Don't name it, her mother warned; just take care of it from now on. Ana fed the chick for weeks, plumping it up with maíz, watching it graze on bits of grass, salivating as it kicked up dirt and ran across the huerta. Her mother, meanwhile, made Ana watch as she cracked the necks or sliced the heads off one bird and then another. Ana watched until whatever was in her belly made its way up her throat, forcing her to run inside their shack. "No corras," Ana's mother would shout. "Your turn will come."

Soon, the nightmares began: those of black, neckless birds catapulting through her bedroom window. Their severed heads cawed as they lay on the sun-butchered dirt outside; their barren eyes fixated on her.

On the day of her twelfth birthday, the nightmares stopped, and Ana picked up her mother's knife. She asked Betty to grab the sandy-feathered bird she'd fed and cared for, and bring it to the tree stub in the middle of the huerta. As her friend held down her chicken, Ana wrapped her thin fingers around the handle of the knife and, with all the might her minuscule body could muster, smashed the blade into its sunny neck. The knife slipped off Ana's fingers, wet and tremulous, and she scurried inside. She almost collided with her mother, who heard the bird's shriek, and had to finish what her daughter could not.

That afternoon, Ana mourned her chicken as it crisped above an open flame in the huerta. She sat in front of the fire pit, her arms wrapped around her scarred and flaky legs. The smoke stung her eyes, but she did not flit away her tears. She let them hit her knees even as she kept her body still.

Her mother was unmoved. "You're going to have to do things like this in life, Ana." Doña Sara did not look at her daughter as she spoke. She turned the chicken, picking at the flesh. "You're going to love and have to do things for love. Sacrifice is a part of life." Ana wiped the tears from her legs. "Better that you learn that lesson now. God knows I don't want you running around here for the rest of your life, like this bird." She turned to face her then. "I need you to fly, Ana."

When she finally sat down for her birthday dinner, she prayed for her chicken. *Diosito,* she pleaded, *que mi pollito esté contigo en el cielo.*

Except her sandy-feathered pollito wasn't in heaven with God. It was on her plate, its yellow skin crisped to gold, and then in her mouth, melting on her tongue.

■ ■ ■

FIFTEEN YEARS LATER, NOT LONG AFTER HER TWENTY-SEVENTH BIRTH-day, Ana was still cooking chicken, only this time, she was in a three-bedroom co-op in a six-story building in Queens, New York. And she didn't have to kill anything. She had taken a frozen carcass from the refrigerator the night before, and let it thaw in the sink. Now, Christmas Day, she simply had to season the bird.

It sat on an aluminum foil pan on the kitchen's pearl-like countertop. A small radio she had placed there three months earlier now blasted a string of salsa songs, punctuated with the occasional reggae en español, a new kind of sound she was not particularly keen on. Her straight black hair, with its shades of dye in Mahogany #10, was tied in a low ponytail by a mint green elastic band she had fished from the ziplock bag where she kept her daughter's hair accessories. She didn't need anyone to find a strand of her hair in their dinner.

Lately, the smell of raw meat had made her nauseous. The thought of eating chicken in particular sent her stomach into a somersault. She opened the overhead kitchen cabinet, eager to throw on whatever spices she could find, anything to mask the smell.

The cabinet housed dozens of spices, some topped to the brim and others still sealed in plastic, but she grabbed only the ones she knew: salt, black pepper, the tall plastic bottle with the red "Adobo All Purpose Seasoning" scribbled across the middle. Her tongue was reluctant to accept the others, some she'd never seen until she came to live with her husband's cousin, just three months earlier. She didn't know where they came from, how they were made, or how they were actually supposed to taste. When she lived in her own home, she never used anything that didn't come from a specific bodega in Queens, but the señora of unit 4D in Lexar Tower didn't seem to mind the spices from the local Key Food or the Pathmark.

Valeria Sosa had not cooked a single meal since Ana, her husband, Lucho, and their two children moved in. Ana prepared her own sofrito the first time she offered to make dinner, spending most of her grocery money on enough beef to feed her own family and Valeria's. She later watched Valeria slide her finger across the meat, swallow a cough, and declare that her son didn't eat spicy food. She then ordered a pizza. Ana kept to salt ever since.

But today was different. Today, there was a package on the counter, one her Tía Ofelia had prepared just days earlier in Lima: a glass jar wrapped in plastic, then covered in sheets from Sunday's edition of *El Comercio*, and inside of that jar, was palillo. Ana had run out of the spice months earlier. As a child, her father had brought home sacks of the plant from the chacra: fat, arthritic nubs covered in the red dirt from the ranch where he labored for weeks at a time. She'd help her mother lay them outside beneath the scalding sun and, once they had shriveled, smash the roots for hours, sometimes over the course of several days, until she crumbled the twisted umber roots into gilded powder. For days, it turned her rusted finger gold.

Ana's pale chicken now ached for color, but the jar didn't belong to her. Hers was tucked away in the bedroom she and her family occupied in Valeria's apartment. She closed the kitchen cabinet and grabbed the package anyway. The newspaper ink bled onto her fingers, their crinkle exuding hints of limeño gasoline and her aunt's vanilla perfume. Valeria's name wasn't on it, but she knew better than to tear the paper open. She needed permission first. Valeria had arrived from her latest trip that morning and was still locked in her bedroom. There was only one other person she could ask.

She walked across the dimly lit living room to the glass doors that led to the balcony, where Rubén Sosa, Valeria's husband, was smoking another cigarette. The man wore only a sweatshirt and jeans, despite the dipping temperature outside. He stood at the center, taking up most of the space on the balcony. He was the kind of man that overflowed—his voice, his chest, his chevron mustache. He wasn't overweight, but he never protested if anyone called him "gordo." Fat was a sign of abundance, and as a man with his own business, he was, by all accounts, a man of abundance. If anyone would let Ana use a mere teaspoon of palillo from that jar, it was Rubén.

"Sí, sí, Anita," he said. "You don't have to ask about those things. Take whatever you need." She smiled and inadvertently bowed her head as she closed the glass doors. He'd opened his home to her and her family. She found it difficult not to be overly grateful.

She was about to return to the kitchen when the blaring of an English-language cartoon coming from her nephew's partially opened bedroom door drew her attention. Michael, the Sosa's ten-year-old son, wasn't hard of hearing. The child simply liked to shut out the world.

"Is everything okay?" she asked as she went inside. The room was the same size as the one she and her family occupied. The walls were white, like the rest of the unit, but the bed covers, the dresser, the bean bag, the oval rug, even the chair by the desk, were coated in shades of blue. The floor was littered with new toys that were given to the children the night before, yet her own, still in their pajamas, were more focused on the television that sat on top of the dresser. She snapped her fingers. "Hey," she said, "is everything okay?"

Her daughter, Victoria, sat cross-legged on the bed. "Sí," she replied, shutting her eyes momentarily before she answered. She was Ana's eldest child, but at the age of six, her eyes carried the load of a dozen lives, always threatening to see more than one was willing to show. Her hair was straight, like her mother's, but softer than either of her parents', and when she was born, it was almost as light as Valeria's. That's how they knew she was Lucho's.

Pedro, Ana's five-year-old son, sat on the floor, his back against the bed. From top to bottom, there was no denying he was hers. His black hair was rich and shot straight up from his scalp. His skin was not copper, but he had pulled some of Ana's brown as he left the womb. He had his father's mouth, a heart-shaped button that he chewed on when he was nervous, as he was doing now. Ana looked at the screen. "What are you watching?" she asked.

"The kid wants a present for Christmas," said Victoria, then in English, "a gun."

"Español," said her mother.

"Una pistola," said Pedro.

Ana grabbed the remote control. "Tonterías," she scoffed as she changed the channel. "Who gives a kid a gun?"

Michael pulled his eyes off the device in his hands. "Hey, it's not a real gun," he said in English, the only language he ever spoke. "And I'm watching that!" He was broader than most children his age, with glasses that made him appear more fragile and scholarly than he actually was. He had been given the anglicized version of his maternal grandfather's name to indicate his Americanness, but he bore no resemblance to his mother. He was not as fair as Valeria, and when relatives saw him, they remarked on how he was trigueñito, the color of toasted corn, like his father.

Ana responded in Spanish. "They're too little to watch that. I told you, just channel twenty-one when they're in here."

"I'm not little," protested Victoria.

"It's my room," declared Michael. "I can watch whatever I want."

She turned to her daughter. "If he changes the channel, I want you to go to our room." The edge of a miniature, lilac dress, partially visible from beneath Michael's bed, caught her eye. She grabbed the plastic, brown-haired doll and asked, "What's this doing here?"

"I was playing with her," said Victoria.

"I told you, Liliana stays in the room."

"I forgot."

"Don't forget again." She pushed a shoe against the door to hold it open, then took the remote control and the doll with her as she walked out and headed to her bedroom.

That bedroom had been their home for the past three months. Lucho had lost his job over the summer, and when September came, the Sosas offered them their spare bedroom. It was bare, except for a vanity set that Valeria insisted remain in the room. They paid the utilities, but no rent. "Guarden su dinero," Rubén had said.

Save your money so you can get back on your feet. There was no choice but to downsize while they lived off of her factory-worker wage and Lucho looked for a job. They saved a bunk bed and a queen-size bed, a dresser drawer, a small television, but otherwise reduced their possessions to whatever else could fit into that bedroom. Ana saved as much of the children's clothes as she could, but she and Lucho each kept only a drawer's worth of shirts and pants. Valeria took the rest to Peru, for Ana's distant cousins and whoever else could fit into the clothes she had outgrown.

Yet despite keeping only the necessities, the move to Valeria's apartment was something of an upgrade. Statues of cherubs greeted anyone that entered Lexar Tower's front doors. Vines climbed its red bricks. A chandelier dangled above its marbled lobby. Although it was almost palatial, Ana at first found its newness uninviting. Those red bricks retracted from the top of the entrance's wide white columns like open lips showcasing a set of clenched teeth. The keypad reminded her of punching in at work. The lobby echoed every sound. There was no secret it could keep.

She wanted to dislike the place and, up until the day Valeria left for her trip, she did. She was a guest there, and so she did what she could to compensate for the lack of rent. She acquiesced whenever Valeria asked her to make dinner or pack Michael's lunch or clean the bathroom since her family outnumbered the Sosas. She said nothing when Lucho took Valeria shopping for her trip to Peru, or when he picked her up from the auto body shop, the business she and Rubén owned. Those were all a husband's duties, but Ana never asked Valeria why Rubén couldn't do those things for her nor did she ask Lucho to stop.

During those weeks that Valeria was gone, Ana was the only woman in unit 4D, and she embraced the chance to care for it the way it should be. She walked barefoot or in socks so she could check her soles for signs of dirt, grabbing the broom at the first hint of a speckle. A forgotten mug in the living room could jolt her out of bed faster than a fire. She washed each plate and piece of cutlery, every pot and pan with her bare hands, convinced the dishwasher was only for those who were too lazy to pick up a sponge. She played merengue and salsa on weekends as she made breakfast, and in the evenings, she lit cinnamon-scented candles she purchased from the 99 cents store.

But Valeria was back, and whatever sense of home Ana felt in her absence quickly dissipated. Her room, however, was still her sanctuary.

She opened its door slowly, careful not to make any noise. The lights were off, the curtains pulled shut, yet from the afternoon sky that crept between the lips of the blinds, she could see her husband's curled, sleeping figure under the blanket. She closed the door behind her. Her pink polyester socks skimmed the oak floors as she made her way to the bed. She put Liliana on the top bunk, in a far corner beside her daughter's pillow. On the nightstand between her bed and her children's bunk bed, Ana had set up her altar. A large white doily covered the top of the stand, and over it was a statute of La Virgen María, a picture of San Martincito, her mother's prayer card, a cauldron where she burned charcoal and incense, and a pair of red and white candles. She kissed her mother's card and blessed herself, then sat on the edge of the bed beside her husband.

She liked to watch him sleep. He'd returned only a few hours ago from his night shift driving a livery cab. The top of his head was visible beneath the blanket. The oil in his hair had tempered its waves, and it laid out flat against the pillow, in desperate need of a trim. She leaned close to his ear, over the brown mole that stood prominently on the right side of his bare neck. His hands were tucked beneath his cheek, and his lips puckered against them. She could smell the fading bergamot in his cologne and the leather from the car that still lingered on his body. She imagined brushing her lips over his eyes, watching them flutter into life, but even when she had the chance to do so, she held back. The time for those kinds of things, it seemed, had passed.

She shook his shoulder gently. He had once told her to never wake a person in mid-dream by calling out their name. "You don't want to pull their soul from wherever it is," he had said then. She did not know where Lucho's soul was now. For some time now, she'd wondered where it had been.

"Despierta," she said as she rocked him. She noticed his burgundy lace-ups by the bed, defying both the house rule that all shoes must be kept by the door and his own meticulous storage practice. He had rebuffed Ana's winter boot suggestions from the outset. Thick-soled, hard-shelled tan boots—he'd look too much like a construction worker, he said. Instead, he wore the shoes he brought from Peru, three pairs that he refused to exchange for any American sneaker or boot: the dark burgundy lace-ups that were by her feet, a pair of black slip-ons, and a set of tassel loafers that reminded him of the kind of shoe his late father used to wear. He kept them each in separate boxes in the closet, and their stitches had been redone several times over the years by the same cobbler. Beside the shoes were the two layers of socks he needed to keep his feet warm in the cold months—a sliver of thin black socks Ana had purchased at a local store for two dollars and the pair of one-dollar, cotton-blend white socks he wore underneath them, the kind that hit the knees with red double lines at the top.

Ana tucked the socks inside the shoes then slid them under the bed. She lay down beside him. She almost always slept with her back to him, a force of habit from sharing the space with both him and Pedro. But she had enough room now to lie on her back instead. His feet almost reached the edge of the bed, but lying next to him, with his legs tucked under his chest and his body succumbing to the long night of driving, he seemed small. She felt oddly strong, as if she could protect him. It was not something she felt often. It was a sensation that only occurred to her in these quiet moments, when no one was looking or could tell her otherwise.

She poked his back. "Despierta," she whispered again. "It's already past noon."

He pulled the covers closer to him and inched toward the window. "It's Christmas, Ana," he muttered. "Mass is at five P.M."

"Yes, but we can't skip this one. If that priest doesn't sign Victoria's sheet, she can't do communion this year. I'd go if I could, but I have to head to Brooklyn later anyway."

There was a slight shift in his body. "Are you going to see Señora Aguilar?" he asked. "I heard you on the phone with her yesterday."

She straightened at the sound of the name. "I called to check in. She wants me to stop by."

He flipped onto his back. "Did she say anything about the deed?" he asked. "We're behind, Ana."

"I already told her we'd be short this month," she said. "But I'm paying her today. It'll be the last time we're short, I promise. Believe me, she hasn't done anything with that deed."

He stared at the ceiling. "I can't have my mother be a tenant in her own house."

"She won't be," she said. "Mama just wants to make sure we don't disappear without paying her, that's all."

"'Mama,'" he snickered. "What a funny thing to call yourself. Mother of what? Debt? Loans?"

Opportunity, she thought, though she wasn't quite sure how to answer him. The word *Mama* was, in fact, so loaded. "Come on," she insisted, shaking his shoulder again. "Valeria's going to be up soon. She's going to start drinking and I really don't want to hear her shit, Lucho."

"Don't do this now, Ana."

She chewed the inside of her mouth. "That's the problem," she said. "You never want to 'do this.'" She jumped off the bed, slamming the bedroom door behind her as she walked out. *Couldn't do this now,* she thought. *Could he ever?*

Valeria's bedroom door was still shut, and Rubén was no longer on the balcony. When she got to the kitchen, she went straight to the package. She tore through the paper and plastic. The powder inside the glass jar glowed and, once the lid popped open, the mélange of tilled earth and sunburned powder stung her nostrils and seeped into Ana's chest like water through tree roots. It was the scent of her mother, her father. It came from the same red earth that snuck between her toes as a child. It had burned beneath the same scathing sun that saturated her skin. Nothing could replace it, certainly not the turmeric she found at the local Key Food. She went back to her pale, naked fowl, and poured a tiny mound onto its center, careful not to use too much. She let the gilded grinds tumble down the sides of the creature's breast before brushing them across its cold skin.

She was too consumed by the memory of a mother and father she'd lost long ago to hear Valeria walk in.

"Is that mine?" she asked.

Ana blushed, her naturally red cheeks deepening. "Yes," she said, without turning. Through the corners of her eyes, she could see Valeria glowing in her fuchsia robe. Unlike Ana, Valeria rarely turned pink, and never red. She was ivory, and proud of her paleness. She never wore anything that didn't make her look like white fire. The water in her hair made it seem heavy and dark, but it was still blonde, the kind Americans call dirty. But rubia is rubia, and Valeria was blonde.

"Didn't you open yours already?" she asked. "Look, I know it's from the chacra, and your aunt had to make a few calls to get it, but she can always get you more. You think I can just call someone up to get this kind of stuff? I practically grew up in my mother's boutique in San Isidro, Ana," she said, as though she lamented her upbringing in an upscale neighborhood in Lima. "It's not like I could go off and make my own spices. Besides, you said you didn't mind, remember?"

How could Ana mind? In the past year, Valeria had made a business out of going back to Peru, making several trips a year, bringing items back and forth. On this most recent trip, she'd left on a cloudy Monday after the long Thanksgiving weekend, dressed in three-inch heels, sunglasses, and a fur-trimmed leather coat. Lucho and Rubén crammed two suitcases and a large army bag into Rubén's station wagon, all filled with items she planned to sell to old university friends and neighbors: clothes from the outlet malls, handbags from the hidden backrooms of Chinatown, diluted perfumes and colognes from Twenty-Eighth Street, lingerie and fruit-scented lotions. She also took encargos, items Peruvians in their circle could not take themselves either because they lacked a green card or simply didn't have the money to ship. Vitamins for ailing mothers, light-up sneakers for nieces and nephews, baseball caps for brothers who worked under the sun. Everyone who sent something usually wanted something else in return. Plants, medicine, spices impossible to find in New York for all the talk of it being the capital of the world. Valeria never asked for cash. Most didn't have much money on hand anyway. But she was happy to barter, and took bits of what people asked her to bring back as payment.

When Ana asked if Valeria could bring back the palillo, her fee was half of what Ana's aunt had prepared for her.

Valeria shook off the water from her hair, drops smacking the wall, the table, and Ana's cheek. She headed to the fridge, the scent of citrus and honey trailing behind her, and grabbed a can of beer from the six-pack she'd purchased on her way home from the airport that morning, even though she'd brought back bottles of pisco and no one had touched the rum and vodka she kept in the cabinet under the counter.

"¿Quieres una cervecita?" she asked.

"It's a little early for a drink, don't you think?"

"This is like water," she said as she wiped the beer that trickled down her chin and sat at the table. "Your aunt looks great, by the way. She's thinner, but she doesn't look acabada like most women do when they lose weight at that age. But she's lonely, poor thing. That cousin of yours is still up in the mountains. He couldn't even spend Christmas with her."

"He can only come down once or twice a month," said Ana. "I know she worries, but he loves what he does."

"I couldn't do it," said Valeria. "Teach in those villages, if you can even call them that. Campesinos are so hardheaded too. Practically unteachable. But I guess you and your family understand your people better than I do."

"That we do," she said, as she finished pounding the palillo into the pink skin and put the chicken in the oven. "There's a lot that most limeños wouldn't understand."

"I suppose so," said Valeria. "There must be a lot that Lucho doesn't."

She was tempted to agree. After all, there was much that a light-skinned man, born and raised in Lima, did not understand about a woman, brown and nurtured in Peru's womb. There was much

Valeria herself couldn't understand, even as a woman, but Ana knew better than to take the bait. If she bad-mouthed her husband, Valeria would certainly tell him. The tone of her voice, however, could be small and disarming at times, like it was at this particular moment, and Ana wondered if perhaps she actually cared to know about all the ways that Lucho couldn't understand.

When she didn't respond, Valeria continued. "How long's it been now," she asked, "since you celebrated Christmas with your aunt? Five years?"

Ana nodded. "Just about. Pedro wasn't even crawling."

"Nineteen eighty-nine was it?" Valeria drew a sharp breath. "How quickly the years go by. And look at you. Still living like nomads."

"This is temporary," said Ana. She could feel the blood race up to her neck and face. "And if it bothers you so much—"

"It doesn't," Valeria interrupted. "But if you don't mind me asking, how is the apartment search going?"

"We're looking," she said. There was, in fact, no rush to rent apartments in the neighborhoods they could afford. No employments to verify, no credit checks. They could've moved in to a one-bedroom railroad with a water-stained ceiling and fading hallway lights the very same month they moved out of their last one. But Ana insisted they wait. She hoped that time might turn up something better. An apartment without torn laminate floors, perhaps, or rooms with light switches instead of single bulbs with strings limping down their sides. More than anything, she wanted a better neighborhood, or at least a safe block for the children. "We saw an apartment in Los Sures last week, but there's no way we can fit both beds in the bedroom."

"You're looking in your old neighborhood?"

"It's close to the school and I can walk to the factory."

Valeria jutted her lower lip. "And my cousin, the cab driver. Is he finding work okay?"

"Things picked up around Thanksgiving. Yesterday was busy. You were his last ride this morning. He's not working tonight."

"What do you mean he's not working tonight? He leased the car for the night shift."

"Yes, but he's not working tonight," she said, "or New Year's Eve."

Valeria scoffed. "Well, it's not his car. It's probably best he stay home on New Year's Eve anyway, with all those borrachos out on the street. The job is dangerous as it is. You always hear about drivers getting mugged or worse. But you need that money, don't you? God knows that seems to be more important than Lucho's safety."

"Of course it's not," said Ana. "But we can't stop working because we're afraid."

"No one's saying that," said Valeria. "But believe me, it could be a lot easier if it was just the two of you here." It was the one piece of advice Valeria offered so readily that Ana wondered if she understood what it was to be a mother. "I know Filomena's getting older, but she's willing to help. And who better to raise Vicki and Pedro than their grandmother?"

The thought of anyone taking her place as their mother made Ana bristle. "With all those car bombs going off in Lima," she said, "and soldiers at every corner? Yes, it sounds like a much better place for my kids."

"The soldiers should make you feel safe."

"Safe? The military is just as bad as the terrorists."

"It was terrible when you left," said Valeria, "but it's not that bad now. And it's not like there are bombs going off everywhere. My aunt lives in a safe neighborhood. Safer than most. You and Lucho can stay here, work, send money back. And Vicki and Pedro can get a good education in Lima. You can send them to private schools if you want. What have you got in Brooklyn? Gangueros, viciosos. Apartments infested with rats and cockroaches. Shitty ceilings, like the one that fell that time, when you lived on Montrose. Remember that?"

"Of course I do, but you're exagger—"

"No, I'm not. You're lucky that ceiling didn't fall on one of the kids. If it had, then what? You'd have an injured child or worse. Child services, the police! And immigration right there, like this," she said, snapping her fingers, "just waiting to put you in handcuffs and back on a plane to Peru." She turned in her chair, leaning her head back against the wall. "Immigration will always be after you. Doesn't that wear you out, Ana? All the running and hiding just because you don't have documents?"

Documents. Papeles. How easy would it be if they had papeles. A well-made green card or seldom-used social security number was a chance for a better job, an education even. Pay for the good ones, she was told, in case someone checks, and she did. She paid hundreds for documents she was told her family needed. She learned quickly that no one really checks.

A person could get by on fake documents, sure, but if you had real ones—an actual green card and social security number—you were practically a gringo. You were almost American. That was Valeria.

"I know you don't want to be separated from the children," she said. "I get that. I'm a mother too. And maybe the solution is that you all go back. There's no shame in that, but you have to be realistic. You have no money. You don't have a place to live. You've got both kids in Catholic school. You don't want them to go to public school, okay, that's your misplaced pride if you ask me."

"It's not misplaced pride," she said. "They're safe there. There's discipline. They're getting a good education. Victoria's speaking English and writing sentences. Pedro's reading. Half the time he's translating whatever his sister's saying. They'd separate my kids from the rest of the class if they were in public school, you know that."

"But how long do you think you'll be able to pay that tuition?" she countered. "What are you going to do when you have to start paying rent again?"

She had no answer. How she'd pay the tuition once they left was something she had avoided thinking about simply because tuition, more so than rent, was something that had to be paid, always.

"You have to get over this pride of yours, Ana. You're just like every other cholo that got here before you. Those few semesters at that technical school mean nothing here. You work in a factory. Lucho drives a car for a living."

Ana held on to the counter as her stomach did a turn.

"Son ilegales, Ana."

Her stomach clenched. "I know what we are, Valeria. But we're not going anywhere. My children aren't going anywhere. I'm not going anywhere. We came here as a family and we're staying as a family. I'll keep sewing curtains and wiping toilet seats if I have to, and so will Lucho." She held on as her stomach settled. "But we're not leaving."

There was no retort this time. Valeria's advice was practical, a solution to Ana's financial dilemma. But she wanted no one else raising her children.

She grabbed the cloth from the counter and pulled the oven door open. A salted cloud emanated from its mouth, stinging her face, then a chair creaked behind her.

Vete, she thought.

But although Valeria was gone, her words clung to the sharpness of the spice that now filled the room. The air tasted bitter with every inhalation.

Ana grabbed a fork. The heat poured into her lungs. She poked through the bird's thick skin. It had already begun its transformation from carcass to sustenance, sucking in the gold powder and crisping in the heat. But its skin was still raw and parts of it still bled.

2

NIGHT SETTLED IN EARLY THAT CHRISTMAS DAY, AND BY 5 P.M., PUR-
ple hues had leaked into the cloudless blue sky. Lucho and the
children, dressed in Sunday mass attire, left Lexar Tower for the
local church they attended since their move. Ana stayed behind to
finish dinner and managed to steal a few minutes to herself before
heading to Mama's building.

She needed to collect herself before she headed to the place. She
sat in front of her altar, dressed in a snug long-sleeved shirt and a
pair of acid-washed jeans. Her hair, now out of the ponytail, was
twisted up into the mouth of a butterfly clip. She lit a candle as she
gathered her thoughts into a prayer. What does one pray for when
one cannot pay a debt? To pay it off, of course, but Ana was fearful
of those prayers, aware that they were often tied to an illness or a
death or some other loss she knew she could not bear. Instead, she
prayed for things the saints could not oppose. Calmness, strength,
the ability to say only what was needed to be heard.

The room chilled. She opened her eyes, expecting whatever had
made her shiver to have also extinguished the flame, but it continued to burn. She blew it out, suddenly overwhelmed by a sense of

being seen. She reached for her maroon sweater, hanging on the vanity's chair. The garment had cloaked her body during her pregnancies in Peru, and it continued to comfort her on cool nights in New York. Beside the chair, laying on the edge of the vanity, was a notebook she recognized. It wasn't the marble notebooks Lucho had begun to fill since he started driving a cab, but the tattered, leather-bound notebook she had given him years ago, over dinner, weeks after he confessed that he liked to write poetry.

She threw on her sweater, then instinctively looked around the room to make sure no one was watching. She opened the notebook carefully, as if its pages might disintegrate at the mere touch of a finger that didn't belong to its owner. She skimmed the sheets bloated with old addresses and crossed-out word search puzzles, pausing momentarily at the ones with lines filled only halfway through, fragments that didn't reach the end of the margins. *Lyrics,* she thought, *or lines from a poem.* Were these his poems? she wondered. It occurred to her that'd it been years since she'd seen the notebook. Had he ever stopped writing?

She shut it, realizing that whatever her husband had written in those pages, he hadn't meant for her to know. She blew out the candle, grabbed the red gift bag with the bottle of hand lotion she'd set aside earlier that day, and headed out the door.

A light rain fell, the late afternoon warmer than she expected. Once she sat on the hard, gray seat of the Manhattan-bound 7 train, she took off her hood and scarf, and unzipped her coat as the train catapulted above the prickly parts of Queens. The view from it was familiar now, and she'd begun to develop a history with some of the stops along the ride. The mall where she had done most of her Christmas shopping. The cemetery where an old neighbor from their first Brooklyn apartment was now buried. Even the pawn shop with the large diamond on its awning was visible when the train passed its station. It was where she'd given up their wedding bands, her mother-in-law's earrings, even the gold ring she'd taken from her own mother's drawer days after she died.

Other than the buildings, which spoke of her memories, the train was silent. She welcomed the time to not think: not think about the money, about work or the kids, not think about staying or going back. She was not going back.

She turned the red gift bag in her hand and noticed the tag still on the handle. It was addressed to Aunt Ana; the gift-giver, Michael. She ripped it off and slid the tag into her handbag. She fished out her address book and pen, then scanned the list Mama had dictated to her over the phone the day before:

- mantequilla
- arroz
- Advil
- bredstic
- té

She had called the woman to say she'd come by the next day, implying that she'd make a payment toward the debt she owed. But she also ran errands for Mama. Ana didn't mind doing so. Mama was in her seventies, with a sluggish walk and gnarled fingers. Their knots stood out despite her polished rings and manicured nails. The curve in her upper back was rounder than her belly. She never complained of any aches or pains, but she took her time whenever she sat down or stood up. Recently, Ana noticed that her hands had started to shake.

And she had that man. He was younger than Mama by only a decade. Still, the difference in age was noticeable, and so was the distance between them. Why she kept him around, Ana did not know.

But Mama's need for help at home wasn't the only reason Ana ran errands for the woman. It was also a quid pro quo. Picking up the occasional groceries or prescriptions meant a lower interest rate on her loan. That was worth fronting a few dollars and giving up an afternoon on a holiday. She picked up the items on Mama's list at the twenty-four-hour deli just off the train station, then headed to her building.

Mama lived on a quiet block, where holiday lights and Christmas ornaments illuminated most windows, even as autumn clung to the trees, forming a canopy over the brownstone-lined corridor. Unlike those just south of it, Mama's block was untouched by the broken bits of glass and rogue garbage cans that filled every other part of her neighborhood. Here, the stoops were empty, and no one lingered by the spiked black gates that sealed off ground floors from the unsettling world. The homes, painted in varying shades of muted fire, looked stately yet ready to engulf whatever wandered past.

Mama was perched at her undecorated window, her pallid face partially obscured by the square frames that sat on the bridge of her nose, stealing the faintest glimpse of daylight. Her rusted lips pressed against each other, and Ana knew a lecture was coming. She lifted the pot of soil by the front door and took the key beneath it.

Mama waited at the end of the hall, the light from her kitchen settling behind her, an aura that bathed her broad figure and floral print dress in its yolk glow.

"Take off your shoes," she told Ana, nodding to the rack by the wall as her hand pressed against the door frame. "Unless you want to mop up later."

Ana placed her sneakers by a pair of polished loafers, careful not to touch their shiny edges. Inside the apartment, the heat from the radiator pounded the scent of a vanilla candle through the air. The kitchen and living room were symbiotic, every object soaked in dusky tones, accented by the copper flowers that climbed the wallpaper. Six chairs surrounded the dining table, which was anchored by an unlit candle and its pillar holder. A single place mat lay in front of the chair at the edge of the table. The living room consisted of a plastic-covered couch and a coffee table with a stack of *Vanidades* magazines, some dating back to before Ana's arrival in New York and all of which she had paged through in her first few visits.

The room then opened to two others: to the left was Mama's sitting room, where she conducted business; to the right, her bedroom, which always had its door ajar. By now, Ana had made out Mama's preference for rose-patterned bedsheets and oversized pillows.

"No umbrella?" Mama asked as she leaned on the back of a chair. "Did it stop raining?"

"No," said Ana, pulling apart her coat and scarf. "Just a drizzle."

"What took you so long then?"

"It's a holiday," she replied. "The trains are slow."

Mama raised her eyebrows, as though she suddenly remembered. "Merry Christmas."

"Merry Christmas," she replied, then handed Mama the red gift bag as she scanned the room. "Where is Don Beto?"

Mama pulled out the bottle of hand lotion. "Out somewhere," she said, turning the bottle with one hand and dismissing her husband with a wave of the other. Her fingers dazzled, even in the dull light. She put the lotion back in the bag, then walked toward her sitting room. "There's water in the kettle. Make some tea and bring us something to eat."

Minutes later, Ana brought a tray of breakfast treats and two teacups into the room. She set it down on a coffee table in front of the love seat. Mama was on one end of it, and beside her was a rolling tray, where she kept her medicine and a water bottle. Ana shrunk into the other end of the couch. The television blared. *El derecho de vivir*, the name of a telenovela, was scribbled across the screen in shades of ivory and tangerine cursive. Ana averted her eyes to avoid a headache.

Mama turned up the volume as the protagonist, María Rosario, sobbed on the screen. "Miguel left her," she explained, as she popped a few pills in her mouth and took several gulps from the bottle of water. "He found out she was pregnant. Do you know this story?"

Ana shook her head no.

"It's the second time I'm seeing it in this country. But the first time I heard it was over the radio back in Cuba." She picked up her cup and blew into the tea. Her glasses fogged and unfogged. "I was a much younger woman then. I had hair like honey and eyes like the sea. Of course, I imagined that María Rosario looked like me." A grin grazed her lips, then quickly faded. "I don't know why these Mexicans picked a morena to play her." She paused as she was about to take another sip. She stared at Ana as the fog in her lenses cleared. "You know, you look a bit like her. Your eyes are on the lighter side, and your hair is just as dark." She traced Ana's face in the air with her fingers. "Except you're more Indian than black."

Ana brought her scalding cup to her lips. She wanted to tell the woman that she wasn't *all* Indian. Her eyes, for example, hinted at some distant European relative. But she knew how ridiculous she'd sound, especially saying this to someone like Mama.

"Anyway," Mama continued, pointing at Ana's hands. "I see you've been cooking."

Ana straightened her mustard fingers in front of her. "Yes," she said with a smile. "My aunt sent me this spice. It's from the old ranch where my father used to work."

"Ah," said Mama. "El desaparecido. Don't tell me you make your poor aunt go back there hoping to find him."

"No, no," she stammered. "I know I'll never see him again."

She hadn't seen her father in nearly seventeen years. But every now and again, a scent or a sound would lure a vague memory that, as the years went by, only seemed to grow more vivid. Every December, the scent of fresh cut trees piled along the street took her back to his embrace, back when she'd sit on his lap and sniff the smell of sap that emanated from the paper-thin skin along his neck. Whenever she heard a whistle, she'd turn almost instinctively, expecting to see him waving to her to come closer to home; she'd wandered too far into the dusty, solitary road.

He worked on the ranch, along with her mother's brother, going deep into the forest to retrieve whatever crop the patrón was harvesting that season. Then, every three weeks, he'd travel down the river on a motorboat, returning home for a few days before going back again. He indulged in their cooking, napped in the hammock in the huerta, and sat with his daughter outside in his rocking chair as the stars appeared in the pastel sky. On the mornings he was home, Ana went to the market early, oftentimes with Betty by her side, in search of the ripest capironas. He liked to drink chapo de plátano for breakfast, and Ana wouldn't settle for anything but capironas, the sweetest of plantains, to make his morning shake.

One night, when her father had already been gone for more than a month, her Tío Marcos showed up at their door, alone. He carried only a single bag with him, and when her mother saw his face, she walked out and crouched beside the door, unable to move for what seemed like days.

"There must always be a man here," he said somberly, as he

unpacked. He handed Ana three palillos, all that her father had been able to stow away under his cot. She made the powder, using it sparingly, and was able to make it last for several months. She reined in her tears even as she used her father's palillo one final time, not long after Marcos himself returned to the forest, despite her mother's protests, and never came back.

Once, she told her mother she'd forgotten what her father looked like. She remembered his smile, the way the froth of the chapo lined his upper lip. Look in the mirror, her mother had told her then, there he is—in your eyes, your mouth. You share the same smile. For some time, this comforted her, knowing she could always see her father this way.

It wasn't until Doña Sara died that Ana wished she'd seen her mother's reflection instead.

"Just as well," said Mama. "Probably better that you don't know what happened to him. Those terrorists are animals. Although it's always nice to have a grave to go to. In any case, I suppose you had a party last night."

Ana cleared her throat. "Just a few friends over."

"No wonder you look beat. Anyway, you should wash your hands better."

"I actually like the color on my skin."

"It makes you look like a cook." She picked up the remote control and lowered the volume on the television set. "I hear your husband is doing well in his new venture."

It was Ana's cue. She dug into her handbag and pulled out the white envelope that delivered Valeria's gas bill that month. The cellophane crunched as she handed it to Mama. "It's going okay," she said, diverting her eyes, hoping to downplay Lucho's luck so far and mask her own discomfort at handing their money to the woman.

"Which car service is he with?"

"RapiCar," said Ana, and immediately regretted sharing that bit of information.

"Why that one?"

"The man we're leasing the car from," said Ana, "he works out of that base."

"I see. I take it your family helped with the lease then?"

"His cousin lent us the money," she lied.

"How long do you have it for?"

"Three months."

Mama raised her eyebrows. "You only wanted one month when you came to me."

"We only have the car at night for now. The owner's going to Ecuador for the summer. Lucho thinks that if he shows he's responsible and a hard worker, then maybe we can work the car the entire time he's gone. We'd love our own car, of course."

"Pay off your debts first." She shuffled through the twenty-dollar bills in the envelope. "You're short again."

"I'll catch up next week, Mama."

"Ana, the only reason I do business with you is because you said I could count on you to pay your debts—"

"And you can," she said. "I *do* pay my debts, Mama. It's just that, Lucho just started working the car. We had to pay his cousin back for some of the bills she covered. Gas, electric. And it's Christmas—"

"Look. This," she said, holding up the envelope, "is better than not getting paid at all. But don't think I'm going to hold on to that deed of yours forever. You miss one payment, you get behind, it happens. But I expect you to catch up. Not for your payments to get smaller and smaller."

"I promise you I'll get back on track next week, and even pay you more."

"Good." She put the money back in the envelope and slipped it in the gap between the cushion and the arm rest. "I'm being very reasonable, Ana, and very patient. I understand the dilemma that you're in. I've been helping women like you since I came to this country. Some in better situations than you, some in worse. Single mothers with no husbands, no family."

Ana had heard about the women Mama liked to help. It was only women, and only those with real estate or other valuable pieces of property to offer up as collateral. But she had a soft spot for a particular type of woman. Undocumented, South American. Mothers. That was what Carla Lazarte, Ana's friend and Betty's eldest sister, had told her. Ana and her family had spent their first months in New York living with Carla and her husband, Ernesto. But when fall arrived that year, Carla hinted that it was time Ana and her family move out. She suggested that Ana meet a woman named Patricia Aguilar. They called her Mama because, unlike other prestamistas, she was more lenient. She wasn't as quick to react when things got difficult for a client. She understood the challenges of being a new immigrant and a woman, having been a single mother herself. She liked young, ambitious women who didn't see obstacles; the kind who want a house in the States, a house back home, wherever that might be, cars nice enough to pose in front of for pictures, and brand-name colleges for their children. She liked these kinds of women because they were prideful, and so they always paid. She was also kinder to these women, so Ana was told.

"I know things haven't been easy," Mama continued, "what with your husband out of a job. But imagine if I had lent you that money for the lease? We both know you couldn't pay it back. I'd have no choice but to take that house."

That house was the one Lucho, as the eldest son, had inherited from his father. It had always been meant for him, but it was nevertheless his mother's. Ana had once believed they could build their lives in that house. She had imagined cooking her meals in its garlicky kitchen, eating in its chandeliered dining room, sitting in the garden with a cup of chamomile tea in her hand as the moon clawed its way behind the avocado tree. Despite his mother's presence, she still believed it could one day be hers.

But right now, it was Mama's.

The woman shifted in her seat. "Besides, your family should help you. Your husband is unemployed, and you have two small children. They know what it's like to be here, so young and inexperienced."

"Mama, Lucho's cousins have a very different experience," she said. "And they're already giving us a place to live."

"That is the least they can do for you. They may be your husband's blood, but he married you. They're your family too." She paused, tapping her fingers on the armrest. "On the other hand, I can understand why they won't help. People come here after everyone else has done all the heavy lifting. That's how you get a job, how you get connected to someone like me. Someone else has found a way in, then you come, and benefit from all they've done. That's not right either. You have to learn to stand on your own two feet."

"I know that, Mama, but Lucho lost his job—"

"And it won't be the last time you run from immigration." Her voice rose. "I helped you then, all those months he didn't work. I helped you. He's working now, and I expect to get paid exactly what we agreed to every week. Are we clear, Ana?"

She pressed her lips and nodded.

"I didn't hear you."

"Yes."

"Good. Clean this up before you go. I've lost my appetite."

Ana did as she was told, threw on her winter gear, then kissed

Mama goodbye, though the woman said nothing to her. As she picked up her sneakers, still wet from the walk over, they brushed against the shiny heels of the loafers she had so gingerly avoided when she first set them down. She wiped them dry with her sleeve.

She descended the front steps, looking over her shoulder to see if Mama had made her way back to the window, but it was empty. The plight of the suffering María Rosario was more entertaining and less costly to watch than that of a suffering Ana, and she was glad for it. She had to pay the woman back. She'd work faster this week at la factoría, and longer. She might even sell some of her palillo to the women.

She made it halfway down the block when she saw Don Beto standing under a black umbrella several feet from her. He was half a foot taller than her, a man composed of spherical parts and corners—a round nose, round hands, curls at the ends of disappearing white hair on a round head. He was thinly dressed: a light jacket in the same shade as that of his living room furniture, zipped only halfway, revealing a translucent guayabera underneath it, and pants stitched of fabric as fragile as the dead leaves that littered the street. His shoes shone in the rain.

"Hola, niña," he said, his voice hoarse and thick. "Been too long." A grin stretched across his face as he walked toward her. He stopped close enough that she could smell the coffee and tobacco that lingered in his breath. "Feliz Navidad," he said, but she didn't respond. "You're not going to say hello?'"

She leaned over and punctuated his cheek with a kiss. "Hola," she whispered. "Feliz Navidad."

His eyes lingered on her mouth as she pulled away. "Where have you been?"

"I've been—" She took a step back. "It's been a very busy week. With the kids. Work. Christmas."

"Ah," he said. "I thought maybe you were avoiding me."

She pressed her lips, pulling her hood over her head as the rain fell harder.

He stepped closer, covering both of them with his umbrella. "Will you come inside then?"

She wanted to say no. Their encounters had become increasingly intimate; their secretive nature alone should have been enough to keep her from coming back. They finally did, but not after the two had crossed a line. For three weeks, she managed to avoid him, coming at different times to pay Mama instead of the Fridays-after-work schedule she had agreed to months ago. He knew that schedule. She needed to stay away, to say no, but it wasn't something she could muster the courage to do. She was too afraid of what might happen if she did.

Instead, she tried to find another way to say it. "I have to go home to my kids. I'm already running late."

"You *are* avoiding me," he chuckled.

"I didn't like where things were going," she admitted.

He inched closer. "It only went as far as you let it."

She then remembered her handbag and began to dig into it. "I'm going to pay you back."

He held up his hand. "I don't want a penny from you, Ana."

"But I have money for you." She pulled out a few folded bills and handed them to him. It was money that should've gone to Mama, but she had set it aside for him. She needed to pay off that debt too.

"Please," he said. "You didn't do anything wrong. We were fine. You were fine. Our arrangement was fine. Why do you want to change things now?"

It was fine for him. Fine for an old man with money. Ana knew men like Don Beto, men who used kindness as a disguise, friendship as a veil. She needed money to lease the car for the night shift.

She needed her husband to get back to work. Talk of sending her children back, chatter about her family returning to Peru—all of it ringing perpetually in her ear. Mama would not lend her the money she needed, not all of it, and Lucho didn't want to ask Valeria, who, as he put it, was already giving them so much, and whom, she suspected, would say no anyway.

And then she thought of Don Beto, the man who always had a smile ready for her whenever she came to see Mama, whom she caught skimming her body with his eyes, and who only greeted her with a kiss when Mama wasn't looking. He told her once as he walked her out, on that very block, that she could come to him for anything, anything at all; that it wasn't just Mama who could help.

Don Beto gave her the money she needed, but she began repaying him almost immediately.

"I miss seeing you," he said. "You've been away so long."

"Three weeks is not very long," she replied.

"For a woman like you, young and beautiful? No. But for a lonely old man like me?"

She cleared her throat. "I appreciate your help, but I never wanted a handout. I said I'd repay you, and I have every intention of doing so."

"I'm sure you can pay me back eventually. Your husband's been driving that car for what? A month? It might take you some time to pay me back, but you don't have to. I'm glad to just have your company."

He was right. She couldn't afford to pay him back. Not now, when she needed to pay back Mama, and when they needed to move out of Valeria's. But she knew where things were headed. "One month of being your—", she searched for the word, "companion is fair, don't you think?"

He reached up and stroked his finger across her lips. "No, I don't."

She pulled away, tightening her mouth.

"Come to the garage tomorrow," he said. "After work."

She set her eyes on the ground, at the stubborn leaf that clung to the edge of her sneaker. She scrubbed it against the pavement, her mind searching for an excuse. "I can't. We're going to see an apartment tomorrow," she lied.

"That's good. I hope it works out. Tuesday then."

She was going to have to see him. Whether it was tomorrow, or the day after, she would be forced to be alone with him again until she paid back the money he'd given her, and even then, she wasn't sure if she could rid herself of him.

"I won't be able to stay long," she said finally. "I have to get home to my children."

"I understand," he said. "Half an hour, then?"

She nodded.

"Good." He tipped his head toward her. "I'll see you Tuesday then." And without kissing her farewell, he walked off. His heels clicked along the empty street as he made his way down the block, their clack never really fading with each step.

He was just what she expected: un sucio. A man with money who preyed on women like her, women he could take advantage of. She cursed him. She cursed Mama for not lending her the money she needed. She hated needing the money in the first place.

When the sound of his shoes finally faded, Ana straightened her spine. The rain pelted harder on the ground, but she kept her chin up and marched on.

3

IT WAS A TEN-MINUTE WALK FROM THE TRAIN STATION TO LA FAC-
toría. Ana always welcomed the walk to work. She lost herself in
the sound of car horns and bus growls, the soft collisions into other
wrapped bodies, the blue that dripped into the winter air. She
could still feel the city's pulse with every step.

The sounds faded as she got farther away from the main strip
in that particular part of the borough. Sparrows flew overhead and
their song became clearer as she got closer to the gray river that
circled the island. When she had first set eyes on it, the color had
surprised her. The rivers in Santa Clara were the color of the land,
tan and sanguine, like the very people who depended on them for
survival. Here, it was the buildings that bled into the water.

On most mornings, she hustled through the crowds, pausing at
the traffic stop signs unnecessarily longer than she needed to. The
world around her grew quiet until it was just her and the flock brave
enough to stay the winter.

But not this day. She woke earlier than usual, somewhere between the moon's retreat and the sun's advance, with a restlessness
she had not felt since before she came to New York; the same kind

that wrestled her from slumber the nights before she first told Lucho about her pregnancies. Only this time, it was the weight of Don Beto's request that sat on her chest. Her promise to return chased her, and no matter how much she walked or where she headed, she couldn't leave it anywhere behind. His mouth, his teeth clung to her like the flock of sparrows she usually welcomed in the mornings, but whose chatter now only gnawed at her ear.

They stayed with her as she turned a corner toward the congealing river. La factoría was the last building on the block, looming over the others, watching everyone in its shadow as though it were a church. Its windows, misted with age and frost, defiantly faced the morning sun.

Outside its main door, women huddled in batches beneath clouds of smoke, tossing "Merry Christmases" at her as she walked by. Despite her mood, she returned the greeting, and as she repeated the words, her chest grew lighter, her steps slowed. Christmas was over; a new year was only days away. Despite the turmoil of the past few months—of the last few years—she reminded herself of her good fortune. She was blessed with healthy children, a job. Her husband was by her side. They were safe. No matter how difficult things were, they were just obstacles; nothing that couldn't be fixed, rectified. There was no reason to believe that the year to come couldn't be a good one. So instead of simply wishing the women a Merry Christmas, she added "y un próspero año nuevo" to her greeting, a genuine desire that they might all benefit from good fortune in the new year.

"I see you're in a good mood this morning, Comadrita," said Carla Lazarte as Ana passed by her and another seamstress standing by a lamppost. Carla had been working at la factoría for years when she recommended Ana for a job there. She did the same for her sister, Betty, when she arrived in the States just a few months earlier.

Betty Sandoval was Ana's oldest friend, a girl who'd grown up in the house next to hers in Santa Clara. She stood now with a group several feet from la factoría's main door. The huddle rumbled in a billow of smoke. When she saw Ana, Betty broke out of the group and walked toward her. A cigarette dangled from her mouth and coffee slipped from the lipstick-stained Styrofoam cup in her hand.

"Don't tell me that's breakfast?" said Ana, pointing to the cigarette.

Betty paused halfway toward her. "Good morning!" she said, her eyes widening though neither the caffeine nor the feigned enthusiasm could shake the look of listlessness that had settled on her gaze long ago. Betty's eyes had once seemed as if they were on the verge of plunging into a dream, a dream so sweet she might never wake up. Now, they were only tired. "How are you?" she asked. "I'm doing great, thanks for asking."

Carla hollered from the lamppost. "Don't bother, Anita. She can't quit now that she's selling that shit."

"No one's talking to you, Sister," Betty shouted. "Don't tell me you're like that one now?" she whispered to Ana. "Are you going to start lecturing me about what I can and can't do? I swear this country turns everyone into a fucking saint." She looked at Carla sideways as she puffed on her cigarette. "She's forgotten all about those nights at the club, hasn't she? She's a señora now. A wife and a mother. Please. This is the only respectable job she's had since God knows when."

Carla had indeed taken her role as wife and mother very seriously. She was close to forty and Betty's eldest sister by fifteen years.

The two had reunited in New York in early summer, when Carla and Ernesto had enough money—and the right paperwork—to finally bring their three children to the United States. By then, Betty had spent the better part of a decade raising them in Lima. She made a case for why she should also join them in New York. She could help the children adjust to their new environment, and also help Carla with the transition from mothering by telephone to mothering live and in person, every day. At the very least, they owed her a trip.

It took several calls before Carla agreed, and although Betty had managed to get a tourist visa, she had already overstayed it.

"I'm just trying to quit, that's all," said Ana.

"Since when?" said Betty, as the two walked to the huddle. "You've always smoked. You think you can give it up just like that?"

"No, I haven't always smoked," she said. "Besides, it doesn't matter if I've smoked a day or ten years. If I want to stop, I can stop."

Betty smirked. "You won't." There was something in the way Betty spoke to Ana, always with a degree of certainty, that unnerved her. She knew more about Ana than almost anyone else; even more than her own husband. They had spent their childhood playing on the same dirt road, in homes separated by only a few yards. While Ana grew up an only child, Betty was the youngest in a family of six children. By the time the last sister left Santa Clara, it was only Betty who remained at home with Doña Sara and two older brothers. She occasionally joined Ana and her mother on their early morning walks to the market, often shared the same bar of soap when they washed their clothes by the river, sneaking in swims as the sun baked the earth red. Betty could only tolerate so much of the sun. Unlike Carla, she was blanquiñosa, white enough that her skin hurt if she was outside for too long. Her hair was castaño, a muted copper in the right light. But she was not full-on white; the indígena was more noticeable in Carla and their other siblings, with their straight, heavy hair and aquiline noses. But Betty had the nutty half-moon eyes of the women who traveled to Santa Clara from deep in the rain forest, and that gave her away. "Even when you were pregnant, you'd sneak in a cigarette here and there," she said.

"Can you keep it down?" whispered Ana.

"Guess you are like that one," she said. "Anyway, you're coming with me to the pharmacy later, right?" They agreed to leave as soon as the bell rang so as not to miss the bus that'd take them to La Farmacia Pérez. They needed oils and medicines, and Betty had business to discuss with the owner.

When Ana told the women she was no longer smoking, they congratulated her, even though Betty was making it difficult for everyone else to quit. "I told you these were good," she said as one of the seamstresses pulled another cigarette from a packet similar to the kind Betty was smoking. "Now, I don't have that many, but I'll have a few for sale next week."

"Is that what Valeria brought back for you?" asked Ana.

Betty gestured with her eye, and although Ana took it to mean that whatever she got from Valeria was supposed to be a secret, Betty had never perfected the art of subtlety. The gesture looked more like a twitch.

"I guess the answer is 'yes,'" said one of the seamstresses, and the rest giggled. She then pointed her chin across the street and said, "Look who's coming." The women turned almost in unison. "Disimula, disimula," someone added, but the person who had caught the group's attention had already made eye contact and was heading toward them.

Nilda, the Ecuadorian, was in no rush as she slinked across the street. Her cranberry leather jacket hit just above her hip, though

Ana thought the color was closer to the hard skin of the aguaje fruit that grew all over Santa Clara. Her jeans choked her rear end and thighs; how she got them on was anybody's guess. Her highlighted black curls were still wet from her morning shower. Ana swore the hint of strawberry in the air came from their bounce.

"Chicas, buenos días," she shouted as she approached, her glossy mouth aglow, but only Ana returned the greeting. Not that there was a reason to be rude to Nilda. She always said good morning, added a smile even when it was clear she was making an effort, and occasionally brought in leftover humitas, corn cakes she said she made whenever her spirits needed a lift.

But she was decadent for a factory worker. She held her hair back in a sparkly red butterfly clip as she worked her machine, not a scrunchy like the others. She never let her golden highlights dull, and her acrylic nails were always dotted with studs that sparkled under her machine's needle. At first, Ana saw all the ways Nilda glittered and was tempted to befriend her. They were alike in many ways. Both were younger than most of the other seamstresses, even though Nilda had been working there for years. They were both South American, undocumented, married with children. They sat on the same island, along with Betty and Carla. Although Ana never saw herself in the sparkly accessories and put-together attire that Nilda was able to pull off every morning, there was a boldness there that she admired.

But then, every Friday, the murmurs swelled. It was the day when, just before clocking out, Nilda piled on more eyeshadow and liner than usual. Everyone knew she was headed to her other job, serving drinks at a nightclub on Northern Boulevard. She might as well have come clean about working in a brothel.

"How was your Christmas?" asked Ana.

"Oof," said Nilda, giving her head a gentle toss. "Exhausting.

I worked Christmas Eve." She rarely mentioned her other job, and so everyone leaned in. "I'll have to work New Year's Eve, too, but I can't complain. In one night I can make what I earn here in a week." Her smile grew wider. "I almost didn't come in today."

"Why did you then?" asked Betty, with such spite that Ana swatted her friend's forearm, catching herself only after she'd done it and unaware that the other women were giving Nilda the same contemptuous look as Betty. She caught Nilda's eyes and felt herself blushing out of shame.

"Because this is my real job," said Nilda, as if pointing out the obvious. "Besides, I have my eye on a ring that'd go perfectly with these." She tucked her hair behind her ear, and the thick, studded hoop that hung there sparkled. "My husband gave them to me for Christmas. Besides, my boy needs a new pair of sneakers, so," she shrugged, "here I am."

No one else asked any questions, and when Olga, the foreman's assistant, arrived at the main door, Nilda followed her inside.

When she was gone, one of the women stepped closer into the huddle and speculated that Nilda's husband hadn't given her those earrings. A neighbor, she claimed, had seen a man drive Nilda home late at night. The man never drives to the door, just parks on the side street. She was certain that he, and not her husband, had given Nilda those earrings.

Ana laughed. "Is it so hard to believe that maybe her husband *did* give her those earrings?"

The woman cocked her head. "Don't be stupid, Ana. If he had that kind of money, she wouldn't be working here. No, she's got someone on the side, for sure. Or maybe she just dropped her panties enough times to buy them herself."

"If that's the case, then good for her," said Ana. "And don't call me stupid again."

A church bell chimed in the distance. The women with cigarettes in hand drew a final, long drag as the others began marching
inside. A man in a fawn-colored coat, with a generous midsec-
tion and a thready Mets baseball cap, pushed past them. "Chicas,
¡avancen!" shouted George Milas as he squeezed through the door.
Ana hurried toward it as Betty and the others trailed behind. The
lobby swelled with women waiting for the elevators. George had
already made his way to the front. Ana and Betty took to the stairs,
like they always did, racing up to the fourth floor.

They were nearly out of breath when they reached it. El piso
de costura—the garment floor—was an ashen room with rows of
lean lights above dozens of sewing machines manned entirely by
women. The stations were arranged in groups of four, forming islands throughout the floor. There was just enough room between
each island to squeeze through sideways. Fans were spread across
the room, flanking its corners, filling it with a lazy hum and a
dusty mist that never seemed to dissipate. Reams of fabric leaned
against the walls and exits. Blinds covered the windows, trapping
in the heat, keeping out the light. In the mornings, the piles of
needles closest to the windows gleamed from the daylight that
somehow managed to slink its way in.

George, still catching his breath from his sprint, eyed the
women as they made their way to their stations. He had a thick accent, and knew only a few words in Spanish, but nevertheless spoke
those words as assuredly as any native speaker. "Vamos, muchachas,
adentro." He handed Olga his coat and cap. She was the women's
go-to if they had any questions about money, hours, materials, running out of toilet paper in the bathroom. She was one of the few
Puerto Ricans on the floor and she acted as George's translator, even
though the Dominicans and Salvadorians thought Olga's Spanish
was atrocious. Ana didn't think it was that much worse than theirs.

By the time Ana and Betty arrived, the other seamstresses near their island were already settling in. Ana greeted them with a "Feliz Navidad" as she hung her coat and maroon sweater on her chair, and although some were disappointed to see the holidays coming to an end, others worried about how they'd pay for it all come January.

"But not Ana," teased Betty. "She's got high hopes for the new year. She's even stopped smoking."

Carla set down the piece of fabric in her hand. "And you're not drinking anymore either, are you?" she said. Ana had refused a shot of tequila from a bottle she'd brought to work the week before. Carla had pulled it out from her oversized bag, shown the women the worm still swimming at its bottom. A pre-Christmas toast with the girls, she said. But Ana refused to drink. What if they got in trouble for drinking on the job? What if she got tipsy, cut her finger, messed up the fabric, or broke the machine?

"No," said Ana, "I said I won't drink *here*. And honestly, I don't drink much as it is. It just messes with my stomach."

"That's because you don't know how to drink," said Carla. "And unless you practice, I swear, each time, it'll be like you're having your first."

Nilda chimed in. "It's true," she said, and Carla immediately tensed. "It's like sex. You don't do it enough, you forget it all. How to hold the thing, what to do with it. You forget what you like. You get lazy."

"Nilda!" exclaimed Carla.

"But it's true! You have to know what alcohol you like and how much, just like sex. What kind and how much. These are two very important things when it comes to sex and alcohol. Otherwise you get it in your mouth or in your culo before you even realize what's happening." She laughed, even as Carla looked around nervously

to see if anyone else was listening. "Anyway, Anita," Nilda continued, "I really do hope the new year's better for you than this one.
Although I didn't hear about any planes crashing, so I guess your
sister-in-law made it back."

Ana snorted. "She's my husband's cousin, not my sister-in-law.
And yes, she's back. She flew in yesterday morning."

"Good, then maybe she can cook for New Year's," said Betty.
"Give you a break after taking care of her house and kid for a
month."

"At least you didn't have to worry about cooking lunch for
today," said Nilda, who had promised to bring humitas for the
women. "I brought a few for your kids too." Her humitas were a favorite of Victoria and Pedro's, and as much as Ana wanted to make
them herself, she couldn't ask Nilda for the recipe. It belonged to
Nilda, and like any beloved meal, no one ever asked the chef to
share her magic.

It was at lunch, as they walked down the hall toward the cafeteria, that Nilda held her back and gestured to the utility closet
beside the restroom. Ana looked about, but the other seamstresses
making their way to the cafeteria didn't seem to notice them. It
made her uneasy to be seen going into a room alone with Nilda, but
she went inside anyway. The closet, stocked with cleaning supplies,
mops, and brooms, was not unfamiliar to her. She often snuck in
there before heading home, stuffing toilet paper and paper towels
into her bag. The stacks seemed to soak up Nilda's strawberry scent,
drenching the room, swallowing Ana whole.

"I have to leave work early a few days next week," she said.
"Wednesday and Thursday. Olga mentioned you were looking for
extra hours." Before Christmas, Ana had indeed asked Olga to
keep her in mind in case there was an opportunity to put in more
than the ten hours she was putting in now. Women who'd been at

la factoría the longest, like Carla and Nilda, had first dibs on any overtime. The more pieces one made, the more one got paid. At a minimum, a seamstress had to work ten hours a day, but sometimes, there was a doctor's appointment, a call from the school, a mother who died back in the homeland, that made it difficult to make the ten-hour-a-day mandate.

If you couldn't, you had to have a damn good reason. And you needed someone to pick up the slack. It was usually a veteran, a seamstress who knew how to do the work and could do it fast. Someone George couldn't say no to.

"I haven't told George yet," Nilda continued. "I want to make sure I have someone to cover for me first. I really can't take another lecture about responsibility and how I don't value the place. And I'd rather ask you than let it go to one of the others."

No doubt there were others who'd made the same request of Olga, eager to try to pay off whatever debt they had accumulated from buying Barbie dolls and Matchbox cars. But here was Nilda, with her shiny Christmas earrings and the prospect of a glorious New Year's Eve, giving her a chance to cut the line.

"It's only two extra hours each day, so not much," she said. "What do you say?"

Just a couple of extra hours. That was four more hours. Four hours for her to work as fast as she could, prove herself as someone who deserved the extra hours when they needed the help. She was struck not just by Nilda's gesture, but the timing.

Dios es grande, she thought.

Nilda took her stunned silence as a yes. "Okay," she said, "I'll tell George. And don't thank me yet. He still has to say yes." She stepped out, turning in the opposite direction of the cafeteria, toward George's office. There was no doubt in Ana's mind that he'd agree, not because he was generous or because Nilda was coming with a backup, but because Nilda was going to do whatever it was she needed to do.

She had to do the same, and so, when she joined the others in the cafeteria, she said nothing about their conversation. Even as Carla leaned over and whispered, "What did that one want?" Ana only muttered, "Nothing," between mouthfuls of mashed corn and cheese. She felt everyone's eyes dig into her face and body, searching for signs of Nilda. She let them dig. Did they see the woman's smirk, her hippy lean? Did Ana smell like strawberries now?

After lunch, Olga pulled Ana aside, once again raising eyebrows. Yes, she told her, she could do the extra hours, and Ana thanked her again and again for the chance to prove herself. The money she made during those hours could go to Mama, get her payments back on schedule. It could even go to Don Beto. Maybe that was the more important debt to pay off. She'd need Valeria to watch Victoria and Pedro while she worked. She wouldn't say no, not after leaving Michael in her care for a month, not when it meant Ana was one step closer to getting out of Lexar Tower.

At the island, the other women shot glances at her, and she avoided Betty's gaze altogether. Then Carla finally remarked, "You look happy." Ana had always been wary of sharing good news. She was hesitant to stir up any feelings of envy, especially at work. If there was anything that could certainly stir it up, it was money and another woman. She decided not to give an explanation. They'd know soon enough that she'd be working a few extra hours when she remained at her machine while the rest of them packed up for the day. They'd understand then.

Yet she couldn't suppress the relief, the sense of hope, that she now dared to nurture. And so she kept on smiling and replied, "You know, Carla, I think it *will* be a good year."

4

THAT AFTERNOON, ANA AND BETTY HURRIED TO CATCH THE EAST-
bound bus toward La Farmacia Pérez. They pushed toward the
back of the bus, away from the teenagers bold enough to blare music from a boombox that one held across his lap. Betty asked what
it was that Nilda wanted. She was surprised by Ana's reply. "She
wants you to cover for her?" she said, her eyes widening. "I didn't
realize you two were friends."

"We're not," said Ana. "But I need the money, just like you do.
Isn't that why you asked Valeria to bring you back those cigarettes?"

She said nothing for the rest of the ride. The bus emptied as it
hauled itself farther east, to a mostly Caribbean stretch two neighborhoods away from la factoría. Christmas lights were strewn above
the street, from one lamppost to another, lit as the afternoon moon
crawled up the darkening sky. Storefronts featuring mannequins,
dressed in sequined red cut-out tops and fur-laced boots, defied
the purified glares of those clad in ivory wedding and quinceañera
dresses across the street. Appliance and furniture stores announced
they were closing, everything must go. A nook at a corner, with a
menu in its window, had the only sign on the strip with an English

word: "Cup." As they got off the bus, only half a block from La Farmacia Pérez, the wind picked up the smell of the birds caged in the slaughterhouse nearby.

Lety Pérez was behind the pharmacy's main register, perched on a swivel chair, pen in hand, flipping through the pages of an overstuffed notebook. Muffled voices emanated from a portable television hidden in a nook to her right. A picture of her daughter, in braces and a checkered uniform, hung on the wall behind her. Ana greeted her in a pitch she normally reserved for her elders or professionals—abuelitas, doctors, priests. The pharmacist's wife held a similar status, even though she was only a few years older than Ana and was close to two decades younger than her husband.

"He's not too busy today," she assured them, her eyes disappearing as she smiled. Navy blue liquid liner ran across their top edges, which made them look too small for her face. Tiny hair clips held back her spiral curls. She had a mole on her cheek, the first thing Ana noticed whenever she saw the woman, but her face was otherwise unblemished, line-less. Lety was a woman who slept, Ana realized, and who slept well. Even with the mole beneath her rice-sized eyes, she was beautiful.

"I don't get what's so great about her," Betty whispered as they walked to the back of the store. Since she'd met the successful pharmacist's wife, she couldn't fathom her appeal. Lety had been a single mother when she met Don Alfonso. Pretty, but enough to marry? "She's got that cockroach crawling on her face."

"It's not all about looks," said Ana. "She's educated. She's got a degree hanging somewhere back there. I've seen it."

"She got lucky," said Betty. "And it's *all* about looks. She'll get some enhancements in a few years, you'll see."

At the back of the store, a handful of customers had gathered beneath the blue sign at the center, with the word *farmacia* written on it in slanted white bold letters. The waiting area was comprised of two chairs, lined side by side against the wall. A man sat in one, while a woman leaned on her cane over the second, where she had placed her grocery bags.

There were smaller signs on either end of the counter. A stout woman dressed in a white robe and holding a white bag shouted, "García," as she stood beneath the sign that read "Recoger." The woman with the cane responded by hollering back, "¡Aquí estoy!"

The other sign said, "Consultas." Standing beneath it, with a medicine bottle in hand and explaining something to a woman with a frizzy gray bun, was Don Alfonso Pérez. He was a slim man with skin that shone like wet wood against his white pharmacist's coat. He had closely cropped hair and a long, inquisitive face. One of his eyebrows always rose above his gold-rimmed glasses whenever he read labels aloud to his customers.

When she was first introduced to La Farmacia Pérez, Ana had hesitated taking advice about her health from a man like Alfonso. He was Peruvian, one of the few she'd met in New York, but he'd grown up in a pueblo joven along the outskirts of Lima, poor and black. And he talked about being black and what it meant to be black and what it meant to be an indio and black. She'd overheard his contained outrage when cops thought a local Dominican boy had a gun or when some of his customers were rounded up like cattle and shoved into trucks. To hell, he'd say, with these abductors, these invaders who killed our fathers, raped our mothers, shoot us like animals, and tell us to get out of *our* land—all of which made Ana uncomfortable.

But he was an actual pharmacist, trained in Lima and in the States. He'd arrived in New York decades earlier, and, with the help of a friend, managed to open the pharmacy even while he was still undocumented. It was Lety, a Panamanian mother trying to finish up community college, who eventually got him his green card. Their diplomas hung on the pharmacy wall, and Ana couldn't help but stare at them each time she was there. They were the only diplomas she'd ever seen.

On that very first visit, Don Alfonso sold Ana thyroid medication, the same kind she had bought in Lima. She did her best to keep her children from doctors, with their prodding tools and invasive questions. With Don Alfonso's guidance, she waited out coughs, filled her kids' bodies with water and sports drinks until whatever infected their systems made its way out. She built up their defenses with daily doses of the good pharmacist's preferred brand of cod liver oil and bowls of caldo de gallina. He was well-stocked with other medications and treatments as well. Herbal pain killers from Brazil; whitening creams from Colombia and fat-burning gels from Venezuela; even small, blue-tinted bottles of oils, his own concoctions, which attracted luck and money and deflected evil eyes. The pharmacy itself smelled like Palo Santo. Chunks of the tree were laid out throughout the space. Its minty sap, he told her once, helped with allergies.

But Don Alfonso also had the unmentionables that señoras and señoritas requested only in whispers: something to help the itch and the smell down there, birth control pills, condoms for the ones bold enough to ask their men to put one on.

"¡Don Alfonso!" Betty exclaimed as they walked toward the Consultas sign.

"Muchachas, buenas tardes," he hollered in his crispy voice. They exchanged pleasantries about the holiday, his relatively quiet but expensive Christmas with his daughter and Lety's nephews, and their plans to go on a boat cruise around Manhattan for New Year's Eve. He assumed they came to stock up on their regular medication, but then Betty asked to speak to him about "something" and threw Ana a look. She excused herself, but lingered by the shampoos and body washes nearby, keeping a close eye on her friend. Betty's face was steady, her lips moving quickly as Don Alfonso leaned in. When he spoke, Betty followed his mouth as if he were a fortune-teller.

When it was her turn, Ana approached Don Alfonso with a nervous smile, said hello again, and fidgeted with the strap on her bag. As if sensing her discomfort, Don Alfonso watched her from over the top of his glasses and whispered, "You came for your pills, right?" She knew he was referring to the right pills. After all, there was no need to whisper about thyroid medication. "When was the last time you took them?" he asked.

"A few weeks ago," she stammered.

He pulled a notebook from behind the counter and flipped through its pages. The notebook had always unnerved her. She wanted nothing more than to stay hidden, untraceable, and here was Alfonso memorializing her visits and what she was consuming. "The last time I gave you any was in . . ." he traced his finger down a list until, apparently, finding the information he was looking for. "November."

She stood on her toes and peered over, hoping, as she always did, that he used some kind of code to track her and her medications, but he shut the notebook quickly and slipped it back under the counter.

"Any chance you could be pregnant?" he asked.

She shook her head no and looked around to see if anyone had heard his question.

"Are you sure?"

"I'm taking care of myself," she said.

"Do you want the full month this time?"

Again, no. "Two weeks. I'll come back for the rest."

"You said that the last time." He raised a single eyebrow over his frames. She fiddled with her strap. "Give me fifteen minutes."

She lingered by the oils as she waited, away from Betty who had drifted toward the pain relievers. She never asked Betty what she got from Don Alfonso. She assumed it was the same thing she got. Or condoms. Although she'd only been in New York since the summer, Betty was never without a lover. When they were children in Santa Clara, it was Betty who taught her about the part that grows on a man whenever he sees or feels something he likes. It was Betty who giggled, as if she were in on some secret, when Colonel Mejía began visiting Ana's mother. He was a stocky, pinkish man, always dressed in a uniform that reminded the girls of bijao leaves. It was only later, when Ana caught Betty watching them through her mother's bedroom window and then crouched down beside her, that she realized what that secret was—what it was exactly that the Colonel and her mother were doing.

Years later, when Ana was already working at the notaría, Betty made the move to Lima, where she lived with Carla and her young children. By then, the Sendero Luminoso and the military had grown bolder, deepening their presence in the jungle. Teachers were rounded up in the evenings, taken and told what it was they had to teach the children the next day. Bullets shot into the night, some purposeful, most at random. Men and women, especially the girls, were stopped and searched, interrogated, held for days. More and more seemed to disappear. The movement needed soldiers; the soldiers needed bodies. They needed women. Betty had to leave before they needed her.

The elder Sandoval sister took in the younger but set rules. Skirts had to hit the knees. No heels or perfume or red lipstick; nothing to suggest she was looking for a fuck. She had to think twice about bringing home any female friends, except for Ana. Ana was a decent girl. She'd somehow managed to get an office job, and it was this that inevitably made her the smokescreen for Betty's rendezvous with whichever boyfriend she had at the time. There was always one; any more than that just complicated things. They're easy enough to get, she'd tell Ana. "They're just animals," she'd say plainly. Despite living once again under Carla's scrutiny and her low opinion of the opposite sex, there was no doubt in Ana's mind that Betty had someone.

She contemplated broaching the subject on the bus ride back when Lety Pérez tapped her on the shoulder, a white paper bag in her hand. Ana followed her to the register, but instead of ringing her up, Lety only slipped Ana's money into a box. "Come back in two weeks," she whispered. "If money's a problem, we can figure something out." She slid the white paper bag across the counter and tapped it as she said, "You need to stay on top of this."

Ana quickly shoved it inside her handbag and walked back between the aisles to grab Betty, waving farewell to Alfonso and giving Lety a quick nod. "No te olvides," she called out as the pair exited the store. The two then headed to the slaughterhouse, where Ana had a hen killed and collected a pork shoulder, before hopping back on the bus heading west.

This time, the bus grew fatter as it pulled itself through the streets. The Spanish dwindled, and soon enough, English overtook the front of the bus. The two sat in silence in the back until they reached the highway underpass, only a few blocks from where Ana was to get off, when Betty asked, "Are you mad at me? About the cigarettes?"

Ana gathered the handles of her bags. "I don't like that you're in business with Valeria," she admitted. "It's just another thing for her to throw in my face. Doing favors for my friends."

"She's not doing me any favors. I'm paying her to bring them over. I need the money, Ana. I have to move out of Carla's. With the way Ernesto treats those kids, I swear, I'm going to lose it one day." She paused, placing her elbows above her knees, scratching her brow. "I need the money for other things too," she said.

Ana looked out the window and realized her stop was next. She pulled the string above her head, signaling for the driver to stop. "Do you want to walk?" she asked. It was during their walks as children that Ana learned what it was like to be Betty. On a Sunday morning walk to the market, she learned that Betty still asked Papa Dios to look after her father, even though she couldn't remember what he looked like anymore. And it was during those morning walks to school, whenever Betty had a fresh moretón on her leg or cut across her cheek, that Ana learned how one could salve a wound by listening to the birds' song or consuming the morning air. She taught Ana how to shut her eyes and breathe.

Betty's stop was still several streets away, but she stood as the bus jerked to a halt. The pair walked alongside each other, down a narrow, residential street, two avenues away from the train station. A dampness had settled on the pavement, the mild winter having laid a shiny sheen on the concrete. The lamppost lights shot through the tree branches, creating shadow webs beneath their feet.

"Do you remember," Betty began, crossing her arms across her chest, "do you remember that time . . ."

After what seemed like too long of a pause, Ana prodded, "Which time?"

Betty shut her eyes as she spoke. "That time I told you I was pregnant?"

Ana slowed her pace. Betty had first mentioned the pregnancy one night after an impromptu party at Tía Ofelia's house in Bellavista. Ana was only eighteen at the time; Betty, sixteen. The pair could get drunk off of a couple of chelas. Betty was too tipsy to go back to her sister's, and the two squeezed into Ana's twin-size bed. It was as Ana was about to fall asleep, her ears still clogged from the pounding music, fantasizing about having Lucho's mouth on hers, that Betty mumbled about why it was she had to leave Santa Clara. She couldn't have the baby there. She couldn't have the baby at all. Ana only listened, certain that, despite the beer and the muffled hearing and the hushed voice, she heard exactly what she thought she heard. She didn't dare ask any questions, however. Betty was tired; she'd been drinking. What if this was something Ana wasn't meant to know? What if this was something she couldn't un-know?

Except for that one time, Betty had never mentioned the pregnancy, and Ana had always hesitated bringing up the topic. She assumed Betty had taken care of the problem. She was, after all, childless.

And so Ana admitted, "Yes, I do," even though she still wasn't sure how much she wanted to know. "I honestly thought maybe I wasn't hearing right. We could barely get through a bottle of beer without getting drunk."

"That was a fun party your tía had that night," said Betty, a smile touching her lips. "I didn't think she'd let us drink like that. But you heard right. I got pregnant back in Santa Clara. That's why I ended up in Lima."

"So what happened?" she asked. "Did you lose the baby?" As soon as she said it, Ana knew the answer, but she hoped her friend would say that yes, she'd lost the baby. She could feel sympathy, even console her friend, for a loss like that. She didn't know how she'd react if the answer was anything else.

"I did," she said, "because Carla helped me." She pulled a cigarette and matchbook from her coat pocket. "You know how it is over there. Here, you can walk into a spot on Roosevelt Avenue or buy a few pills from a clinic or from Alfonso. Even one of these bodegas, ¡y ya! You can get back on track quicker than it took you to get pregnant in the first place." She chewed her lips. "I had to go to the curandero first."

The curandero. The Don Alfonsos of Santa Clara. The chemists who made magic. They were the only ones who could be trusted. They didn't rely on science or medicine. They had the earth, the sun, the saints, and the spirits to guide their work.

"He gave me some herbs," Betty continued. "I made a tea, but I didn't bleed. I didn't feel any pain at all. So then I went to Lima. Carla took me to some place to get it done. It turned out I didn't need to worry about it after all. I have quistes."

"Where?" she asked.

"All over," she replied, circling her forefinger over her abdomen. "In one ovary and in my uterus. It's hard for me to get pregnant in the first place. It's even harder to stay pregnant."

A sudden wave of sadness hit Ana. Betty was good with Carla's children; protective and doting, traits that Carla lacked. She spent years raising another woman's children when, perhaps, she could have spent those years raising her own. She suddenly had a thought she couldn't shake. What if the child was meant to be? If the curandero's potions hadn't worked, perhaps it was a sign that Betty needed to stay pregnant. "Was that your only chance?" she asked, then, quickly added, "I'm sorry. I didn't mean—"

"No, it's okay," she said. "I know what you're thinking. I've thought the same thing." She pinched the skin on her lower lip. "It might have been. But I don't regret it. I was fourteen when I got pregnant, Ana. Fourteen! What was I going to do with a baby at fourteen?"

What *was* Betty to do with a child at that age? Doña Sandoval only had two boys, and was cursed with four girls, all of whom left when they were old enough to make money in the capital or in another province. Betty's future had been uncertain even while in the womb. She'd been an unexpected addition to the Sandoval clan. From an early age, everyone from her mother to the school nuns had declared her to be the stupid, careless child in the Sandoval house. There was, simply, never enough for her or her brothers, and the brothers were, after all, the only ones who could possibly find work to support the family. If she hadn't ended the pregnancy, her own mother might have beaten it out of her.

"Alfonso's helping me with the pain and my cycle. It's kind of all over the place. He gave me some new medication, but he wants me to see a doctor. It's the last thing I want. The pain isn't that bad yet. Hopefully the new medication will work. But they're expensive, even with Alfonso's discount. God forbid I need something more drastic, what am I supposed to do? Borrow money from Carla? Forget it. That's why I'm trying to make some extra money with these cigarettes, Ana."

She nodded, and the two fell silent as their walk turned into a stroll. The gusts had picked up, and the stillness of the empty street would ordinarily have sent Ana racing toward a warmer, more brightly lit area. Neither could make her move faster, however. She was nearly planted into the concrete as she took in all that Betty had revealed.

They reached the train station, and Betty dropped her cigarette butt into what was left of her shadow, pressing it into the ground before lighting another one. "I'm not one to cry about things, you know me. But it doesn't seem fair sometimes, especially when I see Carla and Ernesto with the kids."

"It can't be easy for them either," said Ana, overwhelmed by an unexpected impulse to defend the pair. "They haven't really parented before. They're getting to know their children, and their children are older. It's not like they're babies. Imagine how difficult it must be for them."

"Imagine how much more difficult it is for the kids," Betty countered. "Anyway, I have to go see that bodeguero about the cigarettes. I feel terrible leaving my chiquitines, but the sooner I move out of Carla's, the better."

When they said goodbye, Ana held on to Betty a beat longer than usual. She felt heavier, as if something still weighed on her. It wasn't shame. Betty was never one to lament the circumstance of her life, even if she had every reason to. She was always the bold, strong one. It occurred to Ana that perhaps there was something else Betty was keeping from her.

And so she whispered, "Who was it?" as she held Betty. "Don't tell me it was Pepito?" she joked to lighten the severity of her question. By the time Betty was fourteen, Ana had already been in Lima for two years. Her father had disappeared; so had her uncle. There was the Colonel, who she hadn't seen since her own mother died. She wanted to know who it was; if it was any one of the men who had come in and out of her own life.

Betty held her tighter. "Remember how we used to watch your mother?" she said. An image of the two on their knees beside Doña Sara's bedroom window, the dust clouding around them in the mid-afternoon sun, the boots and revolver scattered on the floor, made Ana's skin rise. "Remember *him*? He used to come for your mother. All the time. It was always your mother, and I'm so grateful to her for that." She looked skyward, shutting her eyes. "And then she was gone."

Ana's body bristled.

"It was gonna be our turn one day," Betty continued. "You just got out before it was yours."

5

WHEN SHE ARRIVED AT LEXAR TOWER, SHE WAS COVERED IN SWEAT
and ten minutes late. Her schedule and Lucho's overlapped for less
than an hour during the week: as soon as she got home, there was
a hand off of unfinished homework, tangled hair, and television
monitoring. Tonight, with her visit to La Farmacia Pérez, there
was even less time to make the swap. "I'm here," she shouted as she
opened the front door, still in a daze from her conversation with
Betty.

Victoria bolted toward her. "¡Mami!" she shouted, wrapping her
arms around her mother's waist then quickly snapping back. She
pinched her nose and pointed to the bags in Ana's hands. "What's
that?"

"It's a hen," she said as she set her items down in the kitchen,
"and pork for New Year's. Don't make that face. You love hen
soup." Victoria shuddered then ran back to the living room.

"What took so long?" Lucho shouted from the hallway.

"The bus was late," she replied as he shut the bathroom door.
She took off her coat and slung her purse back over her shoulder
as she headed to Michael's bedroom to greet her son. Then, she

continued to her own room where she stashed her birth control pills in her dresser drawer before changing into an oversized T-shirt and sweatpants.

Victoria was in the living room, sitting in front of the coffee table. A workbook lay open on top of it, surrounded by several colored pencils. *Me lo contó un pajarito,* a Spanish-language entertainment news show, blared from the television screen. Ana did a double take as Lucho walked in, dressed in finely edged black pants and a pair of loafers that, she could tell, had just been polished.

"Do you know she has homework?" he asked as he pulled a burgundy turtleneck over his head.

"I do," said Ana, turning to her daughter. Victoria's chin was in her palm and her eyes were downcast. "Victoria, you told me you already did your homework."

"Papi," she said, sitting up straight, "that's not true. I said I was *doing* my homework, and look." She pointed to her name, scribbled in twig-like letters across the top of several pages. "I *was* doing it."

"*I'm* speaking to you," said Ana. "Not your father. And you told me just the other night that you already did it."

"But I was doing it, Mami, that's what I'm saying." Her eyelashes fluttered, and her head gave a gentle shake. "It's okay, Mami. You forgot. I forget sometimes too."

Ana shot Lucho a look, but he only smirked, seemingly pleased by their daughter's response. "Let's do a little every day, Victoria. I don't want to see you rushing to finish it all the night before you go back to school. And practice your M's." He pointed to the next letter she had to trace. "Then I'll teach you how to write *mentirosa.*"

Victoria pressed her pencil into the paper. "I'm not a liar," she whispered.

"Don't say that to her," said Ana. She couldn't, in fact, remember what words her daughter had used, and Victoria had a penchant for precision. She needed clarification when it came to bedtime (was she supposed to be *in bed* by 8:30 P.M. or *asleep* by 8:30 P.M.?). She negotiated how much food she had to consume if she wasn't particularly fond of it (only four spoonfuls of tripe stew because it takes a long time for her to chew and it was almost bedtime). It didn't surprise Ana that Victoria's explanation for the incomplete homework was that her mother misunderstood her. Perhaps Ana hadn't asked the question with the particularity her daughter demanded. Still, she'd rather get into the habit of clarifying her daughter's words than have anyone, especially her father, call her a liar. "Maybe I did forget," she conceded.

Lucho took a comb out of his back pocket, then headed to the bathroom. She followed.

"Ana, I can't discipline her if you're going to make excuses for her," he said. He added water and gel to his hair.

"You weren't disciplining her," she said. "You were making fun of her."

"I wasn't. She lied, didn't she?"

Ana leaned against the door. "I've got some good news," she said, eager to change the subject. "I'm working overtime next week. Just four hours. Two on Wednesday, two on Thursday."

"That's good," he said, turning around to give her a quick peck on the lips. "'Hello,' by the way."

She looked at the floor, then said, "I'll be a little late tomorrow too. I have to run an errand for Mama." He combed his hair back, looking intently into his reflection in the mirror. "You dress really well for someone who sits in a car all night," she remarked.

"I like looking like my old self sometimes," he said. "Besides, you have no reason to worry. It's not like I have time for girlfriends."

She wasn't amused even though, in all the years they'd been together, he'd never given her a reason to doubt his fidelity. When they first met, at a dinner his friend was hosting in San Borja, he seemed uninterested in anything but politics. She'd gone as his brother's date. Lucho was there alone. He stood out not just for his height and pale skin, but the force in his voice, the fire in his hands, as if he could march to La Plaza de Armas at that very moment and incite a revolution. The newly elected president, the Sendero Luminoso, all those who were now desplazados—these were all the reasons why he had no faith in the new government, no confidence that it would restore peace to Peru's provinces. It was only a matter of time, he said then, before Sendero displaces limeños themselves.

We're already being displaced, someone else had countered, and Ana felt their eyes land on her. It was, after all, the indigenous of Peru's interior who were fleeing their towns and villages to seek refuge in Lima from both the Sendero Luminoso and the soldiers who had descended to protect the people. That she was looked on as an invader didn't surprise her. She'd been working at the notaría's reception desk long enough that she was no longer fazed by the surprised look on some of the clients' faces, when they came to seek their high-paid lawyer's counsel only to be greeted by someone who looked like the maid they kept at home.

What did surprise her that night, however, was that Lucho, and not his brother, came to her aid. "We're one people," he said then. "It's that kind of thinking that's tearing us up. That you and I are any different from this lady. It's bullshit."

On the drive home, she asked Carlos how it was that Lucho was single. "Are you interested?" he joked, though he took his eyes off the road to gauge her reaction.

"He just seems like the kind of man who shouldn't be," she said.

Carlos explained that his brother was more interested in his research work at the university and the upheaval within the government than finding a partner.

When Carlos began working late and couldn't give her a ride home, Lucho offered to pick her up instead. It was during those nights that he asked about her past. He asked only a few questions about her parents. Were they originally from Santa Clara? Did her father always work en las montañas? How was it, growing up an only child?

Fine, she had replied, though she admitted that she sometimes wished she'd had a brother or a sister.

Then he'd ask about the military. Had they ever knocked on her door? What did they do to the people they arrested? Were they even terrorists? Is it true, the stories you hear about the murders and the rapes of the villagers?

Yes, the military checked in, she told him, but she never mentioned the Colonel's visits. She spoke quietly about the gunshots she'd hear while she lay in bed at night, the occasional high-pitched wail that often accompanied them, but otherwise claimed her nights were quiet. She confessed that one could never tell whether the violence was Sendero or not.

It was enough to cause a temblor under his skin. Pero nadie hace nada, he'd grit. It's only when the pitucos in Lima can't have dinner in peace that anyone cares.

She often found herself searching for those shifts, for that passion that moved him so much back in those days. But it had apparently evaded her in New York. They were far away from that reality, and the relative peace that came with their decision to leave Peru had calmed the upheaval that once seemed to brew just beneath the surface.

"Are you going to ask Valeria to watch the kids?" he asked as he walked back into the living room. "You know she doesn't like leaving the body shop too early."

"I'll talk to her," she said. "I don't know why she's always got to be there anyway. It's not like there's anyone there for Rubén to mess around with now."

Victoria perked up. "What are you saying about Tío, Mami?" she asked.

"Your father and I are speaking, Victoria."

"Okay. Excuse me, Mami, but what are you saying about Tío Rubén?"

"Turn around and do your homework."

Lucho looked at Ana sideways. There were some things that the family didn't discuss. Her relationship with Carlos was one of them. Rubén's affair was another. The children were part of the reason why; privacy and pride were another.

"That's not it," he whispered, a line running across his forehead. "I'm not sure exactly what's going on. She doesn't seem to want Rubén there alone."

"He's not," she replied. "He's got a couple of other mechanics and doesn't need any more help, remember?" She was still bitter about the Sosas' reluctance to give Lucho a job. Was it too much for them to give him something to do while he looked for work? Even if it was just to install rims or upholster car seats, any job and whatever income came from it was better than no work at all.

"Maybe something's going on with the business?" he speculated. The business, Falcón Auto & Body Parts, was a shop that Rubén had bought after years of working as a mechanic and soon after he and Valeria had married, mostly with the money she inherited from her parents and the sale of her mother's boutique in Lima. It was why she insisted on having her maiden name on the awning. The Sosas certainly had a particular lifestyle to maintain— the apartment, the cars, Michael's private school tuition, Valeria's frequent traveling. Ana had never heard them complain about their finances, nor had she ever come across an envelope with a red "PAST

DUE" stamped on its face. But Valeria had begun to notice how quickly the juice boxes disappeared from the fridge. She even asked Ana to cover the costs of paper towels, toilet paper, and cleaning supplies. Ana had resorted to taking whatever she could fit in her handbag from the supply closet at work. Although it seemed petty to her, Valeria's request was not entirely unreasonable. Ana's family did make up most of the household. She wondered now if Valeria's requests were simply a way to cut costs; if perhaps they were signs that the body shop wasn't doing as well as the Sosas wanted others to think.

"I'm not going to ask," Lucho continued. "She keeps her business affairs to herself. I just wouldn't be surprised if she says she can't watch the kids."

"She won't," she assured him. "You watch Michael when they're not here, and I practically took care of the whole place while she was gone. Besides, she wants us out of here."

"Don't start with that again," he said. He turned toward Michael's bedroom and emerged with a beaming Pedro perched on one arm. Victoria jumped on the couch, and he scooped her up after two awkward attempts that the children found amusing. They hugged him so tightly that his face disappeared behind their heads.

Pedro called out, "Ven, Mami, ven," but like every night, Ana stayed where she was, taking in the sight, letting the bouts of laughter that erupted when Lucho made fart noises into their necks carry her back to her own father's arms. It was always her father's arrivals that were momentous, not his departures. Seconds after he first stepped inside their shack, after all those weeks away, he'd swoop her into his thin, tired arms and pepper her with kisses. Her fingers would run across his soft hair, his broken nose, his sunken eyes, the deep lines that swerved like rivers down his cheeks. She'd touch him as if he were not real, as if the toasty smell of his breath and the stickiness of his skin had been something she imagined. She was afraid he might crumble underneath her fingertips.

Lucho let out several exaggerated breaths. "Make sure she finishes her homework," he said as he finally put the children down. He threw on his coat, then kissed Ana goodbye, tapping his forehead lightly against hers before walking out the door.

■ ■ ■

ANA HAD SET THE DINNER PLATES ON THE TABLE WHEN THE SOSAS arrived later that evening. Both opted to shower before they sat down. She waited patiently for them to finish their meals. Then, with Rubén present, she asked Valeria if she could please watch the children the next day and for a few hours the following Wednesday and Thursday.

"I just got back from Peru, Ana," she said. "There's a lot I need to do at the shop. I have to get our books in order for the accountant. I have to chase a few descarados that haven't even paid for the work we did last month."

"I told you I'd take care of that," said Rubén. He smelled like lavender and wood at home, but the shop still flowed through his body, from his guttural voice straight to his blackened fingertips.

"That's what happens when you do work for people like Mosca and Pescadito," she said. "They don't pay. Or maybe the problem is that you have friends like that in the first place."

He ignored Valeria and asked Ana, "What time do you need her here?"

"Lucho picks up the car at six o'clock, so five-thirty," she said, glancing from one to the other.

"Five-thirty!" exclaimed Valeria. "We close up at eight o'clock,

Ana. I'd have to leave the shop three hours early. And we only have one car."

"I thought yours was fixed," said Ana. Before Valeria left on her trip, she mentioned that her car needed a few upgrades, which was why no one could use it while she was away.

Valeria dug her fork into what was left of her chicken and yellow rice. "We're still waiting for a part from abroad," she explained.

"I can drop you off," said Rubén, "or one of the guys," but Valeria kept shaking her head.

"It's only for a couple of days," pleaded Ana.

Valeria swallowed and was about to open her mouth to respond when Rubén interrupted. "Of course, Anita. With all you do around here, it's the least we can do. She'll be here."

Valeria's eyes bore into him, but Rubén stared right back. For all her pushback, it was impossible for her to say no when her husband, a man unaccustomed to the word, was there to answer for her. She dropped her fork with a *clank,* filled her empty glass with orange juice, then stood and opened the bottom cabinet below the counter. She pulled out a bottle of vodka and poured some into her glass before walking out.

"I don't want to cause any trouble," said Ana when Valeria had shut her bedroom door. "We both know she's never liked me and I'm clearly in her way." Valeria had never hidden her disdain for Ana. She had visited Peru twice when Ana and Lucho still lived there, and twice she'd been cool and distant. She never struck up a conversation with Ana unless another person was also a part of it. She never held baby Victoria on those visits, although she always commented on how surprising it was that the child was so pale given her mother's complexion. Ana supposed that this was at the heart of her dislike—a bias because Ana was darker and from a province, without a last name of any significance and no parents; an utterly rootless woman. She couldn't expect to plant her roots here, in Valeria's territory.

"She does miss her privacy," Rubén admitted. He was never one to hide the truth. His candor was what made Ana like him so much in the first place. "There's a lot going on, and with you here, she can't exactly go off on me like she'd like to. I should thank you for that."

She scooted onto the chair beside him. Ordinarily, she would've continued to sit at the other end of the table to keep the appropriate amount of distance between them. After all, there was something inherently improper about two married people, who were not married to each other, being alone together. She had been particularly careful of how others might perceive their relationship. She never dared smoke a cigarette alone with him. There was always a third person, and at Lexar Tower, it was Lucho who accompanied them out on the balcony to smoke. She never accepted his offer to drive her to work in the mornings and even avoided dancing with him at parties.

The fact that he let her live in his home, rent-free, was enough to make their relationship more formal. He was, in many ways, another creditor. Had they been in Peru, he would've been obligated to help her, or at the very least help Lucho, and her by extension. But blood seemed to dilute itself outside of one's homeland, and there were limits to how much family could help each other in a place where everyone was trying to make their own way.

After she moved in, she made a point of always showing her gratitude by making his home feel like a home. She filled it with the smells and sounds of nostalgia through her cooking, the music, even her constant tidying. In the process, she won over his appreciation and friendship. He joked with Betty whenever she visited, and insisted on playing bingo with them, always gambling with his own money on their behalf. He joined the family for dinner on Sunday nights, the only night all five were together, even if he was standing. Still, she had avoided any situation that might be viewed as inappropriate.

But when Valeria left for Peru, Ana began to loosen her own rules of propriety. After the kids were asleep, she and Rubén often found themselves alone at night, and even though she had decided to give up the habit, she didn't object to his smoking inside the apartment when it was too cold to linger on the balcony. Their conversations were superficial at first. The weather, the kids, what did Lucho want for his birthday. Then it turned to gossip. Did she hear about the neighbor who had his car jacked in Jersey, or the viejita down the block who died just a few weeks after her chihuahua? He never understood why Americans were so attached to their dogs.

Then, as if he could finally go beyond the onset of winter days and the plights of neighbors, he began to recount his youth, when he stocked shelves at a supermarket in Bay Ridge and realized he didn't have the discipline to make it through college. He talked about his childhood in Peru, when he spent his summers in the north, counting the boats that lined the edge of the Pacific in Máncora. Sometimes, he disappeared into a memory, one he thought he'd long forgotten but recollected with specificity. Like the time his cousins pinned him to the ground and squeezed his testicles as they forced him to sing the Peruvian national anthem. The asphalt left a burn on his cheek that lasted for days. He almost laughed as he told the story. Often, the memories were of his mother, and of how she walked a different path home on Sundays after church to search the sewers for his sister, a sister whose picture still hung in his parents' living room, but whom he could not remember.

The revelations chipped away at the wall Ana had erected between them, and although he had not confessed as much, she'd known, for some time, that nothing had been good between him and his wife. There was enough familiarity between them now that she didn't feel wary about asking, "What exactly is going on?"

He squirmed in his seat. "It's about my daughter," he whispered. The daughter was the one he had with a Dominican woman who worked for him at the shop. Worse than a chola, she had heard Doña Filomena tell Lucho. Rubén had hired the woman to work the register, keep documents in order, pay bills, send invoices. He had asked Valeria for help at first. It was, after all, also her business. But Doña Filomena, in her years of observing the cunningness of men, suspected that Rubén knew his wife would refuse. Valeria wanted to work in an office, a place where she could wear heels and makeup, and look like a professional. What educated woman wanted to work in an auto body shop? Doña Filomena was certain that Rubén was just looking for someone to sleep with, and the easiest way to do that was to simply hire someone you were attracted to.

Back then, Ana didn't give much thought to the troubles between Valeria and her husband, thousands of miles away in another country. But she felt slightly vindicated by the rumor that Rubén was having an affair with someone Valeria no doubt considered so far beneath her.

What was more shameful than the affair itself was the child it produced.

A look of dejection settled on Rubén's face now as he spoke of the girl. Ana had caught glimpses of the same look in his other confessions, whenever he spoke of his mother's pointless search for his dead sister and the way his cousins fondled him as a child.

but if she could somehow prepare herself, go numb to what awaited her, she might be able to go through with it. She paid no mind to the conversations about this telenovela or that celebrity couple or the failing banks in Venezuela. She caught Betty glancing her way several times, but Betty knew her well enough to know not to ask questions. When one of the seamstresses noticed her reticence, however, Ana explained that she was simply tired. She'd fallen asleep at nearly four in the morning, and didn't even hear Lucho when he slid into bed.

"No te vayas a enfermar," the woman said. "None of us can afford to get sick."

"I told you, I'm just tired," Ana snapped back, and no one said anything to her the rest of the morning.

She sat at her usual table in the cafeteria during lunch, slumping over her leftovers. Her head still pounded. She was about to get up to make herself a third cup of coffee when Carla squeezed beside her on the edge of the bench. "¡Comadrita!" she exclaimed as she carefully set a clear plastic container, filled to the brim with sopa de res, on the table. "I told you I wanted to talk, remember?"

She nodded, unable to suppress a yawn.

"I have good news," said Carla, excitedly.

Betty stopped her fork midway to her mouth and said, "She wants you to move into one of our landlord's buildings. I already told you, Sister. That Irishman. ¡Es un tacaño!"

"He's not cheap," said Carla, eyeing the other women at the table to gauge their reaction.

"Then why'd it take him two months to fix that sink?" Betty asked. "Is it even fixed? There was still a leak this morning—"

"Ya, Hermanita," gritted Carla. By then, they had caught the attention of the rest of the women at the table. Carla cleared her throat as she composed herself. "The man's busy," she said, drop-

He glanced over his shoulder, as if his wife might be listening. "I want to tell Michael. He needs to know he has a sister."

Ana's jaw dropped. "Are you insane, Rubén? Do you honestly think Valeria will let Michael have anything to do with that girl?"

"She's my daughter and Michael's sister. Everyone knows about her now, but I have to pretend like she doesn't exist. I'm tired of it."

"But now is not the time to tell Michael," she whispered. "He's a child. He won't understand."

"Better that he hear the truth from me than from his mother. You know Valeria. She'll try to poison him before I even have a chance to explain."

"She will if the girl's mother is still in the picture." She said this knowing that the other woman was, in fact, still in the picture. She couldn't help but feel sympathy for Valeria. Here was her husband, a man she presumably loved, or at least once did, and he had a relationship—another family—with another woman. What could Valeria do but try to ignore it, pretend like she didn't see it? The alternative seemed too cruel. To wonder where he was, what he was doing, every time he walked out the door or didn't come home.

"It's complicated," he said.

"It always is," she replied. "But she's not poisoning Michael by telling him her version of the truth. You'll tell him yours one day and then he can come to his own conclusion about all this."

He rubbed his eyes with his palms. "I just want my children to know each other, that's all." He wiped his mouth with the trifold paper towel she'd placed beneath his cutlery, then tossed it on his plate. "I know I've made mistakes, Anita. I'm not perfect. She isn't either. But my children shouldn't suffer for what we've done to each other."

She shut her eyes, suddenly overcome with exhaustion. "No,

they shouldn't," she said, leaning back in her chair. "But they always seem to, don't they?"

. . .

SLEEP EVADED HER THAT NIGHT. BETTY, RUBÉN—EVERYONE, IT SEEMED, had kept secrets, including her. She'd had her share of sleepless nights since moving to unit 4D, but none as restless as this one, the eve before she was to see Don Beto. She'd shut her eyes, eager for the darkness to melt away the weariness that weighed down her bones. Yet all she could see were her children clinging to their father, to each other, as if a deluge was about to overtake them and they were each other's only salvation. She could never quite bring herself to cling to them. She always feared they'd slip between her fingertips.

6

SHE WAS IN A HAZE THE NEXT MORNING, HER HEAD POUNDING FROM the lack of sleep. She drank a large cup of coffee on her way to la factoría, determined to move through her day as mechanically as possible, and say as little as she needed to so as to avoid hinting that something might be off.

When she arrived, she headed straight to the stairs, avoiding the usual smokers that were huddled outside. As she began her climb up the steps, however, Carla called from behind.

"¡Comadrita¡" she shouted. "I have some news for you. Something good." She cocked her head and gave Ana a disconcerting look. "You look awful," she said.

"Thanks," said Ana. "I didn't get much sleep last night. Would you mind if we talk later? I really just need to sit down."

"Sure, let's talk at lunch. It's good news," she assured her, though Ana couldn't imagine anything good enough to take her out of the void she was falling into.

All she wanted was to numb her thoughts, avoid thinking about anything but the fabric between her fingers and the rumbling of the machine. The hours would pass—that was unavoidable—

ping her voice to just above a whisper. "That's not the same as being cheap."

And her landlord *was* busy because he had three other walk-ups in Brooklyn, and—here's the good news, Ana—he has a couple of vacancies in a building not too far from la factoría. "The rent's a little high," Carla admitted, "but he's fixing them up. The bedroom's apparently the size of my living room. I can give you the information if you want to check it out."

Ana hesitated. Her family would have to leave Lexar Tower at some point, but she hoped to stay there a little longer. At the very least, she wanted to stay through the winter. She wouldn't have to worry about not having heat or hot water.

"Gracias, Comadrita," she said, "but we're going to wait a little longer. Lucho wants to put in a few more weeks working the car. I'm going to pick up some overtime here. It'll make it easier to leave Valeria's if we have more of a cushion."

"Ya veo," said Carla, then she leaned closer. "I know that's why you were talking to esa huachafa." Ana shot Betty a look, and when she turned away, Ana knew she'd told her sister about Nilda. "Oh, don't blame that one," she said. "We were all going to find out eventually. And we were saying yesterday what a waste of time it is, right Betty? You'd be much better off putting away coats at that restaurant. At least then you'd get paid under the table. And you'd be one step closer to learning how to run the place."

Ana had thought about going back to that restaurant more than she'd ever admit. Regina's was an Italian spot in the Theater District that served mostly European tourists and sleep-deprived lawyers who worked in the building across the street from it. Ana had spent her first New York winter, when she lived with Carla and Ernesto, working the coat check room. Her goal, however, was to make her way into Regina's kitchen. It was run by men, men who spoke their own language—a mixture of English, Italian, and Spanish—and who spit out orders too fast for her to follow. But she couldn't afford to be their apprentice. The hours were too long, the pay was next to nothing, and she was uncomfortable being the only woman in a kitchen filled with men. But she took a weekend job doing coat check, hoping to slowly gain the confidence and trust she needed to make her way in regardless. Lucho initially fought the idea of her taking the job. He worked nights at a meat-packing plant, and although Carla had offered to watch the children, he didn't want Ana working at night, especially not in that part of Manhattan. She convinced him, however, that it was the first step to something bigger, something they could potentially leave one day to their children: a restaurant, a business. He went with her one evening to see the clientele, to speak to the manager, and when he saw that the train station was at the corner, and that it was only a two-block walk from the train station to Carla's apartment, he agreed.

But then winter was over, and as diners lost their coats to the warmer nights, Ana didn't feel quite comfortable asking to be let into the kitchen. By then, Carla had also started to tell this friend or that, and always within earshot, that she had to miss a birthday party or bingo night because she was playing the part of a nanny, again, that evening. Lucho refused to say no to weekend work, and so Ana never made it beyond the coat check room.

That she might one day cook at a place like Regina's, speak those men's language, inject it with her own words and commands, seemed so remote now. What felt even farther away was the possibility of watching her own recipes come alive on porcelain plates and make their way to a table of well-dressed patrons, eager to devour her Escabeche or her Tallarín Verde. They'd keep coming back, keen to try something new on La Inmaculada's menu. La Inmaculada, that's what she'd call it. "Immaculate" because the place would be spotless; the food, perfection. Immaculate as the Virgin herself.

"Yes, Ana, go back so you can learn," said Betty. "Then maybe you can hire us and we can say goodbye to this place."

"That might never happen," said Ana.

"Don't be so negative," said Carla. "You never know. You might actually have that restaurant one day, and then Betty can be your waitress, and the two of you can serve me and Ernesto when we celebrate our anniversary there. First thing you have to do, though, is get yourself out of Valeria's. It's the only way you're going to get ahead." She pulled a pen from her pocket, grabbed a paper towel, and began scribbling. "His name's Bob," she said, "but everyone calls him Sully." She tore the piece of paper and slid it over. Ana eyed the name and phone number. A seven-one-eight area code, a name she would've pronounced "su-yi" had Carla not said it aloud. "Just call him and see the apartment, Ana. What've you got to lose?"

■ ■ ■

THAT AFTERNOON, SHE HEADED TO MAMA'S. SHE'D GROWN NUMB AT THE thought of what might happen once she ended up in the back house behind the main building. In the weeks leading up to the livery cab money, she'd gone to the place twice to see Don Beto.

The first time, he acted as she expected. He was gracious and gallant. He wore cologne and offered her sweet wine. He talked about Cuba. He sat close to her, then closer, near enough that she could smell his sweat and count the small chicken pox scars on his face. He told her he liked her, put his hand on the inside of her thigh, and kissed her. Her body stiffened, and she kept drinking. He kept kissing her, then touched her breasts, and even though she could feel it happening, it didn't seem like it was happening to her. She was outside of herself, watching it from across the room. She had only allowed him to touch her.

The next time they met, he wore even more cologne. The bottle of wine was uncorked, and her glass was already filled to the brim. By then, Mama had said no to the money she and Lucho needed to lease Gil's car. Ana was behind on payments, and Mama didn't want to lose any more money. Ana had to drink enough to let whatever was going to happen happen, but not so much that she'd miss out on the best time to make her request. He'd undone the buttons on her shirt, and was kissing her neck, when she said she needed money.

"For the livery cab?" he asked, and she realized he'd spoken to Mama.

"Yes," she said.

"I can give it to you. Four weeks so you can pay for the month upfront."

Her eyes had widened. "I can start paying you back in two weeks," she promised.

"No, I'll *give* it to you."

He said the words as he slid his hands around her waist and hoisted her back up on the couch. He undid his belt buckle. She hesitated, then reached over, but he placed his hand on the back of her head and guided her face forward instead.

At the end of that visit, Ana had the money she needed to lease the cab.

There had always been a line she was unwilling to cross with

Don Beto. If he'd been satisfied with their encounters to that point, she might be able to bear them a little longer. But she knew he expected more than the petting and the kissing, and all the precursors to sex that she could barely stomach. She was willing to see him again, but she didn't want to cross that imaginary line. She didn't want to know if she could bear it.

Now, as she walked toward Mama's house on a dim afternoon, she relied on one possible out: she could pay Don Beto back. She had enough money stuffed inside her coat pocket to show him she was serious. She could get on some sort of schedule. Maybe not as frequently as she paid Mama, but a couple of times a month. She could figure out a way to pay him back, little by little, but she'd give him back his money.

The truth was that she wanted nothing more than to run back to the train station with the cash still tucked in her pocket. She deserved something for what had happened between them. If she had to live with the disgust of the moment, she should get something for it. But it wasn't an encounter she wanted to repeat, and she couldn't think of a way to keep the money without also having him in the picture. She urged her Virgencita to please ask El Señor to call the man. She didn't even want a tragedy, but a heart attack or a stroke. She asked for a merciful death even though he didn't deserve one. The Lord, however, didn't seem to listen.

She threw on her hood as she approached, but there was no one at Mama's apartment window when she arrived. She hurried onto the cobbled path that led to the back house. A burgundy car, at least two decades old, watched her with its rectangular eyes as she hurried toward the structure. She tapped its cobalt door, and he answered in a cream guayabera and pleated cinnamon slacks.

"Entra, niña," he said, "before the heat escapes." She hurried inside, but kept her hood over her head. The space had been a garage once, but it was now a small studio that Ana found oddly soothing. The walls were cream and mostly bare, with the exception of one wall that had a single large window that faced out into the yard and the back of the main house. Its blinds were pulled shut. Another wall held the black-and-white image of a woman on her back with her palm on her forehead and a leg kicking up. Don Beto had installed a small bar in one corner of the room. A number of tools hung in another and, below them, a table with three wooden orbs that needed to be sanded. A brown futon sat in the middle of the room with a vanilla-colored throw draped across it. Beside it was a recliner decorated with twists of tamed flowers and leaves, the only item in the room that Ana suspected had once belonged to Mama. A coffee table was at the very center. Its ruby wood gleamed beneath the overhead recessed lights. It offered up a bottle of wine, plump red grapes, and perfectly punctured crackers.

"Let me get your coat," he offered, but she didn't budge. She had no intention of staying, let alone taking off her coat. "Don't worry," he said. "Your patrona is not here."

Her head jerked. Mama never left the sanctuary of her first-floor apartment, not even to collect the rent from her upstairs tenants. She depended on her clients to do everything from picking up groceries and refilling prescriptions to dropping off items at the post office. Leaving its warmth to head into the frigid late December air seemed odd. "Where is she?" she asked.

"Go ahead," he urged her. "Get comfortable and I'll tell you." He noticed her hesitation. "You're going to cook in here if you keep that coat on."

She didn't know whether it was the comfort of the room, the fullness of the grapes, or the knowledge that Mama was away, but she acquiesced. Her gloves came off, and then her scarf. She slid off her coat, and then her boots. Her feet were cold inside her socks. She crossed her arms, adding another layer.

"So where is she?" she asked again.

"Mateo's in town," he said. "Here to see doctors with his 'novio.'"

Mateo was Mama's only child, a man in his mid-thirties. She'd mentioned him only once in passing. Mama liked to watch the five o'clock newscast because one of the reporters reminded her of him. "They have similar eyes," she'd said once, when Ana had come by to make a payment. That was all she ever said of him. There were no pictures on the wall, no drawing or ceramic or other childhood remnant to remind Mama or the world that a child had once lived there. That's because he's gay, Carla had whispered when Ana asked her about him. He lives in Miami, she'd said, so he could live his life however he wanted.

"You're surprised too?" said Don Beto, setting her clothes down on a stool by the bar. "So am I. But the prodigal son is back! After all this time, I thought he'd left for good."

"How long has he been gone?" she asked, curious to hear more of Mama's lost son.

"Long time," he said, picking up a bottle of rum and two glasses. "All because she tried to fix him. I told her, there's nothing that needs to be fixing. It is what it is. But she was stubborn. She had him in soccer, baseball, all kinds of sports. He was good at them too. Then she spent all this money on those baths they sell you at the botánicas. Those brujas are just thieves if you ask me. Her brother even took him to some brothels in Woodside. Nothing." He set the bottle and glasses on the coffee table, then walked back to her. He touched her back, urging her to sit. "Then he went to college in Florida," he said as he followed her to the couch, "and that was it. Completely forgot about his mother. Not a letter or a phone call. Not even for her birthday or Mother's Day." He filled a glass with rum then threw it back before muttering, "Ingrato."

Don Beto might have been more forgiving of Mateo's ungratefulness if he'd been his biological father or even his adopted one. But Don Beto had come into Mama's life when Mateo was still in high school, playing on that soccer team that Mama had hoped might set him straight. By then, a string of men had followed the death of Mama's first husband, Mateo's father. None, however, had managed to pull off what Don Beto had done. He married Mama only months after Mateo left.

"He's here to see doctors?" she asked. "Is he okay?"

He shrugged. "Who knows? I didn't ask. It's none of my business." He poured wine into the second glass and handed it to her. "I honestly don't care. He's been a thorn in her side for as long as I can remember. He should just stay away." She held the glass under her nose, its sweet scent crawling up her nostrils as she drew the rim to her mouth. "How did that apartment turn out?" he asked.

"It's not for us," she said, taking a large gulp. "I have your money."

He held up his palm. "I told you it wasn't a loan, Ana."

"I don't just take people's money. I said I'd pay you back when I have the money and I have it." She looked at her coat bundled on the stool and was about to stand when he grabbed her arm.

"Your husband just started a new job, Ana. You still don't have a place to live. I'm sure you spent a lot to make Christmas real special for your little ones. Consider it a gift."

She sat back, relenting. She needed that money. Besides, she had already repaid her debt in other ways. She muttered a thank-you, but she didn't think he heard her.

Her hands, once cold, now sweated. He stared at her. A layer of gel coated his eyes. His smirk made her uneasy, and she did not know what to do with her hands. She rubbed them against her pants to avoid looking at his face.

"How are things at your cousin's?" he asked.

"Fine," she said. "Everything's fine." She grabbed a grape and quickly stuffed it in her mouth. She looked around the room, tucking her fingers into the insides of her sleeves. He moved closer. She smelled the rum on his breath. She could almost find it enticing, if it had come from another man.

"Tranquila," he whispered. "You've gained some weight." She tensed as his hand moved up her inner thigh. He reached higher.

She knew what he expected, but she asked anyway. "What is it you want?"

He leaned in, his breath pressing on her face. "Come on. You know. You're not a child, Ana."

She bristled, and she slowed her breath to keep the anger from turning into tears. His inept attempts to woo her with wine and grapes, his pungent cologne, all turned her stomach. Why not keep it all business? At least then they could get straight to it. It'd be done and over with, and she could go home.

He grabbed her face and wiped his thumb across her lower lip. "I like helping you, Ana." He squeezed her face tighter and brushed his lips against her puckered mouth. "I don't care what you do with the money. It's yours." He loosened his grip, placing a loose strand of hair behind her ear, caressing the curve in her neck. Her body instinctively retracted, but she tried to stay still. His breath swarmed her skin, then his dry lips descended, his hands invaded. They moved from her face, sliding underneath her shirt and up to her breasts. He rummaged through her body, going from one spot to the next, searching like a pickpocket. As her body fell back onto the couch, Ana only looked longer and deeper into the track lights that ran across the middle of his ceiling. He lifted and pulled, and she counted the lights above her. She heard the seam in her shirt split against her skin. *Breathe,* she told herself. He paused as he fumbled with his pants. She noticed the light that had dimmed near the end of the track. It didn't hurt as much to look at it. She clung to it, and when he pressed against her, she buried her eyes in that last light until its gaze blinded her.

7

A DREAM JOLTED HER FROM BED THAT NIGHT, THE SAME ONE SHE'D been having for weeks. In it, wings had sprung alongside her spine, and she struggled to fly as she hovered above a river on a moonlit night. Shrieking monkeys slung from one tree branch to the next; dolphins raced behind her along the river. They chased her toward a wall, a wall made up of something that was moving, though she couldn't quite make out what it was. She woke as she crashed into it.

Her heart pounded against her ribcage. The back of her T-shirt and the undersides of her breasts were drenched in sweat. Her socks had slid off, and her bare feet were numb from the cold. The room was still as an indigo night crept through the blinds, its fingertips touching the top of her rose-covered blanket. She was in her bed, not in that dream, she realized, yet the river's scent lingered beneath her nostrils.

Beneath the blanket, a bump rose and fell to the rhythm of a wheezing breath. She pulled back the sheet, and there was Pedro, his cheek on a pillow, his thighs tucked into his chest. She brushed a swath of wet hair from his forehead and blew air across his face and neck. She wanted to wake him; his eyes always forced her to be stronger than she was. Instead, she turned him onto his side, wiping the saliva that escaped his mouth before pulling the sheet over his chest.

She found her socks near the foot of the bed, but the cold nevertheless crawled through the floor, up the soles of her chancletas, and through her legs. It was the first truly cold night of the winter. She didn't mind the sogginess of summers in New York. Its glue didn't bother her as it did Lucho or Valeria. But she had resented the mild autumn that lingered through December. She had kept the oversized coats, the long johns, and tank tops that she and Lucho had worn the previous winter. But she had to spend money on new clothes for the children. Winter, however, had taken its time, and there was so much more she could've done with that money instead.

She patted the top of the bunk bed where Victoria had turned her blanket into a cocoon. Ana pulled it back just far enough to see her daughter curled into a fetal position—how she always slept— with the two braids Ana had woven together still intact and with her doll, Liliana, beside her. Unlike her brother, Victoria had an almost soundless breath, something that always unnerved Ana. She held her finger beneath Victoria's nose, waiting for a breath to cycle through her body, just to be sure it was there.

The room was otherwise empty. She squinted at the clock on the dresser. Its green light was steady: 2:23 A.M.

She was up again.

She grabbed her maroon sweater hanging on the vanity chair, plucked her address book and pen from her handbag, then stepped into the hallway. All the doors inside unit 4D were shut. Hers closed without a sound. In the darkness, she made her way through the hallway. Her feet skittered over the floor. The ornaments on the

Christmas tree glinted in the darkened living room. Her heart continued to echo through her mouth. She reached the kitchen still shivering, hoping that a cup of tea might lull her back to sleep.

It was her attempt at a remedy for the restlessness of the past month. She'd wake at the same hour, between two and three in the morning, make herself a cup of chamomile tea that occasionally did the trick, and head back to bed before 4 A.M. She often woke as Lucho crawled into bed, lying on the edge of the mattress, his back to her and Pedro. "Sleep," he'd whisper, and sometimes, she did, straight until it was time for her to rise for the day.

Other times, they simply lay next to each other, whispering. She'd ask if he ate something, and he'd say yes. She assumed he ate in the car, though she never knew for sure. He'd tell her if the night was good or slow, ask if Victoria finished her homework or if Pedro was holding his pencil the right way when he wrote out his name. He always lay on his right side, his back to her. Sometimes, she got close enough to wrap her arm around his waist, and sometimes, he held her hand, bringing it to his lips and kissing it almost imperceptibly. It was a welcome contrast to the many nights he had spent on the couch, watching television or re-reading the same newspapers, quiet and distant, back when work had been difficult to find. Now, he fell asleep quickly; his snoring would begin almost instantly. She'd lay there, smelling the remnants of his cologne, the oil that had started to accumulate in his hair, the leather from the car, and him—the very underside of his skin—underneath it all. She knew his smell as if it were her own. It was singular, like Pedro's candied sweat and Victoria's milky breath.

She could recall Don Beto's smell now with the same precision. The coffee and tobacco, the rum and his sour stomach, all a jumble. The smell was permanent and decipherable, separate from any other she knew. She didn't regret sleeping with him that day, but as much as she tried to set it aside, it kept coming back. It was so easy to get the money she needed. Have sex with him every once in a while and he'd likely give her whatever she asked for. Money for the car, the rent, the kids' school tuition. They could move out of Valeria's. They could stay in New York and silence any notion to the contrary. No going back to Peru or worrying about car bombs or anyone in uniform. No need to prove just how far she'd gotten from that orphaned provincial girl. She could go back to Regina's, see if now there was room for her in its kitchen. She could keep her family intact.

Was she wrong, then, to do what she did?

She set a kettle on the stove, and as she waited for the water to fizzle, she leafed through her address book. She'd bought the vinyl-covered book at a discount store just before she moved in to Lexar Tower. It was one of many she'd gone through since moving to New York. She seldom added a person's phone number or address. Instead, she used the book to jot down her grocery lists, her to-dos for the week, whatever errands Mama had asked her to run. These were all listed in the front of the book, at the beginning of the alphabet. She had considered using the book to journal. Her sleepless nights brought all she wanted to avoid thinking about during the day. But there were simply some things she couldn't bear to see on the page. The reflection might be too much for her to bear. So she didn't write any of it down—not her day or her thoughts, nothing about the father who'd never come back, or the mother she knew, with certainty, never would. Not even her recipes.

Her dream, however, was always in the book, scribbled in its back pages under the letter *Z*. On the nights it woke her, she'd sit at the table with her cup of tea, writing down what she remembered to try to make sense out of it. The humidity on her skin, the hum of the leaves, the mumbling water. She listed whatever she could jog from her memory:

- río
- alas
- árboles
- monos
- bufeos

And to that list, she added:

- cayendo

She stared at the new word. Falling. In her dream, she had wings, but couldn't get them to work. She was falling, crashing through lean trees that reminded her of her father's arms, and into the river that smelled so clearly like the one that cut Santa Clara in two. She used to bathe in that water as a child. She expected to see her mother in her dream, sitting on the riverbank, like she did in real life, but she never saw her.

Then there were the monkeys and the river dolphins. Those things, she recalled with a shiver, were going to consume her.

The kettle shook, and though she ran to turn off the stove, she couldn't beat the whistle. Most nights, she tried to make as little noise as possible. There were few moments in her day in which she could enjoy silence and the idleness of time. Tonight, however, time slowed too much, and it quickly filled with too much contemplation.

She didn't mind, then, when Rubén appeared in the kitchen. Squinting, his hair tousled, he looked as if he'd risen from a deep sleep. His voice, however, was full and alert as always. "I can't sleep either," he declared. He stood at the doorway, waiting for an invitation to enter. She gestured for him to sit, then closed the address book and slipped it in her pocket. "I don't want to disturb you," he said as he sat down. "I know this is probably the only time you get for yourself."

"I was just getting organized for tomorrow," she said, adding a smile to ease his worry. "Besides, this is your kitchen."

He chuckled. "You've put it to much better use than me or Valeria. It might as well be yours." She set down a mug with a tea-bag in front of him. He dipped it in and out of the water. "What's got you up tonight?"

"Oh, same as always," she said. "Bad dream. Work. Money."

"You'll always worry about that," he said. "You can be a million-aire and still worry about money."

"Maybe," she said, "but it does make things a lot easier."

"That's true," he acknowledged. "It's better to worry about hav-ing too much than not enough."

"My father would agree with that," she said.

"Then he understood how important it is to work."

"He worked *too* much. Week after week he'd work in the jun-gle. He'd get so dark from the sun, it was like all the blood just ran up to his pores and stayed there. And for what? The basics. Food and our house and that was it. Not that the house was much. Wooden slabs and a metal roof. If we needed a door, we hung a blanket. That kind of house."

Suddenly, she was back there, her feet bringing up the after-noon dust as she walked on its floor, the wood panels that made up the walls long and uneven. The sun poked through newly punched holes, eyes made from the gunshots she heard in the middle of the night, when her mother would hold her so tight, Ana thought she might disappear into her.

"I'm sure he did what he thought was best," he said. "That's what we all try to do."

"Yes, he thought he needed to be out there making money. Like all men. I used to hate seeing him leave. It was worse for my mother. I was a kid, you know. Something else she had to feed and protect. She didn't always have the patience for it." She instinctively rubbed a scar on her thigh. She could still feel the stick coming at her, how she tried to swat it away with her delicate fingers, only for it to strike her wrist as well as her leg.

"It couldn't have been easy for her," said Rubén, "may she rest in peace. Alone with a daughter."

"It wasn't," she said. "She did what she could. It got worse when the kids started coming around. I say kids because they looked young to me. Teenagers. That's what tipped her off. They'd come around asking if we were ready for a revolution. Then my father disappeared. Then my uncle. She knew they weren't coming back."

That realization didn't hit Ana until later; even now, a part of her didn't quite accept that her father was not going to emerge one day from that jungle. She never could bring herself to mourn him.

"Then she died," she continued, "and Tía Ofelia came to get me." Her mother's death was a fact. She'd seen the body; she'd buried it. There was nothing more she could say about it, except that she promised herself to never squander the opportunity it gave her to start over. "I got to leave all that, and you know, I thought I could make it all disappear in Lima."

"No, Anita," he said, shaking his head. "That never happens. It's one of the biggest lies you could ever tell yourself. The idea that you can go somewhere and make something disappear. You can't. The ghosts will always follow you."

"But at least you've been able to make yourself into something here," she said. "I couldn't in Lima and I never would. My mother-in-law made that very clear."

Rubén chuckled. "I'm sure she did. If there's one thing Filomena loves, its making sure people know their place in the world."

"She loves a good last name too," she joked. "And money. You don't have a good last name either, Rubén, but at least you had the money. I have nothing! I remember when I told her that I didn't get my father's last name until I was in grammar school. I was always my mother's daughter. I was Ríos. You should've seen the look on Filomena's face." She shushed Rubén as his body shook with laughter. "It's funny now, but I didn't think it was so funny then."

There had been nothing humorous at all about Doña Filomena Falcón. When Ana first met her, it was for lunch at her gated house on Avenida Las Almendras. The floors were made of polished wood. The light from a chandelier drenched the living room in meringue, and on the edge of a velvet couch sat Doña Filomena. Her face showed the Galician blood that Carlos claimed she was so proud of, with her skin as translucent as powder and her hair as black as the charcoal tablets Ana burned on her altar. A widow's peak peered from her forehead like a third eye. She was older than Ana expected. Her skin hung around her mouth and eyes; her nose arched like a beak. Yet her cheeks were curved and soft like a bird's chest. Her eyelashes stood tall and black above vivid disks of sand. Her hair curled into her head like tiny fists. A whisper of pink lipstick touched her wound mouth.

For a long time, she observed her guest, speaking only to her son. When she finally addressed Ana, it was to ask if she aspired to do anything else besides greeting visitors from behind a desk.

Carlos laughed uncomfortably.

Yes, Ana had muttered, though she dared not tell Doña Filomena or even Carlos about her dream of owning a restaurant, afraid they'd find it silly. Instead, she explained that she was going to school at night to study computers.

Doña Filomena did not know what that meant, and so she asked Ana about her father and mother. What did they do? Who is the aunt she's living with?

My father's aunt, she replied, as a young, heavy-set teenager served them tea and cookies. That Ana had too much color, too much accent, and was too obvious of a social climber became evident when she saw that muchacha, a girl Doña Filomena said was from a small town only a few miles south of Santa Clara. Her skin was lighter than Ana's, the result of both a sporadic limeño sun and long days spent inside Doña Filomena's house. Ana could hear the singsong tail end of her words, an accent which took effort for Ana herself to mask. She diverted her eyes as soon as she saw the girl. But Doña Filomena wondered aloud if they might be cousins, since they grew up so close to each other and were almost as dark as her floors. She said this with a chuckle, and Ana scalded her tongue with her tea to avoid a retort.

A year after Carlos brought her home, Lucho told his mother Ana was expecting his child, and that he was going to marry her. Doña Filomena slapped him; she would never accept that garbage. She was una cualquiera, a nobody who slept through her sons and would've slept with her husband too, if he'd been alive, and when Ana heard this from the kitchen, she ran from the house, unable to hear the rest.

"Now there's someone who will never accept me," she said. "To Doña Filo, I'm just a poor cholita who somehow managed to get a job as a receptionist. That's as far as I was going to get in life, unless I found an idiot to marry me. I couldn't snag one son so I got pregnant just to make sure the other one couldn't get away."

"That's not how it is," said Rubén. "I see the way you look at Lucho."

She raised her eyebrows. "Well, that's not what she saw. It's not what your wife sees. They all see what they want to see. Once they make up their minds, there's no changing it."

"Exactly," he said, shifting in his seat and leaning on the table. "And that's why I think it's time Michael met his sister."

"Ah," she said. "You're back on that again. No wonder you can't sleep."

"It's like you say, Anita. It won't make a difference to Valeria. She's going to think the worst no matter what. But it'd change everything for Michael and Nora."

"Nora?" she repeated. "That's good. Naming the girl after your mother." She imagined Valeria batting away tears, her lashes clumping like burned oil, at the sound of his mother's name on another woman's child. "Honestly, Rubén, I don't know how you're still walking."

"Trust me, if Valeria ever did anything to me, you'd never find out," he snickered. "She can lose control sometimes. She just doesn't ever let anyone see it. Anyone but me, that is."

She let out a defeated breath. "To be honest, I doubt she'll ever leave you. She hasn't so far, and like you said, she's proud."

He sucked his teeth and mumbled something beneath his breath. She had little sympathy for the man. The affair, the lies, the disconnect between the children—he caused it all. And even though he was hurting so many, he still managed to sit there, in his large kitchen inside his own home, a man with money, an attractive wife, and a healthy child, and lament the circumstances of his life. Were she not living under his roof, Ana would've told him how he had no right to feel sorry for himself. How she hoped that his wife might one day get the nerve to leave him and take his precious auto body shop with her; that his children might never love him enough to mourn his absence; that his lover wouldn't waste her years waiting for a divorce he most certainly promised but would never go through.

Suddenly, there was what seemed like an apparition at the door frame. Valeria, in a pink pajama set, her face glistening from a coat of night cream, her hair tied in a loose bun at the crown of her head. "¿Qué hacen despiertos?" she asked.

Rubén's face reddened and he hurried off his seat. "I couldn't sleep," he explained. "Ana here was kind enough to offer me some tea."

Ana stood and picked up his cup from the table, then remembered to ask, "Do you want some? There's still water—"

"No, thank you," replied Valeria curtly.

"Thank you for the tea, Ana," he said, then gestured for his wife to go ahead of him. He followed her silently back to their bedroom. No doubt, Valeria didn't like what she interrupted. Ana knew to keep her distance in the days to come.

She was grateful, however, for the interruption. There were enough revelations for one night. It was clear to her that Rubén only stayed with Valeria out of obligation. He didn't love her. He had no remorse for what he'd done, and he wasn't going to stop seeing the other woman either, no matter how much it hurt those who loved him. He didn't even see how he'd wronged Valeria or his children. Was he blind? Ana wondered.

Was she?

No, she was not like him. She and Lucho were on the verge of getting back on their feet. They had lost their way, but things were taking a turn for the better. He had a job; she had hers. Soon, they'd see the apartment Carla had recommended. He looked at her now the way he once did, and even touched her the way he used to. Kissing her neck behind closed doors, venturing to touch her in front of others. She loved him. What she did, she did for them, not out of lust or greed or opportunity, but out of necessity. None of what they had now—Lucho's job, their children's school tuition, the money for a new apartment—none of it was possible if she wasn't willing to adapt, to understand that sacrifice and silence were necessary for their survival.

Her stomach moaned. The water in her cup had cooled. She turned the stove back on, reheating the water that remained in the kettle, and once again opened her address book. She wondered if it was the cod she had for dinner that now unsettled her stomach.

Fish. There were fish in her dream. Piranhas. That was the wall.

She looked at the list again and jotted down "dientes." They had teeth, pointed triangles that gleamed against the moon's reflection. In her dream, the monkeys and the dolphins chased her toward that wall of piranhas. She kicked and whacked them away as they bit, yet they managed to draw blood.

It was the blood that made her spine straighten. She flipped through several pages of her address book, back to the letter *D*. At the top of the second page, she had scribbled "21/10." October 21. She'd drawn a circle around the date. She then flipped a few pages forward, scanning the top corners for any other circled dates, but there were none.

Did she forget to write down December? she wondered. Had she missed any other dates?

She flipped back to *C* and *B* and *A,* and found 13/9, 1/8, 28/6, each encircled. She had written down the first date for every single cycle before October 21, but none after.

She set down the pen. She jogged her memory for clues. When was the last time she used a maxi pad, took a painkiller, placed a warm compress on her abdomen? Was it in November, before Valeria left for Peru? She had been careful, letting Lucho know when it wasn't safe to have sex. Even when she ran out of her pills, she'd been careful.

The kettle rattled, and this time, she turned the knob with such force that it came off the stove. She looked at the date again. October 21. Circled so clearly. Her body had bled then. She'd bled in her dream too.

Sangre. She could see the word, taste it, but she couldn't write it down.

8

THREE MONTHS AFTER THEY LEFT THEIR LAST BROOKLYN APART-ment, Ana and Lucho drove Rubén's station wagon to the southern edge of their old vecindario to see what could be their new home. The building was in a rougher part of the neighborhood, closer to the warehouses and low-lying, boarded-up buildings that lined the outskirts. As they got closer to the address on the torn paper towel Carla had given her, Ana took note of the stores along the main strip: a Salvation Army, a laundromat, a liquor store, a Chinese take-out spot. Sneakers dangled along electric pole wires above them, a contrast to the lights that hung outside Lexar Tower. She counted the corners with crates outside of bodegas—three—and remarked on the number of men standing next to the doors, their faces obscured by dark hoods and their bodies wrapped in heavy coats. "It's winter," Lucho pointed out.

The building itself sat on a corner beside an empty parking lot, on a block that was too quiet, too desolate even for a late December day. The houses across it leaned sideways just enough that Ana could tell they were on the downside of a hill. The bus stop and subway entrance were just four blocks away; the only downside was that a single subway line served the area. Ana could take either to work, or walk if she really wanted to save money. The walk was probably fine by daylight; walking through the area after dark, alone, was out of the question.

When they arrived at the front door, the man who called himself Sully was waiting for them in the building's vestibule. He peeked his owl eyes and boxer's nose through the square glass on the door. The top of his head sprouted white strands, but the curls that fell on his shoulders were a pepper-cinnamon. Finger-shaped dirt stains caked his gray shirt. Threads frayed from the pockets and knees of his saggy jeans. Ana thought he looked odd for a man who owned four buildings. Then again, Betty had said he was cheap.

Apartment 3R was one of two units on the floor, he told them in broken Spanish as they climbed the three flights of cracked staircases. He'd already found a tenant for 3L, but 3R still needed some work. Ana could smell the fresh coat of paint as they ascended. He'd have the apartment ready in a couple of weeks.

It was a railroad-style unit that ran the length of the building, with doors at each end that led to the third-floor stairwell. The front door opened to the kitchen, large enough to fit a table and four chairs, but with appliances that were at least ten years older than those in Valeria's apartment. The tub and toilet were in the center of the kitchen, in two separate, doorless rooms. He was going to install the doors tomorrow, he told them. At the far end was a window, which led to the fire escape. They were high enough that the roofs of several buildings were visible. She could even see the cars racing through the main drag. She imagined herself sitting on the fire escape in the summer, on her sleepless nights with her cup of tea, watching other drivers, other Luchos, pass by.

A door frame separated the kitchen from an elongated room

with two large windows that faced south. Blocks of waning sunlight punched through each one, bouncing off the dull walls that still needed a couple of layers of paint and the torn laminated floors. He was going to replace those, he said. The living room, she decided, might be too hot on summer days.

They then walked through the only door inside the apartment. The bedroom had three windows, giving them a view of all four corners of the streets below. A bulbless, five-light chandelier hung in the center of the room. The ceiling itself had molding: two large squares, one inside the other. Across from the two windows was the second door that led to the stairwell. Carla had been right; the room *was* as big as her living room. It could accommodate their queen-size bed, the bunk bed, and even the dresser. She'd have to cover the radiator to keep the children from burning their hands. Sully said he'd install window grills. "My last tenants had no kids," he explained.

Lucho walked back through the living room, and Sully followed closely. He explained, loud enough so that Ana could hear, that there was a sewage plant nearby, and so if the wind picked up a certain way, it was best to keep the windows closed; that the warehouses brought a lot of truck traffic during the day, and funny characters at night, so's probably best to get stuff done before then; and that a playground a few blocks north hadn't really been played in for years. People mostly slept there.

She heard Lucho say, "Carla said you had other buildings in the area."

"Cuatro," said Sully. "Carla's building. Two more further north. This right here, though, this is probably more—what's that word I hear people say—cómodo."

Affordable. The amount he had quoted over the phone was indeed still within their budget, though at the higher end of the spectrum. Still, if the apartment was getting a facelift, and it was close enough to the children's school and la factoría, it was worth considering.

Then, as Ana joined the men in the living room, Sully told them how much he wanted upfront to secure the lease. First month's rent, last month's rent, and one month's security deposit. For the kids, he said, and in case they ever left in a hurry. He had people once leave in a hurry, so he learned his lesson. Rent had to be in cash on the first of the month.

Ana was too shocked to speak. "Hey, I'm takin' a risk here," he said. "Carla says you's good people. You work hard and got those little kids. I ain't askin' for W-2s or doin' background checks or nothin' like that. I'm tryin' to do some good is all. But I need to cover my ass too." He paused, then decided to wait downstairs to give them time to talk.

They hadn't planned on giving up so much money at once. First month's rent and a security deposit, yes, but not an additional month. "It's too much," Ana whispered as they heard him descend the stairs.

"What choice do we have?" said Lucho. "Everything else we've seen is too expensive or too far. Or in worse shape than this."

"But look at how much he still needs to fix! And did you see the bolsitas by the curb? What kind of cokeros hang around here at night? And then he says we shouldn't even be out at night? You work at night, Lucho."

"He probably just doesn't want the cops around."

"I can see why. He looks like another tecato with all those tattoos on his arms."

"Be grateful they're not on his face. Anyway, the rent's not too bad. We'd be close to the school. The factory's not far. And you heard what he said. He needs another couple of weeks to finish fixing the place up anyway. Maybe we can bring the rest of the money later."

"He won't like that," she said, but Lucho was already heading for the stairwell.

"Come on," he said, "let's find out."

She waited on the first-floor staircase, on a step high enough that she could see Lucho and Sully through the front door's glass window as they spoke outside. She'd given her husband the equivalent of one month's rent, and when she saw both men's eyes look down and Lucho bobbing his head as he mouthed words, she knew he was counting the money.

Sully came inside and held the door open for her. "I better get to work," he said, smiling.

Outside, Lucho was already by the car's driver's-side door. "He said yes," was all he told her as she hopped in.

So that was it. After all those months, all that sacrifice, this was to be their new home. She didn't expect to find anything close to unit 4D, but she couldn't overcome the twinge of disappointment that came with the realization that apartment 3R was the best she could do. She took comfort in one truth: it'd be just the four of them again. They could be one unit, a single marriage under one roof.

On the drive back to Queens, Lucho talked about the setup of the rooms. The bunk bed could go against the second door in the bedroom; their bed by the window. The dresser, he wasn't sure. Maybe it should stay in the living room. They'd have to figure out how to get the rest of the furniture they needed. A couch, a table set. They'd need another few thousand dollars. He started to chew the skin along his fingertips. He'd adjust his hours, work from 8 P.M. to 8 A.M. instead of 6 P.M. to 6 A.M. so he could drop her off at work and the kids at school. They'd save money on the fare. "No, no," she replied, wary of losing her quiet mornings alone. "That doesn't make sense. We lose more if you switch the hours than just paying the fare. I can take them on the bus and walk from there. It's not too far."

He turned on the radio, settling for an English-language station, and humming along to the songs, even though he didn't know any of the lyrics. He pointed out a sedan that swerved up ahead and the red traffic light that took forever to turn green. It struck her that he didn't once mention how they'd get the rest of the money.

It wasn't until they exited the highway that she asked him.

"What do you mean?" he said. "I told Sully he'll have the rest of the money when the apartment is ready."

"But where are we going to get that money?" she asked. "And the money for the table and the couch? You just said we need another thousand or so dollars." She threw her head back, a wave of exhaustion coming over her. They had so little left. She kept every dollar they earned in a canary-colored envelope beneath their mattress. She paid the children's school tuition, gave Valeria money for the utilities, doled out gas money, had a budget for their food, allocated a few twenty-dollar bills for what would go to his mother and Tía Ofelia, but otherwise, Ana eyed every single dollar that went out of that envelope. Any other expense was only justified if a sale or a coupon was attached to it. Rarely did she agree to a five-dollar dress down Friday at the school, and even then, it was only if Victoria had earned enough extra gold stars on her homework to deserve it.

After what she took out that morning, there was just enough money for a couple of weeks' worth of groceries. "I gave you almost all we have," she said. "Or do you have money hidden somewhere that I don't know about?"

"I give you every dollar I make, Ana."

"Then how are we going to get the rest of the money?"

"We've got until the end of the month," he replied. "I'll see if I can work the car a few more hours. You're going to work overtime next week, aren't you? I'm sure you can work more than that. If we really need it, I can always ask Valeria and Rubén—"

"No," she said firmly. "No, you cannot ask them for money."

"Why not? We've never borrowed money from them. I'd tell you to ask Señora Aguilar, but I don't have any more deeds for you to hand out."

She held her tongue. He was lucky to have property with which he could barter. No one wanted his body, so his body was never something he could offer up. He had never negotiated with Mama; it was Ana. Always Ana because, he had said to her once, she's a woman. Hablen entre mujeres. But this was not a "woman thing;" it was a money thing. There was no bank to loan them money, only Mama. Mama didn't care about green cards or social security numbers. She cared about passports, and when Ana first asked her for a loan, she'd given the woman all four. It wasn't until Lucho lost his job, and Ana asked to borrow more money, that Mama wanted something of actual value, something tangible that would ensure she got paid whether they were in New York, in Peru, or in a grave. Ana had already pawned their jewelry, and so she gave her the only thing they had left that was of any real value: the deed to Lucho's house in Lima.

When he came home that day, she told him that Mama had given her the money, that she'd gone and paid the rent, bought groceries for the week. The chuletas were frying on the pan. The rest of the money was in the canary envelope underneath the mattress. "Just like that?" he asked, surprised at how easily she'd gotten the cash. Then she told him how. "My mother's house?" he said, going white. "You gave her my mother's house?" He walked out, leaving her to the pork chops she still had crackling on the stove.

When they needed more money, she had to come up with other ways to get it, other sources. In her mind, it was the only way to stay; it had to be her burden. That's how she ended up at Don Beto's.

If Lucho had any more deeds, she would've offered them to Mama months ago. "At least Mama doesn't nag me every day for her money," she said. "Valeria on the other hand. I've got to stuff toilet paper in my purse just to shut her up when we run out of cereal."

"Here we go," he groaned.

"Are you tired of hearing this, Lucho? You don't want to hear how she comes home from the shop and goes straight to eat the dinner that *I* make? Then grabs a beer or pours some vodka in her soda and spends the rest of the night in her room watching telenovelas?"

"So what if she does?" he countered. "She can do whatever she wants. It's her home. You should stop pretending like it's yours."

"Because I cook and clean? God forbid I want to eat real food and not live in a mess."

"It's not just the cooking and the cleaning, Ana. It's you planning the holiday parties and inviting your friends over without asking her."

"So she complained to you about New Year's? Am I not allowed to have my friends over to celebrate?"

"No one's saying they can't come. But it's *her* house. You should've asked her what she wanted to do or if she wanted to do anything at all."

"She never said no," she cried. She leaned against the car's door and rubbed her temple. "I don't even know why I bother. I'm your *wife*, Lucho. *Your wife*. But you always take her side, always."

"Ana, listen to yourself. You complain that she eats your food and drinks too much, and that she asks about the apartment search. I would too if I had people living with me for three months."

"Carla let us stay with her longer than that, and she isn't even family."

"Things were different back then! Carla and Ernesto were living alone. They had space. Do you think the Lazartes would even open their door to us now with three kids and Betty under their roof?"

She didn't want to admit that he had a point. When they first arrived in New York, Carla had offered up their home while the family settled in to the city. After all, she had known Ana since she was a child, and Ana was Betty's closest friend. And she was a steady, hardworking woman with several mouths to feed. Lucho was a good man too. So she helped Ana get a social security number and a green card from an acquaintance in Jackson Heights, and then the job at la factoría. Ernesto's friend found Lucho a job at the meat-packing plant. And Carla had offered to watch the children when Ana wanted to work evenings at Regina's.

But even the Lazartes had their limits, and after a few months of hearing Carla complain to friends over the phone about not having free weekends and the constant mess in the apartment, Ana knew it was time to go.

She expected it to be different with Valeria because she was family. But why would it be when in so many ways, she was closer to Carla than she was to Valeria?

"She might not be the easiest person to live with," Lucho continued, "but if we're still in this country it's only because she's helped us. And believe me, we're only staying here because it's what *you* want."

"What I want?" she asked. "I don't even understand what it is you want to go back to, Lucho."

"You don't?" He pounded each finger against the steering wheel as he counted off his reasons. "My mother, my house, my friends. Work. *Real* work, not—" he slapped his hand against the wheel, "this."

The work he'd found in New York had always been an issue. The jobs were menial, and his frustration was exacerbated by his broken English. His Peruvian college degree and his work as a research assistant at a university in Lima meant little in New York. Manual work, something he had little experience with, was all he could find. Cutting up meat, cleaning small office spaces, driving a cab. She suspected he preferred nocturnal work to daylight labor because no one could see what he did for a living.

In her mind, they were fortunate just to have a way to earn a living. "There's no work there," she said, "not even for you." She had never identified herself with a job. A job was a job; it was a way to keep one's belly full and one's head dry in a storm. There were other things, however, that she wished he'd see, things that might make him understand why it was simply impossible for her to go back. "You do realize your mother thinks the worst of me. And that house of yours? It's falling apart, Lucho. Those *friends* are in prison. Is that what you want to go back to?"

"They're not criminals," he said.

"Right, they want to make a difference. Just like every other terrorist."

"Terrorist? You can't possibly compare activism to terrorism."

"They blurred the lines, didn't they? Why else were they arrested?"

"Because they wanted to show the military for what it really is. Soldiers aren't protecting anybody, you know that. They're too busy snorting and getting all that cocaine to these Americans." He turned down the radio. "And that's what I don't get. I don't get why you've bought into this idea that this country's lo máximo. All it's ever done is suck us dry and manipulate our people and our leaders. That's what Marzullo, Perry, and Bautista were standing up for. La patria. That's what I should've done, but instead, here I am." He took a hard left as they turned onto a residential street. A car honked, but he cursed as he sped past it. "This country's made it so bad that we can't stay in Peru, but they don't want us here either. We're fucked no matter where we are."

She didn't pretend to understand his anger. He'd read more, studied more than she, and sometimes spoke with such fervor about the pillaging of Peru and the continent as a whole that no one could argue with him. In his mind, the world had ignored how much his country had bled, whether it was gold, coca, or the blood of its very children. It never labored for its own people; others still held the whip.

Yet in her mind, he could never understand just how much Peru hemorrhaged from within. The promise of a better future, one she'd heard about in the classroom as a child, cut its way into the country. It was a future that was only possible with the blanching of brightly colored clothes, the fading of patterns that had been worn for centuries; in the undoing of braids and the disappearance of tongues for a single, dominant one. That was Peru's way forward. Lucho was criollo, already the harbinger of that future, with his light skin, his gray slacks, and that side part. He was already obsessed with the purity and preservation of the Spanish language. Why else would he spend hours reading the Spanish-language newspapers in New York, searching for, as he put it, the butchering of the mother tongue? That and his last name, so clearly not born of the land, could get him a job with relative ease, and therefore, he could debate the fairness of his compensation, the meddling of outsiders, and what could be done to preserve the house his father had bought.

She could not debate such things. In Lima, she was plainly a woman, dark-skinned at that, from some mountainous province, with only a couple of decades left before she'd be considered too old to hire. She hid her accent and tried her best to remove from her everyday speech any words from Santa Clara that could cloud her Spanish. She didn't have the luxury of debating a salary, and when she got that job as a receptionist, it was as though she'd won el premio mayor. She didn't care to preserve anything tangible from the past. It was enough that the house of her childhood still lived in her memory. She was always willing to adapt, something he didn't need to do back home. She wondered if that, and not his disdain for this new country, was at the heart of his frustration.

"I don't feel like we're fucked," she said. "Things here were good in the beginning. We had work. That's all we ever really wanted, right? To work and provide for the kids. To support our families. We had that. We've never had to worry about food. We can buy groceries without worrying that some lunatic might blow us up. And the kids! They speak two languages, Lucho." The thought alone filled her with pride. "They can do so much more here," she whispered. "*We* can be so much more."

"I'm nothing here." He turned onto another street and pulled into the Lexar Tower parking lot. "I'm doing all I can, Ana. I don't know what else you want me to do."

She inhaled sharply. "Can you ask Rubén if we can stay a little longer?" she asked, but he was already shaking his head. "Just until we've saved up some more money?"

"No," he said emphatically. "I'm tired of living like arrimados. If we're not living with Carla and Ernesto, we're living with Valeria and Rubén. And that's the thing about this place. You always need help. It's not enough that we work hard. Doesn't that tell you something?"

She looked out her passenger-side window. She promised herself, when they left Peru, that she'd never complain. That no matter how difficult it was to live and work in another place, another tongue, she wouldn't lament the hardships that came with it. She'd look forward, always. "We can't go back," she said.

He pointed to Lexar Tower's entrance. "We can't stay there either. And we're not going to move into a place like that. Don't expect neighbors who look or dress like the people who live here." He pulled into a parking spot and turned off the engine. He left the music playing. "We can afford that apartment. I don't know for how long, but if you want to stay here, Ana, then that is the next step. Or we can send the kids back. Because that's the only way we're going to make things work here."

"So you'd send them back?" she said. "You'd take my children away from me? Is that what you're telling me?"

"It's not taking them away from you. It's doing what's best for *us*. Be reasonable. If you lose your job or if this cab driver thing doesn't work out, then we should send them back. And if the two of us still can't make it work here then we can't make it work and we'll go back." He tilted his head against the headrest, indulging in whatever memory he thought they could return to. "We can always go back."

■ ■ ■

UPSTAIRS, SHE HEARD VALERIA URGING THE CHILDREN TO EAT THEIR dinner. She was waiting for a friend to pick up a package she'd brought back from Peru, which gave Ana and Lucho a window in which they could see the apartment. Valeria's trips to Peru had not only become more frequent; they'd grown more voluminous, and Ana expected more visitors in the days to come.

The children forgot their meal as Ana and Lucho walked through the door. "Mami, mira," said Pedro as he jumped from his seat with Michael's game console in his hands. "Look what I can do."

"You have to eat!" shouted Valeria.

Victoria, meanwhile, grabbed ahold of her father. "Papi, can you help me with this?" she asked him in English as she handed him her workbook.

"Háblame en español," he said, holding the workbook out in front of him for an instant then handing it back. "This is easy, Victoria. Start and I'll take a look at it tomorrow." She slumped over like a marionette. "I wouldn't tell you to do it if I didn't think you could," he said "and you can. If there's one language that's more important than any other, it's math. Give it a try."

"You're not going to eat?" asked Valeria.

He spun his hat in his hands. "No, thank you, Prima, I don't have much of an appetite at the moment." He walked into the bathroom, swapped his sweater for a new one, and left for his shift without saying goodbye.

Once Ana was certain he was gone, she pulled the canary envelope from underneath her mattress. It carried part of their journey: birth certificates, diplomas, and what was left of the money they were able to save since Lucho started working again.

It wasn't enough.

She heard his words over and over. *Ellos pueden regresar,* he'd said. *Podemos regresar.* He had no qualms about sending the children back, and he held on to some romanticized notion about what life in Peru could be, not what it was. He could never truly see it with her eyes.

She searched the top bunk of the bed, where Victoria slept. The doll wasn't there and she wasn't on Pedro's bottom bunk or on the floor. Ana's own bed was empty.

She called Victoria from the hallway, and when she came into the bedroom, she asked, "Where's Liliana?"

Victoria ran back to Michael's room. When she returned, Ana reminded her daughter, "She stays here."

Victoria rolled her eyes and pouted.

"Don't make that face," said Ana. "She stays on your bed y punto."

"Sorry, Mami," she muttered in English.

"Don't give me 'sorry.' Se dice 'perdón.'"

She told Victoria to go then shut the door behind her. The doll's squishy blonde head popped easily from its body. Inside it, was Ana's money. It was money she'd siphoned away from Lucho. People always left—it was a fear she carried with her ever since her father disappeared and one that only became more pronounced with time. Her and Lucho's work schedules never overlapped, and she often wondered, on her nights alone, if he'd come back. Would he be tempted away by a memory of Peru, by the escape of a drink or two, or even another woman? When he began driving the cab, it was the fear of an accident or a robbery that kept her up. Now, it was simply the stillness of the night she feared, with its power to drown one in an ocean of thoughts.

It was this fear of his imminent departure that made Ana put money away, a little every time she got paid, in five-dollar bills, tens, occasionally a twenty. She kept the money inside the doll's body, a doll she'd purchased at a discount store only months after they arrived in New York and that Victoria protested smelled funny. She instructed her daughter to leave it on her bed always and, when they moved in to Valeria's, that it should never leave the room. She didn't use the money when Lucho was unemployed, and she wasn't going to give it up now. Not for the new apartment; not after he said he'd consider sending the children back. If it ever came to that, she needed enough money to leave him. She needed to find another source of money for the new apartment, and she had another problem now, one that she needed to fix as soon as possible.

And so she called Mama.

9

THE SUN CLUNG TO THE DARKENING SKY AS ANA TURNED THE COR-
ner onto Mama's street the following afternoon. She had stopped
by a Polish bakery, picking up a loaf of the woman's favorite cake to
help her cause. She suspected Mama would say no to another loan,
but she was going to ask anyway. There was always the chance the
woman might say yes, and if she did, Ana could avoid dipping into
her own money. Asking Don Beto for help wasn't an option. Once
she realized she missed her period, she knew whatever it was they
had simply had to end. There was too much already at risk. She had
no plans to return the money he'd given her. It was hers now.

When she arrived at Mama's, her skin bristled at the sight of
Don Beto's black loafers sitting on the shoe tray. She placed her
sneakers beside them, making sure they didn't touch.

Inside the apartment, she searched the living room for any signs
of the man, but it only had Mama's indelible imprints. The faint
scent of Jean Naté emanated from the bathroom. The radiator
hummed its familiar tune along with the woman's labored breaths.
The issues of *Vanidades* were piled on the table as always. Still, he
came back to her all at once. The scent of rum under her nose, the

sound of his fingers fumbling her belt buckle, his breath heavy in her ear. The skin on her stomach retracted, and she folded her arms across her chest to steady herself.

"Take your coat off," said Mama.

Ana shuddered at the command and held her coat closer. "I'm cold," she replied.

"Then make some tea." Mama turned and headed toward the sitting room. "I already have water in the kettle. Bring the babka too."

Minutes later, Ana set a pot of tea and slices of babka on the coffee table. She sipped her tea as a Cuban judge on the television screen debated whether one neighbor owed another money for a dog bite.

"You're quiet," said Mama, as she brought a slice of babka to her mouth. "You just paid me so I know you're not here for that. Tell me what it is you came here to say."

Ana looked straight at the television screen. "We found an apartment."

"That's good," replied Mama, her eyes widening. "That cab business must be going well then."

"Not as well as we'd like," said Ana. "See, we found an apartment. Close to the children's school. Not too far from the factory. The landlord's painting it. Fixing it up. The rent's reasonable. The neighborhood is real quiet too."

"Then what's the problem?" said Mama, tapping her fingers on the armrest.

"The landlord wants an extra month's rent," said Ana. "We've only got enough for two. I was hoping you could lend us the rest."

Mama threw her head back and let out a sound, a single "ja" that was meant to be anything but a laugh. "You're behind on payments, Ana. Why would I give you more money?"

"Because I can pay it back," she said. "Lucho's going to work longer hours. He's worked it out with the car owner already. He's signed up with two bases now. I'm going to work overtime. I know we're still catching up, but the rent is affordable, and we can move in by the end of the month."

"I think it's better for *me*," said Mama, "if you stay at your cousins'. You don't pay rent there. You can pay me back faster. Then maybe, once you're caught up, we can talk about another loan for you to move out."

"But we'll lose that apartment."

"There'll be others. I can make some calls for you when the time is right."

She was taken aback by her response, but Ana didn't want Mama's help either. If she lived in one of her buildings, or in one that belonged to a friend or a client, then what? She'd be far from cutting ties with the woman or Don Beto.

"I appreciate the help, but this apartment is good for us, and the timing is right. I can pay you back, I promise."

"Why the rush to leave now anyway?" she asked. "You've been at your cousins' for some time, I know, but what difference does another month or even two make? Have you worn out your welcome already?"

She had, though Mama didn't need to know that nor how much Ana actually wanted to stay at Lexar Tower. But Lucho was right—it was Valeria's home, and while she was away, Ana could pretend and play house all she wanted. Now that Valeria was back, she had to face reality. She was homeless, and that put her in a precarious spot. She suspected that in the moments she wasn't looking, Valeria was whispering to Lucho, filling his head with doubt about her, about their lives here, and how much easier it would be if the children were in Lima. Lucho's threat to send the children back, or go back altogether, was real enough that Ana was prepared to move into a cave if it meant keeping her family in New York and intact.

She didn't want to appear ungrateful, however, especially toward her own family, and so she said, "My cousin has been very good to us. Generous and patient, like you. But it's not easy, finding a place to live. Especially when you tell these landlords you've got kids. If we don't get this apartment, Mama, then who knows when there'll be another one like it."

"You're right in that sense," said Mama. "You're going to be undocumented for a long time. Unless there's some sort of amnesty, you might never get your residency. Your kids might never have their papers either. You're better off settling somewhere." She became quiet, eyeing Ana for several seconds, then asking, "Have you thought about going back?"

"Everyone in our situation thinks about it," she said. "But there's nothing for my kids there."

Mama set her cup down on the table and folded her hands over her belly. She fixed her eyes on Ana, digging. "You know, I never did ask why you left. I assumed it was the same story as always. No work there, better future for your children here. It's like a script. But I never got that impression from you. I always thought maybe there was more."

"We did come for the kids," she said quickly. It was the first time she heard herself say it so unconvincingly.

Mama thrusted her lower lip as if to sputter. "You're a terrible liar, Ana."

She blushed, suddenly exposed. *Is this what she needed to do?* she thought. It seemed unfair, that she had to give—to show— more than she wanted to in order to get what she wanted.

"I came here because there really is nothing for me in Peru," she said. "Nothing. I lost everything I had back in Santa Clara."

"Because of the terrorists," said Mama.

"Not just Sendero," she said, "although that's why we can't go back now. I mean the soldiers. From the capital." She pulled her legs up on the chair. "Sent in to save us."

She recalled how her mother used to sit on her father's lap, sweeten her voice, hold his face in her hands as she kissed him in his rocker, when they thought they were alone. Ana used to crane her neck, peer from the kitchen or bedroom as she swept, and watch.

After her father and uncle disappeared, it was her mother and Colonel Mejía whom she watched from outside her mother's bedroom window. Unlike her father, the Colonel would grab her silent mother's face with his broad fingers and press his lips onto hers even as her mother kept her mouth shut.

Then one day, the Colonel saw Ana at the window. She tried to hide, but her mother found her in the coop and beat her, weeping as she smacked her. She promised to break her teeth if she ever said anything to anyone about what she saw. Even now, just hinting at the truth so many years later, felt like a betrayal.

"I could've had a brother or sister, if it hadn't been for the soldiers."

Mama crinkled her brows. "What are you saying?" she asked. "Was your mother pregnant?"

It was on one oppressive afternoon, months after Colonel Mejía's visits had begun and as the sun bore through the kitchen window, that Ana heard her mother wailing in the bedroom. She called out to Ana and asked her to bring an olla. The big one, Doña Sara had said, and Ana brought the largest pot they had to her mother's bedside. Doña Sara drew up her skirt, told her daughter to leave, and to pull down the curtain behind her.

That evening, Ana watched her mother amble toward a corner of the huerta where she patiently dug a hole with a small shovel. Beside the hole was the pot, its metal skin reflecting the light from the star-drenched sky. She shook the pot, and whatever was in there slid into the hole. When she was done burying it, Doña Sara knelt beside the mound and wept for only seconds, but even now, her whimper was as blue as the heavens had been on that cool summer night.

"No, no," she said, reprimanding herself for hinting at her mother's secret. "I just think, if the soldiers were really trying to protect us, then they would've done more to protect her. She'd still be alive."

Weeks after the burial, when the mound had nearly flattened against the rest of the earth in the huerta and as Ana returned from school, she noticed that her mother was not waiting for her at the door, as she always did in the afternoons. She tiptoed inside, unsettled by the hush that filled the dim shack. A hen cackled, and she followed the sound to the huerta, gleaming under the cloudless sky. She walked toward the coop, where the cackling had grown louder. Behind it, almost obscured by the wood and leaves, was her mother's dead body. Her eyes bulged from her face; her underwear was at her ankles.

"But she was a poor woman and she was alone," Ana continued. "And then I was." It was only with the passage of time, with motherhood in particular, that she began to see her mother for what she was. She did what she had to do to keep them alive. She adapted—to her father's work and absence, his disappearance, to Colonel Mejía. Her mother began to reveal herself in unexpected ways. Whenever Ana rubbed an egg over her children's bodies after a nightmare in an effort to pull away their fear, just like her mother had done to her. Or during her morning walk to la factoría, when the air still held on to the coolness of the night, so reminiscent of their quiet walks to the market. Or those late evenings when she sat on a fire escape, wondering if her mother was finally at rest among the passing clouds in that starless sky. "Anyway, they didn't care enough to protect her, why would they care about protecting me?"

"You feel unsafe there?" she asked.

"That, and because unless you look like that judge or have a last name that sounds nothing like Ríos, you don't matter much," she said. "And I come from nothing. My father cut down wood and planted crops. My mother washed the neighbors' laundry for a living. What your name is, who your parents are. What you look like. Where you come from. Those things matter more in some places than where you actually want to go. And I can't go anywhere there."

Mama shrugged. "If you say so. I have to tell you, Peru doesn't sound much different than here."

"But there's work here," she said.

"There is, which is why I'm better off if you stay put."

Ana bit her lip then took a shot. "Does this mean you'll lend me the money?"

Mama scoffed. "I meant stay put at your cousin's. I'm not an ATM, Ana. The answer is no. Unless you have something else to offer as collateral."

"I just have the deed—"

"No, *I* have the deed to that house in Lima. Anything else?"

Her shoulders fell, her gaze shifted to the floor.

"Then I won't be lending you any more money."

She spoke plainly, as if it didn't matter that Ana had no place to live, or that she might be separated from her children. It was black and white. She owed the woman money. There was no chance of her lending Ana any more until she got paid.

But who else could she ask? She wasn't going back to Don Beto. No more of that. She wasn't going to lose her children either. "Mama, I need that apartment," she pleaded.

"Then you should've paid me. And you shouldn't have disappeared like you did. You realize I could've done some real damage to you, Ana. I could've sold that house in Lima, but I didn't. You know why? Because I actually have some compassion for you. I understand you're in a difficult situation. That's why I'm being patient, but understand that it's not my way. If I lent out money to every pobretona with a sad story then I'd be penniless myself." Her voice grew louder. "Now, I could be just like others in my position and give you that money. I'll wait for you to miss a payment, which you will, and then I'd have no other choice but to sell your house. Because that's the business that I'm in. That's the agreement you and I have. And I'm starting to think that you have a really hard time understanding what it means to not fuck around with other people's money." She peered over the top of her glasses, her eyes boring into Ana. "But see, I'm giving you the benefit of the doubt. I'm telling you to get caught up, keep up your payments, and then we'll see. I'm doing you a favor. If you can't see that then that's a very big problem for you."

"But Mama," Ana whispered, "it's not a lot of mon—"

"It's *my* money!" she hollered. "And every penny I lend out is a lot to me. I earned every dollar I lend you and people like you. That's my money that you're using to fuel whatever ambition you have here. It's not insignificant to either of us. If it were, you wouldn't be asking for it. So don't trivialize it." Her cup hit the table with a high-pitched clank. "Pay me what you owe me. I don't care what you or your husband need to do to pay me back, just do it. Do it on time and exactly in the amount you said you'd pay each week. Then maybe we can talk about another loan. Until then, don't come asking me for more money, or believe me, I'll start making a few phone calls. The first will be to my new tenant in Peru. Filomena, was it?" She settled into her seat and turned her attention back to the middle-aged male defendant and his Pomeranian. In seconds, she was cackling as the plaintiff showed pictures of the dog's alleged bites to a befuddled judge.

This was a joke to her, thought Ana. She—Ana—was an absolute joke.

She resisted the urge to leave, though she wanted nothing more than to run out and scream. But Mama hadn't said she could go. She was fettered to the woman. Until she repaid her debt, until she could reclaim the passports and the deed, she was shackled to her. Even when she did pay off the debt, she'd still need her. Who else was going to lend her money when she needed it? Who else but Mama?

She needed to make sure things between them were fine. The judge ruled in favor of the neighbor, and as the newscast began, a familiar face appeared on the screen—that of the reporter who looked so much like Mama's son.

And so Ana cleared her throat and asked, "How is your son?"

Mama's head snapped. "My son?" she repeated, tilting her left ear toward Ana as if she'd misheard.

"Yes, your son," said Ana, a little louder. "When I called last week, Don Beto said you were out. He said your son was here. I was just wondering how he was. I don't remember him visiting before."

"Why are you talking to Alberto about my son?"

Ana felt her face flush. "He just—he mentioned him when I

called the other day," she stammered and pointed to the television. "And the reporter. You once said he reminded you of him."

Mama stiffened. "Why do you care?"

"I don't," said Ana. "I mean, I just thought I'd ask since he doesn't visit much, right? And like you said, everyone has a reason for coming here."

Suddenly, Mama bolted from her seat, her sluggishness gone. Her hand was up in the air, ready to strike. Ana gasped, recoiling into the chair. Mama stopped short of hitting her. She panted as she loomed over Ana. She had a reputation of being lenient with her clients, more so than others in her line of business. Perhaps because her clients were mostly female and immigrants. But there were also rumors about what happened to those who crossed her. She sold property; she destroyed passports. But she also had men show up at schools, at work, at a parent's nursing home. Sometimes, her clients got beaten and robbed. Sometimes, they were told to go to Mama's to recover whatever was taken, and they were always told to think twice about going to the hospital. Going to the police was never an option.

She was close enough now that Ana could feel the heat of her body, how it was on the verge of exploding. All she could do was turn her face away, curl her legs closer to her chest. She could let Mama break anything but her face.

Instead, Mama set her hands on the arms of the chair, caging Ana in. "What do you want me to tell you?" she said menacingly. "What do you want to hear? That he's gay? Is that what Alberto told you? Or that my son has cancer?"

Ana shut her eyes, her head stayed low.

"His," Mama began to say, then struggled as she said, "*friend* told me. He thought I should know. He thought I should see my son before he dies." She straightened, her body as still as the air. The reporter signed off as he wrapped up his story. The anchorwoman thanked him for the report. "Get out," she said, and Ana sprinted from her seat. She grabbed her coat and shoes, putting them on as she scrambled to the building's front door. It wasn't until she heard the door slam behind her that she remembered to breathe.

10

SNOW DESCENDED AS ANA HURRIED TO LA FACTORÍA. THE STREETS already slumbered under a thick blanket of white, as the first snowfall of the season fell overnight. She had left Lexar Tower nearly an hour before her usual time, squeezed between the doors of a packed number 7 train, forgetting her lunch in the rush, all in an effort to get to la factoría early and speak to Betty. Time was not on her side. The longer she took to take care of her problem, the harder it'd become to fix. Mama's refusal to help left her with only one option: she had to use the money she'd tucked away inside Liliana.

But she needed Betty's help. She needed something to make the blood come.

When she arrived, the snow had become lighter. The usual crew of smokers was standing outside, huddled and listening intently to the latest bit of gossip. Betty, however, wasn't in the crowd. Then she heard a car horn honk twice. Ana looked in its direction and recognized the green van immediately. It was Ernesto Lazarte's. Carla waved from the seat on the passenger's side.

Ana crossed the street and headed over to the driver's side to greet her son's godfather just as he rolled down his window.

"Surprised to see me, Comadrita?" he asked, showing off his tall, bright teeth. His silver-striped black hair was gelled back, unmovable. The tint in his aviator glasses was a shade lighter than the golden Lady of Guadalupe pendant that banged against the graying hair on his chest. For as long as Ana could remember, he never seemed to find the top buttons on his shirts.

"I am, Compadrito," she said, nodding to Carla and Betty, who was sitting in the back seat. Ernesto worked at night, as part of the maintenance crew of an office tower in midtown Manhattan. When she lived with the Lazartes, he was rarely home before midnight. "I thought you'd be with the kids."

"Hugo's watching them," he said, referring to his twelve-year-old son. "That boy's got to learn responsibility someday. Why not start now? Besides, I couldn't let my queen here walk in all this snow." He then pointed toward Betty. "Or that princess over there."

"I told you, I can walk," said Betty.

He threw his head back. "You can never win with that one," he said, smiling. "¿Y mi Compadrito? When's he gonna get permission to come watch a game with me?"

"Lucho doesn't need my permission," said Ana.

"Oh, come now," he chuckled. "You've got the poor man practically locked away in that little room of yours. You should let him out sometimes."

In truth, there was little the two men had in common. Lucho had only a passing interest in sports, while Ernesto liked to reminisce about his childhood playing soccer on a dirt field along the edges of Callao; how he dreamt, like every other little boy, of one day making it onto the national team. He had never finished high school, unlike Lucho who had spent several years studying economics at the university. Ernesto had spent his youth working alongside his widowed mother, peddling flowers and pictures of saints to those who came to mourn the dead at Santa Rosa cemetery, where his own father was buried. He eventually found work as a bouncer at a nightclub, the kind of place where only men were allowed and where the women working inside were encouraged to do whatever they wanted, short of prostitution. At least that was how Carla had described it to her once. The nightclub had been Carla's first job in Lima and it was where she and Ernesto met. He wasn't a physically intimidating man, and Ana thought it an odd job for someone with his build. He had neither the height nor the frame to elicit fear. But he was a hustler, exuding an eagerness and do-anything attitude that was charming and almost chilling.

"You'll see him tomorrow," said Carla. The Lazartes were celebrating New Year's Eve at Lexar Tower. "Then you can invite him to your little soccer parties yourself. Though I'm sure el Compadrito has better things to do than waste his time drinking cheap beer and lamenting stupid World Cup dreams." She snickered and Ernesto tightened his smile. She then leaned over her husband. "Anita, why don't you and Betty go on ahead? I'll meet you upstairs."

Carla hadn't finished speaking when Betty began exiting the van.

"I'll see you tomorrow," Ana said to Ernesto as he cleared his throat. She had lived long enough with the Lazartes to know when they were arguing.

When she and Betty got to la factoria's door, the smokers were gone. Olga was standing outside. "Get upstairs," she said briskly.

"Is everything okay?" asked Ana, surprised by her tone.

"Everything's fine," she said. "I just need you to get upstairs." Betty ran back to the van to get Carla.

George was already on the fourth floor when they arrived. He held a rolled-up sheet of paper in one hand, which he used to shepherd the women inside. "Vamos, muchachas, adentro," he said.

Minutes later, Olga took her place beside him like a sentinel. The bell rang, and the two began to make their way through the room. He tapped the paper into the palm of his hand as he stopped by each island. Olga translated. Since she'd been at la factoría, Ana had only seen this scenario play out three times: once, when George had to let go of some workers, then again when the boss was coming for a visit. The last time was after the raids in June, when immigration rushed into a nearby meat-packing plant, stuffed men and women into vans, and made them disappear. It was the same raid that had spooked Lucho's boss and prompted him to let him go.

But Ana always assumed immigration didn't matter much to George. It was Carla who'd gotten her the job there, and although she now had her green card, she'd been working at la factoría for years with fake documents as she waited for Ernesto to divorce the American he'd married for papers. Ana's hand had quivered as she tried to give George her documents. She had memorized the numbers on the social security card, repeating them to herself and pausing where the dashes were. At the time, remembering the address where she supposedly lived was much harder. But George only pointed at Olga, and Ana handed her the documents instead. Olga made copies, then handed them right back.

When they reached Ana's station, it was Olga who spoke. "Something happened with one of the girls," she said. Ana glanced at the other women, but their eyes were glued to the floor.

Olga continued translating. "I don't ask too many questions. Mainly because I don't know if you're lying or telling the truth. What you do outside of here is your business. All I ask is that you don't do anything stupid."

George had given a similar speech after the June raids. "Behave" was the takeaway from that lecture. Don't do anything that's going to get everyone into trouble, like getting arrested. If your papers didn't check out, and immigration got involved, and an officer asked where you lived, and where you worked, it could be a problem for George, who didn't ask too many questions and simply wanted good seamstresses who could be invisible outside the factory walls.

It was then that Ana realized Nilda's station was empty. Was she late or had she decided to be visible?

"It's very simple," Olga continued, "just don't do anything stupid. That includes your husbands and boyfriends."

When Olga finished translating, George slapped the rolled-up paper into his palm. "Do we understand?" he said. The women nodded, and he slapped the paper one more time against his palm before he moved to the next set of stations with Olga trailing behind him.

When they were far enough away, Ana asked the women who it was he was talking about. "Your friend Nilda," said one. "Remember how she came in here the other day, flashing those earrings?"

"The ones her husband gave her?" said Ana.

"¿Ese hambriento?" replied the seamstress. "¡Qué va! It was that man, the one who gave her a ride home the other night. Well, her boy saw them this time. Can you believe that? She let her kid see them. Apparently they were kissing right outside their building. Qué descarada."

"What was that boy doing up that late?" asked Betty.

"He was waiting for his mother, of course," said the seamstress. "He told his father. He hit her, she punched him, the other man got involved. Someone called the police, and of course they all got arrested."

"Wait, so her husband hit her because someone else gave her a ride home?" asked Ana.

"A man that wasn't her husband," Carla pointed out.

"So what?" said Ana. "If he cared so much about appearances, he should've picked her up himself."

"But then who would watch the boy?" said one woman.

"If I worked at a bar, I wouldn't want my child to know," said another. "And we all know what kind of bar Nilda was working at."

"She should've been more careful," said Betty, sympathetically. "She's got that boy and no papers."

"I thought her husband had papers," said Ana.

"He does," said Carla, "but she never got them. After all these years and a kid, she's still undocumented." The women began to mumble. Why had it taken so long if they were married? Maybe the boy wasn't his, some speculated, or perhaps filing the paperwork was too expensive. Then she should've spent that bar money on a good lawyer instead of highlights and getting her nails done, said others. Now, she's got herself arrested and soon she'll be on a plane back to Ecuador.

Ana went pale. "She's getting deported?"

Carla nodded. "She's had a deportation order from God knows when. So yes."

Ana's mouth was on the floor. *How does a mother get deported?* she thought. Stupid, stupid Nilda. Why had she let herself be seen?

She then looked toward the windowless gray door, near the corner, several islands away. It was only partially visible. Rolls of fabric leaned against it.

Betty whispered, "Do you think she told them about this place?"

Carla cocked her head toward George. "That one is obviously nervous. But I wouldn't worry. This country's got better things to do than deport a bunch of seamstresses. All the rapists and murderers out there. All those idiots with money putting coke up their noses. No, I don't think she'd say anything. She's got no reason to."

The fans' whirr grew deafening. Some of the women on the floor had papers; most had husbands. If the husband acted up, those with papers could call the cops if they wanted. The others had to remain quiet to stay in the country with their children.

"What about her boy?" asked Ana.

"With her husband, I imagine," said a seamstress. "Hopefully that other man of hers can get her back. Otherwise, who knows if Nilda'll ever see that boy again."

They didn't speak of Nilda for the rest of the morning, yet Ana couldn't stop thinking about her. The thought of Nilda's son being motherless made her chest tighten. She focused on the fabric between her fingers, on each stitch that galloped across the terrain. *Some things are meant to be together,* she thought. *Like these pieces of fabric. Like mother and child. Even Nilda and her son.*

She glanced at the gray door again. On her very first day, it was one of the few things Carla had pointed out, along with the bathroom, the lunch room, and the supply closet. It was mostly unremarkable, painted the same impenetrable gray as the walls. Its knob was round and small, as if it were made for the hand of a child or a small woman. La factoría's first laborers, Ana concluded, were smaller than her. The workers were different now, but she realized the knob was made for someone with a hand much like her own. She had never ventured through it. In fact, she had never seen anyone use it. But on that first day, Carla had told her that the door led to the basement which had a cellar door that opened to the street on the edge of the river.

For days after Lucho lost his job, she kept a close eye on it. But it wasn't until now that she noticed the rolls of fabric that seemed to block it. Had they always been there?

She walked over and began to move them. Betty helped her lay the rolls against the others that had accumulated by the wall. Ana turned the knob, cold and dented, and the door clicked open. It was heavy, and she struggled to open it. Betty slid her hands between the door and the frame and helped her pull. "Esta puerta está más pesada que un matrimonio mal llevado," she said, and the women laughed nervously. Ana peered into the stairwell. Dark, but there was enough light that she could see the steps that led down to the floor below.

She went back to her station, satisfied that she could fit through the narrow spaces between the islands and make her way to the door in a matter of seconds. And then there were the handbags. If only the women kept them underneath their feet instead of in the gaps. But the handbags were easy. She could simply kick or jump over them. It was the other bodies that worried her. If immigration came, would she have to shove her way around dozens of women in a panic, or just sweep past those frozen in fear? There'd be other workers on the stairs, from the third, second, first floors. She'd have to maneuver around them as well. And they weren't all un-documented. Some had papers, like Carla. Maybe they'd step aside to let her and the others through. Whether bag or body, she'd do what she needed to get out of there, claw through the Carlas and even climb over the Bettys in the room if she had to.

Soon, the trilling of the machines and the moaning of the fans drowned her thoughts, and she raced through fabric after fabric. By lunch, Nilda was already forgotten. Instead, the women chatted about a Colombian telenovela, far better than the Mexican one that played at the same time on another channel. They spoke of the relatively mild winter. This snowfall was the first of the season—at least now all that money spent on coats that looked like caskets wouldn't go to waste. They wondered if George and Olga would spend New Year's Eve together. No one spoke of Nilda. It was pointless to talk about someone they'd never see again.

■ ■ ■

THAT AFTERNOON, AS THE WOMEN LEFT THEIR STATIONS BOUND FOR home, Ana managed to grab ahold of Betty. The snow had stopped falling, giving way to a clear, reddening sky. The air was still, except for the occasional gust that interrupted the flow of costureras making their way to the bus and train stations. She and Betty marched along with them, walking past the train station's entrance. They leaned against the white letters and hot pink borders that ignited the black facade of the graffitied bodega wall.

"Is everything okay with Carla and Ernesto?" she asked.

Betty unwrapped her scarf and took off her gloves, digging into her pocket for a cigarette. "Same as always. He likes to spend money they don't have. She'll do whatever just to keep him happy. That's love, I guess."

"But he treats her well," Ana said. "From what I saw back when I lived with them. They argued like every couple does, but they always seemed to work things out."

"I guess." She shrugged.

"Sad, no?" said Ana. "What happened with Nilda?"

"That's what happens when you're sloppy," she said as she lit a cigarette. "But you didn't ask me here to talk about her or Carla. Is everything okay? You sounded a bit agitated on the phone last night."

Ana cleared her throat. "Yes, and no," she said. "We're going to take Sully's apartment."

"He sucks, but congratulations!" She nudged Ana gently on her arm. "Starting off the new year right."

"I hope so," she said. "The building *is* old, but he's fixing up the apartment. It's a railroad, but a good size. Close to everything. The problem is he wants three months' rent. We've only got enough for two."

"Three months? I knew he sucked," she said. "You should ask George for overtime. I'm sure he'll need it with Nilda gone." Then she whispered, "You could use some of that money you've set aside."

Betty knew about the money. It was, after all, something she'd advised Carla to do years before, in case Ernesto never came through with his promise to marry her. What if he left her there in New York, alone with no papers? What if she was deported, sent back to Peru and saddled with the three children? What was she supposed to do then? It was a concern Betty had expressed to Ana over and over during Carla's early years in New York. Carla sent back money every month for the children and, eventually, each remittance included a little bit extra for Betty to set aside in case Carla ended up back in Peru with no green card and no husband. It wasn't until a year after he divorced the American woman and had his green card that Ernesto finally married Carla.

"I don't want to," said Ana. "But I don't have much of a choice. We've been at Valeria's for months. It's clear she wants us out. I was hoping we could wait a little longer, but Lucho's set on leaving. And he's right. The longer we stay, the longer she'll try to convince him this is a bad idea. She keeps talking about how we should send the kids back to live with his mother. Lucho actually thinks we should."

"I can see why," said Betty. "It'd be a lot easier if it were just the two of you. You could rent a room or even a studio. You wouldn't have to pay that tuition. It'd be a lot cheaper to educate them over there."

"Betty, no one's raising my children but me."

"Then go back with them. For a little while at least."

"Why do you all of a sudden want me to leave?"

"I don't," she said. "I just see Valeria's point, that's all. I know why you don't want to leave the kids. They're not that little anymore. They'll remember that you left them. And I can even see why you don't want to leave Lucho. Men forget their responsibilities unless they're right in their faces. You see how Ernesto practically forgot he had a family. And my sister was here!" She paused, tapping lightly on her cigarette. "But Lucho's not Ernesto. He wouldn't disappear on you."

"Exactly, so I'm not going to disappear on him."

"Okay," she said. "So why'd you bring me out here if you don't want my advice?"

"Because I need your help."

The street grew quiet, even as passing trains rumbled beneath their feet. The sound of a shovel scraping against the concrete echoed rhythmically somewhere in the distance. For Ana, the world seemed to slow.

"What is it?" Betty asked.

Ana's palms began to sweat. She swallowed the cool, sharp air. "Can you get me those pills?"

Betty cocked her head and pursed her lips. "What pills?"

"The ones you talked about the other day," she said. "The ones that make your period come."

Two lines formed between Betty's eyebrows. "How long has it been?"

Ana pressed her lips. "End of October."

"So two months?" said Betty. "You missed two periods and now you want to take care of this?"

"I've never been regular," said Ana. "Can you keep your voice—?"

"Does Lucho know?"

She bowed her head as a gust suddenly hit them, picking up snow from the ground. She lifted her scarf, covering half of her face, and mumbled, "No."

Betty whispered, "Can you tell me why?"

Ana looked at her, puzzled. She never had to explain herself to Betty. Even when she confessed, all those years ago, that she had been seeing Lucho, Betty only listened and never gave an opinion. When Ana told her she was going to marry him, Betty didn't question how fast the proposal came, not even after Ana gave birth to Victoria seven months later. She never had to justify her actions to Betty and had no intention of doing so now. "Does it matter?"

"I just want to understand why," she replied. "It's not like you're a kid. Nobody raped you. You're married. You've got a family. You have a job."

"Yes, and those are all the reasons why. You see how my life is here. Do you think I need to add to that?"

"Is that why?" she asked. "Or are you messing around again?" Ana glared at her. "Oh come on. It's not a new thing for you. That's how you ended up with Lucho. You cheated on your boyfriend with his brother." She snickered. "How original."

"I never cheated on Carlos," she said firmly. "We were over."

The accusation had been leveled at her before, in the months after Carlos left for Madrid. Their relationship had only lasted a few months, but in that time, he'd introduced her to his mother and Lucho, a step that indicated a level of seriousness that she hadn't expected. She didn't quite feel for Carlos what she saw between her mother and father. He was formal and serious, devoted so much to the study of law that she came to accept her place in his life, behind his profession and his mother, and possibly a couple of his friends. He was curious about her life in Santa Clara. He had a calmness about him that made her feel at ease, but never enough to speak to him about Colonel Mejía and the other men who visited her mother after her father disappeared. He never asked her about what she envisioned her life to be in the future. It was a contrast to the ferocity she saw in Lucho, who was not the intellectual that his younger brother was. He understood that rules and orders can only do so much in practice. It wasn't love exactly that she felt for Carlos, but there was a cautious affection, one she thought could perhaps grow more certain with time.

Then a university in Madrid offered Carlos a scholarship. There was never an understanding that they'd keep the relationship going after he left. He had to focus on his post-graduate studies to keep his scholarship, and although the program was only for two years, he had every intention of finding work there afterward. Their relationship ended awkwardly but cordially.

It was how quickly she and Lucho got together later that gave everyone pause.

"You're starting to sound a lot like Valeria," she said.

"Valeria," Betty repeated. "She was gone for a whole month and you were spending all that time with her husband."

"Don't start making up stories, Betty," she said. "There's nothing going on between me and Rubén, so get that idea out of your head. Besides, I shouldn't have to defend myself to you. You, of all people! You've been here long enough now. You see how it is, everything you've got to do just to keep food on the table. And now Lucho's talking about sending the kids back."

"Back to live with his mother. Of course, you can't do that. Not with your past."

"At least no one here looks at me like I'm a cockroach."

"Everyone here looks at us like we're cockroaches, Ana."

"I'd rather strangers look at me that way than my own children." Her throat tightened. All her life, she'd been made to feel small and inconsequential. Whenever the feeling was too much to bear, she ran. Outside of Santa Clara, her skin, her hair, the way she spoke—all of it only exacerbated those feelings. She couldn't help but fall into the trap. Lose that accent, lighten those strands. Marry up. Marry light.

But marrying Lucho only reinforced how little the world thought of her. She was now the chola in the family. His mother, she feared, would make her children feel small because of their hair and skin; she'd most certainly make them feel that their mother was nothing.

And so Ana had to run again, this time, from Peru entirely. New York was another chance at reinvention. She could be some-one new, her marriage something different, something better in a new place. Where she was born didn't matter; who her parents were or weren't didn't matter. She could stay outside in the sun and burn to crisp if she wanted to. All that mattered was how hard she worked, how she kept her home a home, that she might someday, however unlikely it might be, open up that restaurant. It might all, somehow, erase the very things that made her seem so discard-able to others, including Doña Filomena and the rest of los Falcón.

"Betty, please," she said. "Carla helped you. She got you out of that situation and now I need to get out of mine. Don't judge me for making the same choice you made."

"It's not the same, Ana," she snapped. She compressed her lips, shut her eyes for a moment to steady her breathing. She then pulled out her packet of cigarettes. "The Colonel and his men," she said, as she gave it several hard taps against her palm. "After your mother was gone, after you were gone, I was the only one left." Her jaw began to quiver. "You think they gave me a choice?" She put a cigarette in her mouth and lit it. She took several deep drags as her breath steadied. She rested against the black wall, the white letters swirling around her. "You got to leave. Right before things got bad. You left. You're the one who has a choice, Ana. I never had one."

The ground shuddered as a train barreled through the concrete below. After she'd found her mother's body, Ana ran to Betty's house and the next day, her Tía Ofelia came for her. They were on a bus to Lima in a matter of days. The trip along the carretera— the road that cut through the Andes toward the Pacific—was more than twenty-four hours long. It was not a place for a woman or a child, Tía Ofelia had told her. The bus might get stopped, the passengers raped or robbed or worse, but it was what she could afford.

All Ana wanted was to get out. She kept her mother's prayer card in her pocket, clutching it whenever the bus stopped to pick up passengers along the road or when the driver needed to step outside to defecate. He drove through the night, a jagged jaunt through the mountains that made the only other child on the bus vomit.

When they got to Lima without incident, Ana kissed her mother's card and vowed to never look back.

It was only when Betty moved to Lima and called her that Ana thought of her again. She hadn't had a choice, she wanted to tell Betty. She had to forget. She didn't have a choice now either, not under the circumstances. But what was that choice compared to what Betty had gone through?

"I'm just asking for your help," she pleaded. "Help me stay here and take care of my children. They need me, and I need them."

The church bell rang, and Betty let out a long, deep breath. Ana wondered now if she'd made a mistake asking her for help. They were still, in most ways, confined to the same world they left behind. They were still the cholitas, the invaders. Still unwelcome. Yet neither was the same person. If the circumstances in their lives were different, Ana wondered if they'd still be friends.

Betty tossed her cigarette on the floor and bit her lower lip before relenting. "Give me a day or two," she said. "I'm not sure how much—"

"Thank you," said Ana, clasping her hands together in prayer. She then pulled out her wallet and handed Betty several twenty-dollar bills. "Let me know if you need more."

"This should be enough," she said. She tucked the money in her pocket, then rewrapped her scarf along her face, a sign that she was ready for the long walk home.

"Can you tell me," said Ana, holding her back as she was about to turn, "what it's like?"

Betty didn't look at her when she spoke. "The worst will be the first day or two. You'll have to start taking the pills after the kids are asleep. Valeria and Rubén'll be in bed too. Lucho will be gone. No one will notice."

That night, Ana gave the rest of the money in Liliana's hollow body to Lucho. She told him Mama had agreed to lend them the money. He looked surprised, but didn't question her. They had enough now to pay Sully.

She took a moment to light a candle and kneel in front of her altar. She placed the doll beside the Virgin Mary and her mother's prayer card. She'd have to start saving all over again. She closed her eyes and prayed. She prayed for Nilda and her son. She prayed for her own children. She prayed that Betty would get her what she needed soon.

She prayed for a way to stop running.

11

ON NEW YEAR'S EVE, ANA SAT IN FRONT OF THE VANITY MIRROR IN
her room, dressed in a thin-strapped, blood-orange dress that hit
her knees and wearing gold impostors that sang in her ears. Her
reflection was encircled by a halo of yellow bulbs that surrounded
the oval mirror. She didn't recognize the woman she saw. The lines
on her face insisted on staying put, even when she didn't smile or
squint. Her cheeks sprouted two new pimples. She'd covered the
cracks on her lips with petroleum jelly, and the blisters on her hands
with freesia-scented cream, but her skin still peeled, and her fingertips were still dented.

She was in there somewhere, but the effort it'd take to lure out
the woman she thought she was already exhausted her. It wasn't the
makeup application or the hair styling or forcing herself into her faja
that was daunting, but how much longer it took to fill in her eyebrows, how more and more eyelashes clung to the rim of her curler
each time she pressed it, how the stretch marks that ran across her
lower abdomen crept closer and closer toward her belly button. She
noticed tiny hairs sprouting along the edges of her forehead. She
hadn't realized that she'd lost so many strands.

But she was determined to make the most out of the night. She'd say goodbye to whatever sadness and worry plagued the end of her year. That, she decided, was something to be grateful for. At least she'd do her best to pretend everything was fine.

She was pinning back her curled hair when Lucho entered the room. "¿Y adónde vas tan bien vestida?" he asked. His eyes stayed on her as he shut the door behind him. He walked behind her chair and leaned onto the edge of the vanity, locking her in. The mint in his bath soap clung to his T-shirt and flannel pants. He traced her neck with his breath. His lips skimmed her skin, and she shifted, subtly, away from them.

"Are you okay?" he asked.

She cleared her throat and forced a smile. "I think I might be coming down with something," she said, looking away. She couldn't look at the reflection of his eyes beside hers in the mirror.

"Sully's away for the holiday," he said as he walked to the bed. "But we should have everything settled by the end of the week." He inspected the black trousers and the ivory sweater she'd laid out for him, then opened the shoebox beside them. His black tassel loafers were inside. He scrunched his face and traced a finger along the edges of the pants, edges so sharp she thought they'd still burn from her iron.

She looked into her mirror and watched him undress. She couldn't remember when she'd last seen him take his clothes off in the light. The skin on his arms was still taut and smooth; the hair on his chest still black. His stomach fell but did not frown. It occurred to her that he looked as though he had not aged, as if the years here—years they've spent raising children in a land not theirs, hiding behind numbers and addresses not their own, cutting out animal innards and sewing fabric together for a dollar—had done nothing to him. He didn't care for this place. Maybe that was why he didn't wear their struggles. Was that her burden? To wear these years, to pile them on because she was the one who wanted to come in the first place, the one who insisted on staying?

He blew onto the tops of the shoes and rubbed them with his sleeve. "The Lazartes are already downstairs. Rubén went to have a look at their car."

She quickly sprayed her wrists and neck with the eau de toilette he'd given her for Christmas. "The chicken is done," she said, "but the pernil needs more time. I still have to put out the chips and the fruit. Rubén's coming back with the soda bottles. Then I need to get the champagne glasses—"

"Ana," he said as she gave herself a final look in the mirror.

"I told Victoria to take them out, but she was playing on that *thing* Michael got for Christmas."

"Ana," he repeated, louder this time. "We spoke about this. This is Valeria's home."

"And I made dinner. I'm not taking over, Lucho. I just need to set the table, and our guests are already here." She rushed to the door, but he tugged on her arm gently.

"This is Valeria's home," he repeated. "Let her greet the Lazartes. Let her bring out the food and set the table. That's her place, not yours."

"Right. I'm just the cook."

"No, you're not. But we'll be out of here soon. After all she's done for us, making New Year's Eve dinner is the least you could do."

"The least *I* could do?" She held back from saying all it was that she'd done ever since they moved in with Valeria; ever since he'd lost his job. She had never once reproached him for all the things he didn't do. She wondered if that had been her mistake; if he'd been willfully blind to it all. "I've done more than my part," she said as she walked out.

In the hallway, the air tasted like rosemary and cinnamon. From the living room, she could hear Joe Arroyo's voice pleading over a cacophony of trumpets and drums as he sung a salsa that reverberated from the stereo system. The glow from the Christmas tree stretched from its corner in the living room through the hallway. The place was primed for a celebration.

She didn't want to start the new year arguing with Lucho. She had avoided Valeria ever since the night she saw her and Rubén talking over tea in the kitchen. She didn't expect her to answer, but Ana knocked on Valeria's bedroom door anyway. She could at least tell Lucho she tried.

To her surprise, Valeria opened it. Her hair was in a ponytail; her makeup only half-applied.

"The Lazartes are downstairs," said Ana.

"Yes, I know," she said. "I'm almost done." She opened the door wider, and scanned Ana from tip to tip. "You look nice. I have something that might work with that." She disappeared into her room. Ana waited by the door, craning her neck as Valeria shuffled through a drawer.

She jumped when she heard Michael wail, "Mooom!" behind her. "I'm hungry," he groaned as he walked past her and plopped onto his mother's bed.

"You have to wait," replied Valeria in an accented English as she approached the door. "We have to wait for everyone to get here." She stretched out her hand. In it was a bracelet, gold and woven, with wide chains that undulated like crisscrossing rivers. "It's too big for my wrist," she said, going back to Spanish. "I bought it when I was pregnant and blew up like a whale. It'll look great with that dress."

Ana blushed as she took the bracelet in her palm, tracing its smooth curves with her thumb. It was heavy and bright, even against the glitter of the hallway. She felt a sudden pang of gratitude that anyone, especially Valeria, could think she could wear such a fine piece of jewelry. She cleared her throat, but couldn't find a 'thank you.'

"But I'm hungry now," shouted Michael, and Ana promised the boy food if he'd go with her to the kitchen so that his mother could get ready. He bolted from the bed. She mustered a smile, but Valeria had already turned away, shutting the door behind them.

As they headed down the hallway, Ana peeked into Michael's bedroom to make sure Channel 21 was on the television screen. Victoria got off the bed and rubbed the edge of Ana's dress between her fingertips. "You look so pretty, Mami," she said. "I like your lipstick."

Pedro grimaced. "I don't. I like your lips better when they're clean."

"Then you're not going to like this," she said, as she planted kisses on his face and neck. He fell back on the bed, giggling even as he wiped the lipstick off his cheek.

As she walked past the living room, she flicked on the light. The furniture, including the kitchen table, were pushed against the wall, creating a dance floor in the center of the room. Stacks of cardboard plates, napkins, and plastic utensils filled one corner of the table. The white Christmas tree lingered beside it, draped in alternating lights of red, blue, and green, with a rosy-faced baby Jesus at its foot, reaching up to touch its glass spikes. Cumbia now blared from the stereo. She had left a large pot of purple corn, swimming in pineapple bits, cinnamon sticks, and cloves, simmering on the stove, and the sweet smell of the Chicha Morada had filled the room. Unit 4D was aglow.

The dining room chairs were still in the kitchen, and Michael waited patiently on a seat by the refrigerator. She scooped cilantro rice into a bowl and told him he could eat as much as he wanted so long as he ate there or in his bedroom. She didn't want to risk having any stains in the living room before the party even started. He jammed a spoonful of rice in his mouth as he hurried back to his room. She leaned against the counter and clipped the bracelet around her wrist. She twisted her arm this way and that, and it swung against her fleshy palms, nipping at her wrist. She poured herself a cup of Chicha Morada, then pulled Valeria's bottle of rum out from underneath the counter. She hesitated, then reminded herself of her promise to forget. She poured the rum into her cup. She sipped as the bracelet danced around her skin beneath the fluorescent light.

■ ■ ■

THE FRONT DOOR OPENED, AND RUBÉN'S VOICE BOOMED THROUGH THE hallway. "Come to the shop tomorrow," he said, almost burying the sound of the footsteps that followed him inside. Carla and Ernesto had already taken off their coats while Betty helped the children remove theirs. "You look exhausted," said Carla as Ana kissed her cheek. Her bronze skin, typically bare and shiny, was covered with a pinkish foundation, so thick that it resembled clay. "Don't tell me you've been cooking all night?" she whispered.

"Two nights," said Ana. "You dyed your hair?"

Carla flicked a lock back. "A fresh start for a new year."

Ana then greeted Hugo, the eldest Lazarte child, with a peck on the cheek. "Your first New Year's in New York," she said. "Are you excited?"

"It's the same as every New Year's everywhere," he replied with a crackle of adulthood in his voice. He plopped into the recliner as his younger siblings scattered.

"Don't bother talking to that one," said Ernesto, handing Ana his peacoat. He smoothed out his pastel pink button-down shirt. "Kids these days. They don't appreciate anything their parents do for them. Malcriados."

"He's not being rude," said Betty. "He's just being a teenager." She wore a royal blue dress with geometric cutouts above the chest, sheer black pantyhose, and heels she was clearly uncomfortable walking in. Carla threw her a look, but Betty adjusted one of her false eye lashes, purposely avoiding her sister's gaze. "It smells great, Ana," she said as she blinked her lashes into place. "You look nice." She kissed Ana, but her embrace was stiff. "That's a beautiful bracelet." She grabbed Ana's wrist to inspect the piece before letting go and saying, "I really need a drink."

"There's Chicha," said Ana, pointing to the glass jar on the table filled with the purple liquid. "You can mix it with pisco or rum, but in your cup. The kids are drinking it too."

"Don't worry, Betty," said Rubén, lowering his voice as he talked into her ear. "Anita put me in charge of the drinks. Let me put these sodas away and then I'll make you a pisco sour that will keep you moving all night!"

Betty blushed. Rubén had a way of making her do that, even though Ana couldn't quite see why. She preferred not to know if there was an attraction there. It would only complicate matters with Valeria.

"Come," she told her friend, "help me with the coats." She gestured toward the hallway closet, but spun her head when she heard Ernesto shout, "¡Compadre!"

Lucho strode into the living room, smiling broadly. She'd been right about the sweater and the pants. He managed to light up an already illuminated room. He greeted Ernesto, and then, as Betty made her way to him, he extended his arms like he was Jesucristo himself. For a moment, Ana thought he might actually take Betty in those arms, but he only gave her a quick embrace and dotted her cheek with a kiss. He offered to take the coats they were carrying, but they refused, and as he and Betty chatted, he placed his hand on the small of Ana's back. Her neck flushed when he touched her.

Then Valeria stepped outside her bedroom door. "I see the sisters are here," she said when she saw Betty. Her hair was pulled back in a chignon, highlighting the precision of the divine hand that had cut her cheekbones, and the mortal one at the hair salon that had tattooed her eyebrows. Her lips were a bright rose, a contrast to the flared black dress she wore. The sleeves hit just above her elbows, revealing the marble skin on the back of her forearms. A white band accentuated her flat waist. Ana searched, in vain, for an outline of a wide strap or a row of hook-and-eye closures, any sign that, beneath it all, Valeria was being held together by a faja.

"I don't want to stain your cheek," she said as she gave Betty an air-kiss. She looked at the coats in Betty's arms. "So the whole tribe is here. You can put those in Ana's room. They're not all going to fit in the closet." She slid her arm on the hook of Lucho's elbow. "Come, Primo. Let's go say hello to the chusma." She snickered, but no one else laughed. "It's a joke. America is the great equalizer. Rich or poor, black, white, cholo, chino. We're all the same here."

Once the coats were set aside, Ana filled the table with the food she'd prepared: a tray of cilantro rice with corn kernels and carrots; bowls of velvet gold sauce and inch-thick cuts of boiled yellow potatoes topped with quartered hard-boiled eggs; and an oven-roasted chicken whose skin she'd kneaded amber with her palillo. She brought the pork shoulder out last, just as Valeria asked the Sandoval sisters if they could take care of business now.

"Better to get it out of the way before we forget," she said as Rubén handed her a pisco sour. They went into Valeria's bedroom to discuss their arrangement in private. Once they returned to the living room, Ana invited everyone to eat, but only the women approached the table. Carla filled a plate of food for her husband, while Betty filled them for the children. Valeria served herself, and when she sat down, Betty asked Rubén if he wanted a little bit of everything.

"I want a lot of everything." He smiled, but it quickly disappeared as he caught Valeria's face. "Don't worry, Betty, I'll get it myself."

Ana ate last. She sat beside Betty on the love seat, keeping her cup of Chicha at her feet. It was only her second, but she already felt lighter. She thought of Nilda, how right she'd been. Drinking was very much like sex.

They danced, first the married couples, then the women among themselves. Ernesto was the first to ask someone other than his wife to the floor. He took Ana's hand, led her to the center of the room, and as Tito Rojas belted on the radio, the two showed off with S-turns and one-eighty spins that made Ana forget, for those few minutes, the heaviness of the last several months.

At the end of the hour, when everyone was on their second helping of food, Rubén recounted a story of a customer who brought his car into the shop earlier that week. The car's seats were freckled with cigarette burns. The man's wife, he told them, had found him in the back seat with another woman. It was a story only he and Ernesto seemed to find amusing.

"He's lucky she didn't burn the thing with the two of them in it," said Valeria.

"Be glad she didn't," said Rubén. "That antic is going to pay for that little trip to Peru."

"Pay for my trip?" said Valeria. "Do I need to remind you that the body shop is *my* business?"

"It's ours," he said, but everyone in the room knew that wasn't true.

Ana looked around, hoping someone might interrupt. "Would you like some more pernil?" she stammered as she went to take Rubén's plate.

"I think you've had enough," said Valeria, looking at his belly, but Rubén headed to the table and filled a new plate.

Ernesto then cleared his throat. "I'm surprised you're not working today," he said to Lucho.

"That's because that thief Gil wanted the car tonight," said Valeria. "I don't understand, Primo. On the one hand, it's good you're not out on a crazy night like tonight. But he has the day shift, you have the night shift. That's the arrangement. He can't just pick and choose which nights he wants to work and which he doesn't." She then turned to Rubén, who was still at the table, picking at the food, and said, "You realize your friend is taking advantage of our family."

"It's between Lucho and Gil," he replied. "I'm not getting involved."

"You *should* get involved!" she said. "Lucho's already paid for the month and now that ratero isn't letting him work."

"He's not a crook," said Rubén. "He charges less than the bases to rent that car."

"There'll be other nights," said Ernesto. "I used to drive a cab myself when I first got to this country. I know how it is. Yes, you could probably make a decent amount of money tonight, but do you want to ride around with drunks in the back seat? It can take days for the smell of vomit to go away. So maybe you're out some money, but at least you get to stay home and enjoy good company and your wife's food. Maybe even enjoy her later."

"Ernesto, don't be vulgar," said Carla.

Lucho looked into his empty cup, as if he were reading tea leaves. "I could help you again," he said to Valeria, "at the shop."

Rubén chuckled. "No, no, Primo. We tried that once. You're not made for mufflers and engines. You're much better off driving cars than fixing them."

"I can help manage the place," he said.

"What can I say," replied Valeria after an awkward pause. "I prefer to run my business myself." She fanned herself with an empty plate, beads of sweat trickling down the side of her neck.

Lucho straightened, as if shielding himself from the rebuff, then disappeared into Michael's bedroom. Ana fought the urge to follow him. Months earlier, when Lucho lost his job at the meat-packing plant, she believed he could find another one quickly. There was no shortage of odd jobs: men who needed help installing floors, moving furniture, or gutting apartments. But by their nature, the jobs were inconsistent and so was the pay. Sometimes, he was paid in full on the day he did the work. Other times, he had to wait a week or two, or never got paid at all. There was less work as the summer came to a close. Then he began to retreat.

He spent hours reading the same newspapers, pointing out every spelling and grammatical error he found and redoing word search puzzles in his notebook. He'd read the same weekly Peruvian newspaper well into the night, as he waited for the next one, more for what he didn't read in them than for what he did. What had happened to the medical students that were arrested that autumn during a military raid? Who were the people Sendero had executed in this pueblo or the other? By then, the Túpac Amaru Revolutionary Movement MRTA had also done its fair share of killings, invading remote towns in the jungle and shooting whatever threatened the decency of Peru's youth. Was it even MRTA or Sendero that was terrorizing the country, or was it the soldiers?

He'd pace the length of the one-bedroom apartment they could barely afford, his feet sticking to and unsticking from the laminate floors each night. It was as though he'd gone back to the days after the military raided the university. When Rubén said his friend, Gil, needed someone to drive his car at night, Ana urged him to do it. She'd find a way to get the money to lease the cab, and in the end, she made the necessary concessions to make it happen.

"It must be hard for mi Compadrito," said Ernesto when Lucho was out of the room. "All those years at the university to come here and cut pig limbs and drive a cab for a living."

Ana's head spun. "And what's the alternative? To stay in Lima and hope the bombings end? Or that a job would somehow fall from the sky? Or should he have left his family in Peru like you did yours?"

"We're here now," said Carla, flushing.

"He should at least make an effort to learn English," said Valeria.

"Right," said Ana, "because we have so much time and money for that."

"Muchachas, muchachas," said Rubén. "It's almost midnight. Let's not start the New Year like this. We're family. We're together. We're here! We should thank God every day that we're here."

As the final minute of the year descended, Ana poured champagne into glasses while Betty handed them out with cups of green grapes, a dozen in each. Lucho returned to the living room with the children, and the group counted down the seconds to the New Year. He let out an exaggerated grunt as he picked up Pedro. "You're getting too big for me," he said. He wrapped his free arm around Victoria. She leaned into him, barely able to keep sleep at bay. "We'll call your grandmother after this," he said, and Ana knew better than to walk into the kitchen after the clock struck midnight.

When it did, Lucho cheered along with Pedro, and kissed both of his children before turning to Ana. She kissed him just long enough to feel the soft flesh of his inner lip. She emptied her champagne glass, but didn't eat a grape with each stroke of midnight, as was the custom. Instead, she went around the room, wishing each person, even Valeria, a year of health and happiness. She refilled glasses as Lucho took their children into the kitchen to call his mother.

No one noticed that little Jorge Lazarte was in the room until he nearly crashed his plate of cold, uneaten food into Betty's chest. Ernesto scolded him for not eating his dinner.

"He's tired," said Betty, as the boy buried his face in her chest.

"I'm talking to my son," said Ernesto as he stood up. By then, the champagne, the beer, the pisco sours, were coursing through his legs and feet. He steadied himself on the recliner, but Jorge ran back to Michael's bedroom. "You see. That's what happens when you don't have a man to discipline these kids. My father would have knocked a tooth out of my mouth."

"We're not in Peru, Ernesto," said Valeria. "You can go to prison for doing something like that here."

"I'm not raising un maricón," he replied. "Better I do it now than someone else do it later."

"Is that what you did when you were younger, Cuñadito?" asked Betty. "Beat up the gays at the club?"

"I kept them all out," he said. "Los gays, los negros. None of them got past me."

Valeria snickered. "I see the club owners kept the serranos out of the brothel by making them work the door."

Carla sat up straight. "Ernesto was born in Lima."

"But his mother is from Cuzco," replied Valeria.

"My grandmother was from la sierra too," said Rubén. "De

Huaraz. I still have family there, but I haven't been since I was about Jorge's age."

"In any case," slurred Ernesto, "I'm raising a man. That kid is lucky I haven't given him a beating yet."

Betty blinked repeatedly, her eyes already glassy from the alcohol. "I guess no one ever beat you, Cuñado," she said, "since you're running your mouth like you are."

"I think Ernesto always runs his mouth when he drinks," joked Lucho.

"Now, me and Ana," Betty continued, "we know beatings. Maybe if you ever had a good one, you'd think twice about hitting your son."

"I know enough," said Ernesto. "Besides, I don't want my kid blown up because some asshole thinks he's a degenerate."

"There's no MRTA here," said Valeria. "And we are far from any revolution."

"That doesn't make me feel better," he said, his eyes sharpening as he turned once again to Betty. "Just remember, Cuñada, I have two sons and only one daughter."

Betty forced a smile then went into the kitchen. Ana quickly followed her, but Betty already had the bottle of rum in her hand when she walked in. "Hijo de puta," she mumbled as she poured the liquor into her cup and took a shot. "He thinks he's a father. What does he know about being a father?"

"Betty, he is very traditional—"

"Es un machista," she gritted. "He wants *me* to remember that he has two sons and a daughter. What about him?"

"Please lower your voice."

"You're right, you know," she said. "What were you supposed to do? Leave your kids back in Peru like they did? So that someone else can raise them?"

"I shouldn't have said that," said Ana. "They did what they thought was best."

"You know one year he forgot it was Jorge's birthday," said Betty. "They both forgot. He waited all day for their call. He didn't care about the cake or his presents. He just wanted to talk to his parents. You know when those idiots called? Two days later. Two days! They didn't even apologize. They think a four-year-old is too stupid to realize when his parents forget his birthday."

"I'm sure they didn't mean to—"

"They think sending money every month to the niñera made them parents." She poured more rum into her cup. "Because that's all I was, right? That's all I still am. The fucking nanny."

Ana grabbed Betty's forearm before she could take another gulp. "Cálmate."

"You see why I hate living with them, don't you?" she said. "I love my niece and nephews. And my sister is my sister. I can't do much about that. But that idiot she married." She threw back her cup, and nearly choked when she realized Carla was in the room.

"That idiot paid for your flight here," she said. "You wouldn't be here without him."

Betty pounded her chest as she cleared her throat. "It wasn't a gift, Sister. I'm working to pay him back." She grabbed the bottle of rum. "You know what? It's a new year. I'm not going to let any of you ruin it for me." She went back into the living room, her arms raised and her step a beat behind the salsa that blared from the stereo.

Ana tried to follow but Carla held her back. "Anita, wait," she said. "I didn't want to ask in front of everyone, but tell me, how'd it go with the apartment? It's a good one, right?"

Ana nodded and smiled. "We haven't signed yet, but we're taking it."

"You see, Ana!" she said, taking a hold of Ana's arm. "I told you. I know Sully's strange, but he's been a good landlord, I don't care what Betty says. He does most of the work on his buildings himself so if you ever have any trouble with anything, you can just give him a call. Lucho should double-check the work, just in case, but Sully's better than most. And you'll be close to the school, to work, to me." She beamed. "We can even throw our own parties and not invite these pitucos," she joked.

When they were back in the living room, it was Betty and Rubén who took over the dance floor. He held her hand and swayed his hips as she spun around, slower than what the music called for. Ana glanced at Valeria, who was eyeing the pair. She approached Lucho and suggested he ask his cousin to dance. But when he did, Valeria refused. "That food isn't sitting too well with me," she said, and her eyes stayed on Betty and Rubén.

Ana grew anxious. She went back to the kitchen to retrieve the crema volteada and arroz con leche she had prepared for dessert. She passed Betty each time, and each time, she asked her for help, but Betty kept dancing. Finally, when the deejay cut the music short, Ana grabbed her by the arm. "Your nails," Betty protested as Ana shoved her into the kitchen.

"What is wrong with you?" she said. "Why are you flirting with him?"

"With Rubén?" asked Betty. "There are only two other men I could dance with and Lucho doesn't look like he's in the mood. And I'm certainly not going to dance with Ernesto."

"Then ask Valeria! You know she's the jealous type. You don't think anyone noticed how comfortable you were with him out there? You don't think *she* noticed?"

"I don't care what Valeria thinks."

"Well, you should. She got those cigarettes for you, didn't she?

And you might have to live with Ernesto, but I have to live with her." She opened the cabinet and took out plastic containers, tossing them on the counter and slamming the drawers as she searched for something to scoop up the food.

"What are you doing?" asked Betty.

"Getting people's food ready. The party is over. Everyone's already drunk, and I don't want any more problems with her." She found a measuring cup and began to pound the remaining rice into each container. "Can you please help me? I need the potatoes from the table. If I wanted someone to just hang around like an ornament, I would've asked Valeria for help."

"I'm a guest here, Ana, not the help." She was about to walk out when Ana lurched forward. She steadied herself on the counter, then bolted into the hallway.

"¿Qué pasó?" she heard someone say as she slammed the bathroom door closed and vomited into the toilet. Purple. *The Chicha,* she thought, and vomited some more. She splashed cold water on her face as her throat burned. Her tongue tasted sour.

She stepped out of the bathroom, and Lucho and Ernesto were waiting in the hallway. She said she was fine, and she heard Valeria say something about the food. "There's Alka-Seltzer in the cabinet," she called out.

"She just needs to lie down," said Betty. She and Lucho took the coats and handbags off the bed. Betty held on to her pocketbook. Rubén came in with a glass of water. She was in the middle of packing the leftovers, Betty told them as she recounted what happened just before Ana dashed out of the kitchen. She suggested that Lucho finish packing up the food. He agreed—it was time to call it a night—and when the two were alone, Betty sat beside Ana on the bed.

"I have something for you," she told her. She took a small,

plastic bag from her pocketbook. Inside it were several white, hexagonal pills.

Ana sat up, squinting as she tried to focus on what Betty was saying.

Start with three, she heard her say. Just three. You don't want to bleed to death. Then again every couple of hours, three at a time. "Don't put them in there," she said, pointing toward Ana's crotch. "I heard of a girl in Chorrillos who did that and ended up burning her uterus."

Ana held the plastic bag, rolling the pills between her fingertips.

"Start tomorrow if you can," said Betty. "The sooner you start, the sooner you can forget."

■ ■ ■

THE NEXT DAY, ANA TUCKED THE PILLS INSIDE THE FRONT POCKET OF her jeans so she could feel them each time she moved. They poked her as she cleaned up around the apartment, then as she prepared a lunch of leftovers. They bulked in the crux of her hip when she sat down to eat with her children. She was constantly reminded that she needed la regla—to regulate her body, get it under control. Tonight, the first day of a New Year, she'd get it back on track.

She waited until the children were asleep, then until Valeria and Rubén retreated to their bedroom. She wanted a shower. She let the water hit her, and for a brief moment beneath the spatter of the showerhead, standing in the steam and in the pool of foam that had collected around her ankles, she wondered what if. What if she threw the pills in the toilet? She thought of her mother then.

She wrapped her head in a towel, covered her body in mango-scented lotion, and sat on the toilet seat, sipping a bottle of Malta.

She put each pill underneath her tongue and chased them with the drink because she remembered hearing somewhere that it helped the blood come faster. In the early morning, under the fog of another sleepless night, she did it again, putting the pills beneath her tongue when she normally burned it with tea while sitting at the table and fiddling with her address book. She chased these pills with another bottle of Malta. The third time was just before Lucho came home. She did not lock the bathroom door, and was startled when Pedro walked in, crying because he woke up and she wasn't beside him. She went back to bed with him, curled into herself, and was in some pain by the time Lucho came home.

Her period, she told him.

He placed a hot towel on her abdomen and made her chamomile tea, but Ana refused any pain killers. He woke the children, fed them, dressed them, told them she was unwell and that they should stay in the living room or Michael's bedroom while she rested. But Pedro still snuck into their room, asking her where it hurt. "Ya pasó, Mami, ya pasó," he assured her, holding her hand and kissing her forehead before he and Victoria went back to school that morning. Lucho napped in the lower bunk of the bed, while she laid on theirs, cringing occasionally and making regular trips to the bathroom. It was a bad cycle, she told him, and she'd had a very long week. She found herself touching her mother's prayer card and asking her to please let it pass. She wasn't lying about her period. That's what was coming down, she told herself.

As it came, she did not know what to expect. She didn't know how she'd feel. All she knew was that she couldn't look, but she bore the labor of it with relief.

12

FOR TWO DAYS, ANA PRETENDED TO BE IN MORE PAIN THAN SHE WAS actually in. The bleeding subsided, so had the cramping, and even though she could have stepped outside her bedroom door to cook, clean, spend time with the children, she secluded herself inside her room. She slept for longer stretches than she had in months, cuddled with Victoria or Pedro whenever they came into bed, reading whatever newspaper or magazine Lucho brought her, getting up only to eat and for intermittent trips to the bathroom. She let herself be sick, because that's what she was. It's what happens to a woman when she gets her period. Se enferma, she told herself, and she had finally gotten sick.

She spent three days at home, two of which were work days. On that final day, she got out of bed, stumbled through the morning chaos of a calamitous breakfast and sloppy bickering as she got the children ready for school. Rubén dropped them off, as he did every morning, then came back to the apartment to pick up Valeria before they headed to the body shop.

Lucho slept until noon, and when he woke up, she handed him a grocery list. He could find most of the items at a supermarket, but he'd have to venture out to the more nuanced parts of Queens for the purple corn, the pineapple, and cheap dried apricots that made their way onto her list. She had a craving for purple pudding, she told him. The list was long enough to keep him out for at least a couple of hours. She was rarely at home alone during the day. She wanted, more than anything, to eat something without interruption in front of the television screen and pump her mind with nonsense for once.

When he left, she ate two bowls of the leftover pork from New Year's Eve and downed a can of beer. Valeria, no doubt, would notice it was missing. She'd seen her only once since she was in bed, the morning of New Year's Day, when Valeria came into the bedroom to see how she was feeling. She insisted that Ana see a doctor, in case she needed antibiotics, but Ana assured her it was bad menstrual cramps, that's all, from her fibroids. "Carla's been calling," she told her. "I told her you were fine. Lucho said you're moving out. I'm glad, Ana. Hay que seguir adelante."

"Adelante," Ana had mumbled, as she drifted back to sleep.

Outside of her room, nothing in unit 4D had changed. Stacks of unopened mail were still piled on top of the table. Plastic bags, a towel, and a stained T-shirt hung on the chairs, and the sink was filled with tea-stained mugs and food-crusted plates. Life at Lexar Tower continued as usual, and this gave her comfort. She managed to fix a problem that threatened her ordinary, quiet life, and she had done so without the world noticing. She imagined that she too would soon forget.

She lathered up the sponge and, one by one, scraped away the crust on the forks and knives, scrubbed away at the stains on the plates and the brown circles on the inside of the mugs. It'd all be worth it when she had her own place to live, she told herself. When her children were in college; when she could go back, shine as brightly as Doña Filomena underneath her living room chandelier; when she could take Tía Ofelia out to dinner in Miraflores; when she opened the doors to her own restaurant. She could even go back to Santa Clara, back to her mother's grave to tell her all she'd managed to do with that one lesson: do things for love, even if it hurts you.

If she hadn't made the blood come, then what? All the years and sacrifice would be for nothing. They couldn't stay in New York, not with another mouth to feed. And if they did stay with three children, then what? She could provide three children with a mediocre future at best. The restaurant would remain a dream. Now, Victoria and Pedro had a better shot. So did she. Had she not made the blood come, she would've preferred to go back. Going back would've been easier than staying and knowing that her dream would've been possible had it not been for that decision. Now, they could keep moving forward.

Adelante, she told herself.

After she cleaned up the kitchen, she peeled herself an orange and took it, along with a glass of water, into the living room. The fruit wasn't hers, but there was no one in unit 4D to tell her to stop eating it.

She was halfway through watching a talk show when she heard keys rattling the door. She expected to see Lucho, but immediately straightened when she heard Valeria grunting by the door.

"Ah!" she exclaimed as she walked into the living room and unwrapped her scarf. "I see you're feeling better." The shock on Ana's face was obvious. "I decided to come home early," Valeria explained. "That's the good thing about having your own business. Sometimes—not always—but sometimes you can say 'no' to work." She took off her wrap coat. Beneath it, she wore a plum wool turtleneck and a smoky A-line skirt. Her sheer black pantyhose glistened. She didn't need to dress up for the body shop, but Doña Filomena had spoken the truth about her niece. She wanted to look like the professional she was. She didn't need that get-up to fix mufflers, but she was La Dueña and made sure she looked the part.

She took off her wet boots and slipped into a pair of garnet slippers. She went into the kitchen, then came back to the living room with a glass of orange juice that Ana suspected had a splash of vodka in it.

"You do look well," she said as she sat on the recliner. "I used to get terrible backaches. Migraines." She sipped her drink. "But I don't get sick anymore, so it's one less thing to worry about."

"Since when?" asked Ana, shocked that Valeria would reveal something so intimate.

"Since the summer. Just before you moved in." She picked up the remote control. "Do you mind if we talk?" she said, turning off the television before Ana could reply. "I know you weren't expecting me, but I really needed a break."

"You have been working a lot," said Ana, eager to get back to her room.

Valeria smiled, the same forced smile she gave Betty or Carla when she greeted them. "I need to get the place back in order."

Rubén had hinted about the state of the business. It was why Valeria didn't have her car back. She wondered how Valeria had come home now, but she didn't dare ask.

"Anyway," Valeria continued, "I wanted to talk to you about something. You've been so sick lately, I didn't want to bother you. You looked much better this morning, so here I am."

"Is something wrong?" she asked, though she suspected she knew what it was that Valeria wanted to speak to her about.

"This may not even matter since you'll be gone soon," said

Valeria. "But I don't like how friendly you are with my husband." There wasn't a hint of anger in her voice. Instead, Valeria was calm, poised. It was as though Ana were catching a glimpse of the woman Valeria once was. A well-traveled translator who looked more like a pastel-porcelain souvenir, the kind of recuerdo handed out at lavish weddings and quinceañeras, than she did an academic. Valeria had always had an obsession with language, enunciating words with a precision that could cut a tongue. There was no argument she couldn't win, largely because no one understood what she was saying. She was sharp of mind and soft of face, and carried herself with enough pride and confidence to fill a village.

No one was surprised, then, when she caught the eye of a Peruvian who lived in America during one of his visits back home. Rubén was bold, walking right up to her when he spotted her, dressed in a fuchsia bikini and a pair of aviators, along the beach in Punta Hermosa. Soon, he was driving her around Lima, showing off his Japanese car as much as he was showing her off. Although Rubén didn't lack flash, he lacked her polish, but this didn't stop them from marrying only six months after they met on that beach.

Time had tempered whatever passion had driven her to Rubén, and as the seams of the marriage came undone, so did Valeria. She began to lose her words, forgetting how to say this in Spanish or that in English. Instead, she relied on the right adornments to make her feel empowered, things she could point to and say where she bought them and how much they cost. Her gaze was often lost in some thought, falling deeper into a void every time she drank. It was her marriage, Ana concluded, that had done this to her. Of course she was threatened by her. Rubén had cheated on her in the past; he still did. How could an infidelity not change a person? Why wouldn't she be suspicious of Ana?

But she wondered if there was a deeper reason for Valeria's suspicion. Would she feel threatened by someone that was more like her, an educated white woman? Or was she only suspicious of women composed of a different clay?

Ana tried to mimic Valeria's calm when she said, "Valeria, Rubén and I were just talking."

"I know," she said. "About my marriage. About that woman." She stood, rubbing the back of her neck as she walked to the sliding glass doors of the balcony. She stared out over the rooftops and into the gray sky, her arms crossed at her chest. "You know about her," she said. "You know about the girl." She was matter-of-fact, as if there was no shame in acknowledging her husband's transgression, except that she couldn't face Ana when she said it.

Ana wished she could have said yes and told her everything it was that she knew. Not just about the affair or the other child, but how it came after years of Valeria trying to have another one; how Rubén's betrayal was likely as painful as the deaths of her own parents because here she was, alone again, this time in a foreign country with a young child and no family to catch her; how she suspected that Valeria wasn't all right after she had Michael, and hadn't gotten the help she needed.

But Ana couldn't say these things. Valeria would only mistake her sympathy for pity.

There was a long silence before Valeria straightened. "I know he's still with her," she said. "I wish I could say that I don't care."

It was the first time Valeria had ever seemed vulnerable to her. Ana could tell that she loved Rubén, despite what he'd done. Valeria's gaze always stayed on him whenever he danced with other women. She laughed at his jokes even though she objected to their vulgarity. And whenever she passed by the television, her fingers sometimes lingered on the picture frames beside it: snapshots of the couple in a limo on their wedding day, on a boat as it passed in front of the Statute of Liberty one summer night, of the family poolside while on vacation in Miami.

"I can't do much about the situation," she continued. "He's a man, and that's the kind of thing men do. But I treated her well. I thought she was a friend." Her eyes were downcast, then as if catching a mistake, she said, "I never should've trusted that prieta."

Ana cleared her throat. "We don't always know people, Valeria."

"That's true," she replied, "but I know how some women are. I want to think that you're different. So I'm asking you not to meddle in my marriage."

"I never have," she said.

"Then why does my husband want my son to meet that whore's daughter?"

Ana stammered. She hadn't expected Rubén to tell Valeria about their conversation. It was clear that Valeria didn't want the children to meet at all. If they were going to, why tell her? Why not keep it a secret?

She wondered what else Rubén might have told her.

"He brought it up the other night," Valeria continued. "I said 'no,' of course, and to never mention it again. He said I was being unreasonable. Do you know why? Because *you* didn't think there was anything wrong with it. *You.* He said I was unreasonable because I don't want my son to know that whore or that girl, or how his father humiliated me."

Her voice was even, but a blue vein swelled beneath the thin skin on her temple. There was no point in arguing with her. In a matter of weeks, Ana would be out of unit 4D anyway. If all she needed to do was nod and apologize to get through the next few weeks in peace, then she'd keep her head moving and set her mouth on repeat. "You're right," she said. "I'm sorry. I should never have said anything to him."

"No, you shouldn't have." Her ice cubes clinked as she threw back her glass and walked back to the recliner. "I've tried to look past what you did to my family. To Lucho and Carlos. God knows the whole situation brought enough shame to our family."

Valeria had only alluded to Ana's relationships with the Falcón brothers, never asking her about what happened with Carlos or how it was that she came to be with Lucho in the first place. Instead, she viewed it like the rest of the family. The whole mess was an embarrassment for them, and so they avoided speaking about it in the first place. Don't say anything and it's like it never happened. A criollo from a good family getting involved with a chola, probably another terruca. If it happens, the how and the why isn't talked about. His brother then falling in love with her could never happen. Growing a bastard in her belly never really happened. Because Ana had married the child's father, a forced marriage in the eyes of his family, but at least that had righted the wrong.

"Valeria, por favor," said Ana, shaking her head. "You know as much about what happened with Carlos as I know about your marriage. I didn't love him, and he clearly didn't love me. He left me. I wasn't going to wait for him."

"He went to Spain to get a better education," she said. "It wasn't an excuse for you to pounce on his brother."

"I didn't 'pounce.' I fell in love with Lucho. We fell in love. And that was years ago. It's not Lucho who keeps his distance now. It's Carlos."

When Lucho first spoke to his brother about Ana, it wasn't to make sure he didn't have any lingering feelings for her before he began courting her, or even to say that they'd already started a relationship. They were in Tía Ofelia's living room, on the ground floor of her house in Bellavista. By then, they had told her aunt and Doña Filomena about the pregnancy. While the news drove his mother into silence, Ofelia only wanted to make sure she wasn't going to have another mouth to feed. She'd done enough for Ana; she couldn't do anymore. Lucho reassured her that Ana and the child would be taken care of, and so Lucho was welcome to visit his fiancée as often as he liked.

It was there, in Ofelia's living room, with Ana by his side, that Lucho called his brother to tell him that he'd been seeing her and that she was pregnant.

Carlos didn't speak to Lucho until he returned to Lima for a visit nearly a year later. It was then that he held a lanky Victoria, with the same widow's peak as his mother, for the first time. The phone calls eventually became more frequent, coming always on birthdays and sometimes on holidays. He married a woman from Sevilla, one neither Ana nor Lucho met but whom they saw in the pictures Doña Filomena occasionally included with her letters to her son. For a time, whatever it was that Carlos resented fell away. It wasn't until Carlos found out that Lucho had taken the deed to their childhood home that the phone calls stopped.

"Lucho *should* reach out," said Valeria. "He's the one who made the mistake."

"Being with me wasn't a mistake," said Ana.

"Well, God knows you were not what we expected my cousin to marry," she said. "But he's a dutiful man. You're his wife and the mother of his children, and that's not going to change, is it?"

"No, it's not," Ana replied, and darted up. One more insult, and she might regret whatever she might say or do next, and there was so much she wanted to say, so much she wished she could do. Douse Valeria with the water that remained in her glass. Tell her that she had no marriage. That the only reason Rubén didn't divorce her was because of the business and the money and the shame it'd cause her. Talk about duty. Rubén was the one who stayed out of a stupid sense of duty. He owed her something for having had the affair; that *something* was saving her from the embarrassment of a divorce. She should've let the affair go long ago, and she hadn't. She let it sicken her, and now look at her, a borracha, drinking her woes away. *Stupid,* thought Ana. Stupid for letting *him* win.

But Ana didn't say these things. Just a few more weeks, she kept telling herself, and so she apologized once more and reassured her that it would not happen again.

"I know it won't," said Valeria softly. "I don't like you, Ana. I just hope that Lucho might one day see you for what you really are. Maybe then we could finally be rid of you."

A smile she had no desire to suppress touched Ana's lips. "That's too bad, Prima," she said. "I might be leaving your home, but believe me, I'm not going anywhere."

■ ■ ■

SOON AFTER, RUBÉN DROPPED OFF THE CHILDREN AND VALERIA WENT with him back to the body shop. Lucho still wasn't home, and Ana was in the middle of preparing toast with cheese for the children's afternoon snack when the phone rang. It was Carla on the other line, which came as something of a surprise. There was never a need for either one to call the other. Whatever they needed to tell each other was almost always said at work. Carla, however, was clearly annoyed that Ana hadn't returned her calls. "Didn't Valeria tell you?" she asked, and Ana remembered then that Valeria had mentioned Carla's phone calls while she was still in bed. She simply hadn't thought to call her back. She was going back to work tomorrow, she told her. She thought it could wait.

Carla's breath was heavy. "I saw Mama on New Year's," she whispered.

"Oh," said Ana, distracted as she searched the refrigerator for slices of cheese. "How is she?"

"Frustrated," said Carla. "She said you haven't been paying her."

"I have been," said Ana. "I've just been a little short, that's all. You know Lucho just started working again and then it was Christmas—"

"I get that," she interrupted. "But I vouched for you, Ana. I told her you were dependable, responsible. It doesn't look good when someone I refer doesn't pay."

"Will you calm down?" she said. "I'm paying her, Carla. I'm just a little behind, but I'm catching up."

"How? With the few hours of overtime you're supposed to do this week? You need to make up for what you missed today. And then you're supposed to move? How do you expect to do that, Ana? With what money?"

"That's not your problem, Carla."

"But it *is* my problem," she said, her voice hushed as she spat into the phone. "I need her help too. I've got my three kids now and Betty. It's not good for either of us if you keep falling behind." There was genuine concern in her voice. Carla had introduced Ana to Mama, but after that introduction, she had never spoken to Ana about her, let alone about her dealings with the woman or Ana's payments. The fact that she knew Ana had fallen behind was unsettling. Her words sounded more like a warning than a reprimand.

She hung up and sat at the table, butter knife in hand. She

remembered that afternoon, when she cowered in Mama's armchair as the woman glowered over her. It was the first time in years that she thought she'd get hit. Something held the woman back. Ana thought it was her age; after all, how hard of a blow could a sick, elderly woman actually give? But she realized that wasn't what held Mama back. It was simply that there were other, stronger ways she could strike.

She plated the sandwiches and let the children eat in Michael's bedroom. She needed to catch up with those payments, and she wondered if perhaps staying with Valeria a little longer was the best thing to do. Living with her had certainly taken its toll. It was not unlike living with Lucho's mother. There was always that truth that hung over them: that she had once been with Carlos, and that Lucho married her only after she got pregnant. Each woman, in her own way, made sure Ana never forgot that, no matter where she was.

Still, after her last visit with Mama and now Carla's phone call, she hoped that Sully might have found another tenant, one without children and with all the right paperwork, who didn't blink when he asked for three months' rent. If they stayed a little longer, she thought, they could see the Valentine's Day decorations go up, and maybe even celebrate Victoria's communion in the communal recreation room.

But then Lucho finally came home, gripping bags filled with the items on her grocery list, the ingredients of the Mazamorra Morada she craved, and an envelope. "I called him before I left," he said as she unfolded the document inside. "He got back last night. I wanted to surprise you." The long, trifold document was printed on thickly stocked sheets. A shorter piece of paper was stapled on its left-hand corner, the word RECEIPT printed across its top in block letters. She lifted it, and underneath was the address to Sully's building. Lucho and Sully's signatures were scribbled on the bottom of the second page.

They were leaving Lexar Tower.

As he got ready for his shift, she went into their bedroom and placed the lease and the receipt inside the canary envelope. Two more additions to the collection; proof of the next phase in their journey. Adelante, she thought, yet Ana couldn't help but feel a sting over what her departure meant. In one way, Valeria was getting what she wanted. She was getting rid of her.

She tore a piece of paper from her address book and wrote down the street address for Lexar Tower in large letters. She lit the red candle, then held the paper by the flame. She let the fire burn in her hand for a few seconds before she set it down on a small white teacup saucer and watched it turn to cinders. She said farewell to her temporary home.

She then tore another page from her address book. This time, she wrote the address of the new apartment, and set the paper on top of the ashes. She picked up her mother's prayer card. The picture printed on its face was the only one she had of her mother. It was the one used on her mother's government-issued identification card, taken several years before she died. Her eyes were steady; her smile, reluctant. She was younger in that picture than Ana was now. Ana stroked the image. All her mother ever tried to do was to protect what she loved.

She set the prayer card down beside the saucer, then touched the statute of La Virgencita and traced the sign of the cross across her body. She gave thanks to La Virgencita, a short prayer of gratitude for a new beginning. She then asked her mother to intercede on her behalf, to ask God to bless the home they were going to live in; to give her patience. To silence las malas lenguas. *The evil tongues,* she thought. *They never seem to stop wagging.*

13

WHEN ANA RETURNED TO LA FACTORÍA, IT WAS WITH AN URGENCY
and vigor that had eluded her ever since Lucho lost his job. She
walked onto the fourth floor, smiling even with her eyes. She was
relieved to be back at her station, back to her simple and uncom-
plicated days. She felt fine, she told anyone who asked. It was just
the food, she explained. Me cayó mal. No one doubted her. It was
always easy to blame food.

"¿Cómo te sientes?" asked Betty when she saw her that morning.

"Bien," she replied.

"Did you finish all of them?"

"Yes," said Ana.

"You have to take a test again," she told her. "You want to be
sure everything's back to normal."

"I will," Ana whispered, "and thank you."

"Don't thank me," she replied. "Just make sure you take care
of yourself."

She understood what it was that Betty meant, and said, "It
won't happen again."

She then told her and Carla about the lease. By the end of the month, she and her family would leave Lexar Tower.

Carla was stone-faced. "Aren't you tight on money, Ana?" she asked.

"It'll be tough for a bit," Ana admitted. "That's why I have to keep the money coming in." Carla said nothing more, and during lunch, Ana asked George for more hours and reminded him that she also did housekeeping work on weekends, in case the building or a friend of his needed a good cleaning to kick off the New Year. She charged a flat fee for each floor, not by the hour.

Each day, she prepared for the move. Before she left la factoría for the day, she'd sneak into the supply closet with her saddlebag and stuff it with black Sharpies or rolls of wide tape. On her walk home, she'd ask the salvadoreño at the frutería for any empty boxes he was about to toss. At night, in her bedroom at Lexar Tower, she'd sort her children's clothes into those fruit boxes, setting aside the ones Victoria and Pedro had outgrown, now destined for Tía Ofelia's grandchildren. In the sorting and the packing, she realized how little they came with to Lexar Tower, and just how much they'd given away. The clothes, the beds, the dresser, and the television were all that remained of their possessions. Whatever jewelry she still had before Lucho lost his job was pawned; whatever furniture they couldn't fit into that bedroom was sold. She thought of asking Carla for their couch back, a futon that was already tricky to open by the time they offered it to her. But Carla had given Ana some money for it. Una miseria, she recalled bitterly, but even if the amount was paltry, Carla had paid for it. She couldn't ask for it back now.

Between her sorting, packing, tossing and the constant cleaning and cooking, the Sosas became almost invisible. Whenever she saw Valeria in the apartment, they spoke only to exchange gruff greetings. In the evenings, they each disappeared almost completely into their respective bedrooms. Occasionally, Ana heard Valeria pass in the hallway as she headed to the kitchen or to check on Michael.

Rubén was just as evasive. She greeted him in the mornings, before she took off to work and he with the children, but otherwise said nothing more to him. There was no small talk, no jokes like there once had been. He often returned home just as she was getting the children ready for bed. Her talk with Valeria was enough to justify her distance, and she assumed it was enough to justify his. *Better this way,* she thought.

Despite Betty's help, Ana's only regret in all this was that she had asked her for it in the first place. There was always the possibility that, after a few too many drinks or even if she was drunk on love or guilt, Betty might say something. Ana wondered if she herself might one day talk about it. Not now, but in five, ten, twenty years. Would she always wonder what would've happened if she'd flushed the pills down the toilet; if there had been another way? Would it even matter?

But no one made it more difficult for her to close this chapter than Lucho. Her sleep was still restless, and she'd wake in the middle of the night to seek comfort in her chamomile tea and her address book. She never did write the word *blood* on her list. Eventually, she'd go back to bed, just as Lucho came through the front door. She'd always turn her back to him, shut her eyes, and pretend to sleep.

Then one night, he opened the door, and caught her as she turned.

"¿Estás despierta?" he asked.

Without turning around, she said, "You make a lot of noise." She moved closer to Pedro, his breathing thick and gluey. The pillow beneath his head was soaked in sweat. She blew air onto his face, then flipped him over as his breath galloped. She settled her head back down on her pillow, hoping Lucho might let her slip into sleep.

Instead, he whispered, "I'm going to eat. Will you join me?" He didn't wait for her answer. The door creaked as he closed it behind him. She lingered in bed, her son's breathing quiet now, the orange light from a lamppost seeping between the blinds. She wondered what it might be like to leave it all behind. If she went for a walk now, down those empty streets, could she disappear? Would anyone notice? Would he?

She walked into the kitchen, the cold of the hardwood floors brushing against the soles of her slippers. At first, she thought the children or the Sosas were turning down the heat in the unit; it never seemed to be cool enough for any of the men, young or grown. But it was the cooler nights that managed to leech into the wood. She held her maroon sweater closer, and squinted, her eyes adjusting to the light as she sat beside her husband at the table.

The microwave purred. "¿Tienes hambre?" he asked, as if it were the middle of the afternoon instead of nearly dawn. His yellow button-down shirt, its creases still visible along the length of the sleeves, hung on a chair. His tank top, faded with mostly minuscule holes, made her feel that much colder.

She yawned.

"Were you really trying to sleep?" he asked, and his choice of words made her curious. She really did wish she could shut her eyes, escape, even if it was to that dream and the hunger of its forest. But like all things, that was only the partial truth. Did he know that she'd been lying all along?

He didn't wait for a reply. "I wanted to talk about the furniture," he said, popping the microwave door open. He adjusted his grip on the steaming bowl of sopa de sémola she'd prepared and set aside for him the night before.

"We've got the beds," she said, "the dresser and the TV. We need a table and couch."

"We can get folding chairs for now," he said. He unbuckled his pants, blew on a spoonful of soup. "But yes, we'll need a table and a couch. Did you talk to George about working more hours?"

"I did," she said. "He's got a new girl now. This Nicaraguan. He said he'd let me know." *More hours,* she thought. He wanted her to work more hours. As if that soup he was slurping had appeared magically. As if it hadn't taken her hours to make with two children pawing at her side. She'd already spent hours hunched over the sewing machine, her fingers stiffening, her lower back flaring up, just to buy the meat between his teeth. There were only so many hours in a day, so many pieces of fabric that her eyes and hands were capable of sewing together. "Did you talk to Gil?" she asked.

He blew into the hot soup. "He said no."

The spoon clanked against the bowl. Once, at a dinner they had at his mother's, when Ana was already well into the last months of her pregnancy with Victoria, Doña Filomena served her that very same soup. It was thick, creamy, too heavy for her taste, but one that Doña Filomena prepared in the cooler months because her sons, she claimed, liked it from the moment they were in her womb. Ana prepared it every winter they'd been in New York, even though she'd feared that it might make him homesick. He never did thank her for making it.

"January's been slow," he went on. "Everyone was going here and there for the holidays. Now winter's turned everyone into hermits."

"I've noticed," she said, although she wondered how much of

the slowdown was the weather and how much was of his own doing. She recalled one particular early morning conversation, when she was still between sleep and wakefulness. He told her how he sometimes got bored in the car. When he did, he'd park by a bodega near the base, go inside to chat with the cashier and whoever else happened to be gathered beneath the overhead television, and talk about baseball or pretend to follow Mexican soccer, things he had no interest in, just to pass the time as he waited for his next ride. She wondered how many calls he had missed during his bodega breaks. But she was not inclined to argue with him, out of both exhaustion and relief that he was finally working. He was making some money, so there wasn't a need to say anything at all.

"I did speak to Valeria," he said. "She can watch the kids if you end up doing overtime."

He had picked up on the tension between them, and when he asked Ana if something had happened, she said it was just Valeria being Valeria. He didn't press her; he was never one to entertain confrontations, much less ones with his family. Besides, Valeria, it seemed, could do no wrong in Lucho's eyes. If he expected Ana to be the workhorse, then the least he could do was ask his cousin for the favors.

"I'll talk to George again," she said. "Is that it? Did you just get me out of bed to tell me to work more?"

"That's not why. We're moving, Ana."

"This isn't about the move," she replied. "It's about money. I know we need it. You don't have to pull me out of bed to remind me."

"We need more than we make," he said. He let out a long exhale, turning a bright red. He put his face into his palms as he tried to compose himself. "Everything costs money here. Money costs money. No matter how much we work, every penny we make goes right out to someone or something else. La luz, el gas, el teléfono. Mamá—"

"And *your* mother," she mumbled.

"I don't complain when you send money to your aunt," he countered. "And she's got her own children who can take care of her."

"So does yours," she said. "You're not her only child. Your mother's got Carlos too. That money you send her should stay here, with us."

"Are you telling me I can't even send my own mother money? Money that I break my—"

"No," she interrupted. "It's money that *I* break my back making. These last few months? That money's come from me."

She couldn't silence the pounding in her chest. He never stopped sending his mother her mensualidad, even though he'd lost his job, even though they no longer had a place of their own. He sent her the same amount of money every month, no matter how much Ana scrambled to pay the bills. She never asked him to stop. This was, after all, his mother, and in one way or another, that money was tied to her house, the house Ana had given as collateral. A house that didn't really belong to her or to Lucho. Though she'd never admit it, Ana hoped that the money might, in some way, atone for the rift she'd caused among the Falcóns.

He pushed his bowl away, slouching into the chair. He rubbed the back of his neck with his left hand and laid the fingers of his right one on the edge of the table. A band of skin lighter than the rest of his hand encircled his ring finger. He'd worn a wedding ring when they were in Peru, on his right hand, as was the custom. It was a slim gold band that eventually grew tight. He stopped wearing it in New York altogether, afraid he might lose it between taking it off for the meat-packing plant and home, or that someone

might actually steal it. He told her to take hers off for the same reasons. The rings were one of the first things they pawned when he
lost his job.

She put her hand on the table. "I miss how things used to be,"
she whispered. "Not Peru. I don't miss it at all. But between us."

She wondered if that's what was missing. If Peru might somehow bring back what seemed lost between them. The possibility
of returning was never as ominous to him as it was to her. No
ghosts clung to him; no mother's death, no father's disappearance.
There were too many things she could not unsee. Unlike her, he
had things to return to. People paid attention to him there. Every
preconceived notion was in his favor, even how it was that their
marriage came to be. It was always her seduction, a trick on her
part. But Peru was also where their relationship had begun, and
the luster of New York hadn't rubbed off on their marriage.

"Things will never be like that again," he said.

"Why do you say that?"

"Because a lot has changed. We've changed. We have kids now.
They're like roots. They plant you down and force you to grow up.
It's funny how much you take for granted when you only have to
worry about yourself."

"When you could do anything and everything seems possible?"
she said. "You wanted to write, remember? All those poems you
had scribbled in your notebook."

He smiled. "I started re-reading that notebook. The one you
gave me." She feigned surprise. "I go back and read it sometimes. I
had some good memories from back then." He smiled. "I remember when I asked you what you wanted to be. You didn't say teacher
or nurse or anything else I expected. You wanted to open a cebichería."

"I'd still like to," she said.

He laughed. "Ana, you make one kind of cebiche."

"But that's all you need," she said. "If we were in Peru, I'd open it in Miraflores. Serve all those rich Japanese and American businessmen."

"Even Fujimori?"

She shrugged. "A customer is a customer." She chuckled at how ludicrous it seemed now, to have that kind of goal in Lima with nothing and no one—no background, no apprenticeship, no money—for it to even be a possibility. "I had some money set aside for it," she confessed. "I'd take a little out of my paycheck every week. Not much, but just enough so that I felt like maybe it might happen one day."

He grinned. "I remember you wanted to call it 'Ají.'"

"'¡Ají!' Because a good cebiche has to be spicy."

"Except you want everything to be spicy." He grinned. "I still don't know how you haven't burned a hole through your stomach."

"Remember when we had dinner once in El Centro? I poured all that ají over my Lomo Saltado, and you said—"

"'Just go ahead and drink the thing.'" He let out a soft laugh. "I thought you were going to get sick. I knew I was. That smell! There had to be at least three or four different types of peppers in that thing."

"It wasn't that spicy."

"It'd be too spicy for Americans, that's for sure," he said. "They can't take that much heat. And the name wouldn't work either. They pronounce their 'j's like our 'll's."

"That's why I'd have a restaurant and not a cebichería," she said. "We'll call it 'La Inmaculada.' I'd serve only the purest and finest ingredients. As immaculate as the Savior's mother." He chuckled and she continued, "Although we could just put phonetics beneath 'Ají' so the gringos get it right. I'm sure we can get Valeria to help us with that."

"I'm sure she would," he said in all seriousness, although she'd meant it as a joke.

"That's when I first told you about my restaurant dreams," she said. "I never even told Carlos that."

"It's when I told you about my poems," he said. "Then my birthday came around and there was that notebook."

She smiled. "I remember you didn't want to have dinner in the first place. You thought someone might see us. Like we were doing something wrong. But as soon as we sat down, it didn't matter. It was . . . liberating."

"Liberating?" he repeated. "We weren't really free to do anything, Ana. We didn't even know what we were doing."

"I knew what I was doing," she said, putting her hand over his. "I knew I was with you. I knew I loved you."

"That cost us something, didn't it?"

She looked up. His eyes were crestfallen, dimmed by the years. She found those brown eyes alive once, vivacious. They'd melt at the sound of an accordion on the radio, or a string of carefully chosen words in a song or poem, and even, what seemed like a lifetime ago, her own laugh. He was so unlike his brother, who chose his words carefully, who planned and considered the consequences of his actions. Lucho seemed always on the verge of leaping, as if he was prepared to live for the pursuit of a goal instead of the goal itself. Yet convincing him to leave Peru proved to be more difficult than she expected. He had resisted the idea, even though his brother, after those early years in Madrid, seemed content abroad and had no plans to return. But Lucho spoke passionately about La Patria and Apristas and against terrorism. His place was in Lima, ready for whatever change might come.

Pedro's birth, however, changed his mind, and after the move to New York, the differences between his experience abroad and

Carlos's became more acute. Carlos didn't have to run or hide, he'd say, or speak another language in a country that did not welcome him. He had only a wife to worry about. There was nothing, really, for Carlos to lose as he chased whatever dream he had. There was no need for him to concede to the circumstances of his life the way Lucho had to, reduced to a ghost in a foreign land.

He couldn't get past this, and her insistence that they stay seemed only to embitter the life he now led.

"Why can't you see what we have," she asked him, "instead of what's missing?"

"I do see," he replied. "We made the choices we made, and we have responsibilities now. To ourselves, to the children. I just wonder sometimes . . ." His voice trailed off. Sometimes, he reminisced about the life he left behind. He'd talk about the Sunday afternoons he spent by the beach, eavesdropping on the ocean as it spoke to the rocks below, and the algarrobina ice cream he treated himself to on Sunday afternoons. Whenever he helped Victoria with her homework, he was reminded of the fatherless boy he helped go from mediocre scores of fifteens to a succession of perfect twenties on his math exams. Sometimes, he mentioned a former colleague or classmate, or this genius who just got a position at an American school in Monte Rico, or that imbecile who became principal. She listened, but always with a pang of worry that there was nothing in this life that gave him any joy. He talked about how difficult life was here, but rarely mentioned having any regret, which made her think that perhaps he regretted it all.

It was with trepidation, then, that she asked, "What do you wonder?"

"About our choices," he said. "I just wish things could be different. I never expected our lives here to be easy, but we've spent the last few months living in someone else's home. Who's to say we won't be here again? And the job? Do you think I like being some-one's chauffeur? Driving around in the middle of the night just to pay for the basic things we need? I do it because I'm a father and a husband and that's what I'm supposed to do. Pay the rent, pay the bills, give my kids a good education. Take care of you."

"You don't need to take care of me, Lucho." Her chest tight-ened. She had no doubt that, if she needed to, she could do it alone. Here, she could hustle, work as many jobs as she needed to make ends meet, something she couldn't do in Peru. Even with the children, there was more opportunity to earn a living in a decay-ing New York than there was in a fractious and lawless Lima. If he ever left her, or if she needed to leave him, she could make a go of it alone. She could make it here without him, even though the idea pained her. She wanted her husband, not someone to save her from the world. She already knew the world too well, better than he did, though she couldn't tell him this.

"I can take care of myself," she said. "I can take care of us."

"I've no doubt you can," he said. "You're strong. But Victoria and Pedro? They need their father." He didn't speak of love, only of duty. Was that what kept them together now? she wondered. Was it just the children, or did he stay with her to save face, like Rubén? Would he stay no matter what she did?

"Anyway," he continued, "I hope this apartment is a step ahead. I don't know if being here makes sense in the long run. There's never any money. We work and work. They won't even let us work in peace."

"We can't think about going back," she said. "Not now, Lucho. We're so close to starting over."

He nodded, and after a long pause, she stood, ready to return to bed, utterly exhausted by the conversation and in a daze about why it was he was saying all this. As she turned to leave, however, he said, "There's one other thing."

She leaned against the door frame, suddenly overcome with sleep.

"Valeria said you've been talking to Rubén out here. Late at night."

"Of course she did," she said. "She's always trying to make something out of nothing."

"Were you?" he asked.

"Yes," she said defensively, "we had some tea and we talked, that's it. I can't believe you're really asking me this."

"Were you talking about that other woman?" he asked. She didn't respond. "I know Valeria," he continued, "and I know she tends to exaggerate, but can you blame her, after all he's put her through? She chose to stay, I know. She still thinks and acts like she's in Peru sometimes. You know that if she were there . . ."

He let the words hang, and although she knew what he implied, she finished the sentence for him. "She'd have no choice but to stay. But she doesn't need to. Not here."

"It doesn't matter," he said. "It's her marriage. I told her, and I know, that this won't happen again."

She nodded. She was expected to follow the rules, to refrain from doing anything that might raise doubts about her fidelity. She was treading the line of what was considered acceptable behavior for a married woman, of what was acceptable behavior for *her*. Late-night talks with a married man about his marriage wasn't one of them.

He stood and said, "I'm going to shower." He kissed her forehead as he walked by her, and she suddenly felt a pang of guilt. She'd done nothing wrong with Rubén. She felt no need to keep their conversations a secret, yet she didn't feel obliged to tell Lucho about them either. She didn't feel the need to tell him much of anything, and it was the secrecy more than the acts themselves that made her stomach drop at his kiss.

She waited until she heard the bathroom door shut, then headed to their bedroom. She lay in bed, motionless even after he lay down next to her, her eyes wide open as the winter's night receded.

That morning, while Lucho slept and as she dressed the children, she realized it'd been days since the bleeding had stopped. She had only bled for a day and a half. She tiptoed into the bedroom closet, pulled a black plastic bag from behind a pile of sweaters stacked on one of the shelves, and headed to the bathroom. She was already late for work, and she had to breathe deeply just so the muscles in her body could relax.

She waited a few minutes, then several more just to be sure. She shook the stick, as if she could shake off the second line. But it was deep and static, and the two lines, together, matched the pair on the box.

14

SHE RUSHED TO LA FACTORÍA, THE COMMUTE AN UTTER BLUR. ALL she saw were the two lines staring back at her like a pair of eyes. She debated whether or not to tell Betty. A part of her wanted to keep as much of the affair to herself as possible. After all, Betty had only helped because she concluded that the children need their mother more than they needed a sibling. But she'd gotten Ana the pills, instructed her on how to use them. Why hadn't they worked? Ana wondered if perhaps they had, and she only needed to wait a little longer. Betty would know.

By the time she arrived, the women were already settling into their stations. She pulled Betty aside, into the same closet Nilda had taken her nearly two weeks earlier. She told her the test was positive.

"And you took the pills?" Betty asked as she leaned against the door. "All of them?"

Ana nodded. "Just like you told me."

"And you bled?"

"For two days," she said. "Is that enough? My periods are never more than three or four days anyway."

Betty rubbed the back of her neck. "We have to talk to Lety."

"Lety?" Ana repeated. "Lety Pérez?"

"She's the one who sold me the pills. We can go there after work. She'll know exactly what to do."

Ana swallowed hard. "So Alfonso knows?"

"So what if he does?" she exclaimed. "Ana, you just took a bunch of pills—"

"Pills you gave me," she said.

"Because you asked me to get them for you. I don't know what they're supposed to do or not do. I've never taken them. If Alfonso knows, that's a good thing."

Ana crossed her arms. Her leg shook as she thought of Alfonso Pérez flipping through his notebook, going down the list to find her. She should've spent the money, taken the full month's supply.

Betty reached out and held her arm. "Okay," she whispered. "We'll talk to Lety first."

■ ■ ■

WHEN THEY ARRIVED, LETY WAS PERCHED ON THE SEAT AT THE FRONT register, her eyes on the portable television. She grinned at something on the screen, and greeted them with the same smile she greeted everyone who entered the pharmacy. Betty approached the counter, leaning over to whisper that this was the friend who needed the pills. Lety's grin contracted and her eyes went into focus as Betty explained that Ana had bled for two days and took a pregnancy test that came back positive.

"Mi amor," she said to Ana, "come closer. Take your hat off." She placed the back of her hand on Ana's forehead then on her cheek. "You don't have a fever. Give me your hand." She put her fingertips on Ana's wrist. "Have you vomited?"

"No," she replied.

"Your pulse is fine," she said as she let go of Ana's hand. "Well, I told your friend here exactly what to do. If it didn't work, it didn't work. There's not much else I can do."

"But why didn't it work?" Ana demanded, her voice louder than she expected.

"Mi amor, no lo sé," said Lety. "Maybe you skipped a dose. Maybe you're farther along than you think. I don't know. But what I do know is that you need to see a doctor. Even if that test came out negative, I told you," she said to Betty, then turned back to Ana, "I told her you needed to see one anyway, once it was over. They've got to see what's going on inside."

Ana held her breath. She didn't want to know what was going on inside. She was terrified of what she'd see, what she'd hear.

"Can we talk to Alfonso?" said Betty. "He's got to have something back there he can give her."

Lety grinned once more, only this time her eyes blinked repeatedly as she leaned over the counter. "Amiguita," she said to Betty, "this was supposed to be between you and me, remember? You were getting them for a friend, you told me, right? I respect people's privacy. I think you do too. That's why you came to me. So, really, I think this should stay right here." She made a circle with her index finger as she pointed to each of them. "Among friends. Understand?"

Lety then reached beneath the counter. Ana heard something unzip, and Lety licked her thumb as she counted. She handed Ana several bills. "That's what your friend here paid. We understand each other, right?"

Ana shoved the money inside her pocket. She understood that whatever it was Lety was doling out from behind that counter, it was her own affair. It wasn't something she wanted Alfonso to know about and, like Lety, Ana would rather it stay that way.

"Now what?" said Betty as they walked into the waning day. The rush hour commute had begun, and a crowd had gathered at the bus stop. A few blocks away, trains squealed as they pulled in and out of the station.

A doctor, that's what Lety had said. She'd wanted to do it all on her own terms, in private, with only a trusted friend to help and guide her. It was too late now to try to fix it how she wanted to. She needed to go back to that clinic, and the money in her pocket wasn't enough for whatever it was she needed to do next.

"You go home," she told Betty. "I've got something to do."

∎ ∎ ∎

SHE SQUEEZED INTO THE TRAIN, HER SKIN STICKING TO HER CLOTHES IN wet patches, as she headed to Mama's street. Her head thumped, her gut was in a tumult. It didn't matter if Mama was perched at her window when she got there. She didn't even know if Don Beto would be in the back house, but if he wasn't, she'd wait. And if Mama happened to see her, she'd make up some excuse for the visit. Whatever it was didn't matter—she needed to see him.

She shot down the block, the trees silent except for the wind that rustled the leaves too stubborn to die in the winter. The florid first-floor window of Mama's building was empty. Ana spun into the alley, toward the back of the house and passed the aged burgundy car. The back house was lit from the inside.

He was there.

On the train ride over, she'd thought about how she'd tell him, then decided she didn't need to tell him anything at all. It wasn't his business, and no one else needed to know. She'd just ask him for the money and repay him later, however it was he wanted her to.

But as she stood outside, watching his shadow pass across the window, doubt crept in. What if he refused? She'd already slept with him. What if he didn't care to repeat it? What if he'd had enough, and that form of payment wasn't an option anymore?

She tapped on the door twice before he finally opened it. He greeted her in a navy satin robe and a pair of dark flannel pants. A patch of slate hair peeked through his white V-neck top. He wore slippers, black with red trims and no backs. His teeth, still new and broad, bit into the end of a cigar; the lines along his lips like strings, holding his mouth open. Whether he was preparing for an evening in or had never gotten out of his pajamas to begin with, she couldn't tell. "Ana," he said, shocked when he opened the door. "What are you doing here?"

This time, she didn't hesitate to go inside. "We need to talk," she said as she squeezed between him and the door frame. She had always stepped inside the place with trepidation. Everything in it seemed to have eyes. This time, there was no throw on the couch, and she could see a stain on one of its cushions. A nearly empty glass of brown liquid sat on top of the coffee table, nothing more. A pair of women's voices ping-ponged from the television screen, relaying news about a Colombian election as the coffee maker gurgled on the counter. The scent of his cologne was so faint that she could not distinguish it from the musk that had settled in the room. Even the woman in the picture that hung on his wall, with her palm on her forehead and her leg up in the air, seemed too bored to pay her any mind. It was as if the room went blind.

Don Beto's tepid reception was itself disarming. He didn't greet her with a kiss. There was no offer to take her coat, no hand on her back as he spoke. He did remember to ask her to sit, but she declined. He was taken aback by her abrupt entrance, and this emboldened her. This was business, and she could treat it as such.

"¿Todo bien?" he asked as he walked past her.

"No," she said quickly. "I need to borrow some money."

"Oh," he said as he sat on the couch. "What for?"

"Does it matter?" she asked. "You said I could ask you whenever I needed it, no questions asked, and I need it."

He shrugged. "I'd like to know all the same. You come here all of a sudden with that look on your face like you've just robbed a bank and you demand I give you money." He laughed. "I'm curious. Is it for your husband again?"

"It's for me," she said curtly. "I can pay you back any way you like." She hoped that was enough to end his questioning.

"I see," he said, raising his eyebrows. A smile formed on his mouth. "Well, now I *really* want to know! Tell me. Have you run into some trouble?" He scanned her body, then, as if finding the clue he was looking for, his eyes settled on her stomach. "You have gained some weight, Ana. Don't tell me you're not taking care of yourself?"

The question hung in the air, between the drip-drip of the coffee maker and the ja-jas of the anchorwomen. Its weight pinned her to the floor. "You can't even say it, can you?" he said. She felt the rush of blood to her face and averted her eyes. "Well, Anita, I can't give you money for an abortion. Even I have to draw the line somewhere." He picked up the remote control and turned up the volume, spreading his legs wide as he sat back and settled into the cushions, his cigar still plugged in his mouth.

Her voice faltered. "I need the money, Don Beto."

"I understand you need the money," he said, "but don't ask me for it. It's not like it's mine. Now, I don't know who's it is, but I suggest you go ask the father for that money instead."

"Just because I've slept with you doesn't mean I'll sleep with anyone."

"I don't know that," he said. "I don't who's been between your legs. I thought you were one of the good girls." He picked up the glass with the brown liquid and drank whatever was left in it. "But even if it is your husband's, that's still not my problem, and I don't want that on my conscience."

A vibration moved through her body. Something—her heart, her stomach—jammed in her throat. Contrólate, she told herself. She needed to stay calm. There was no one else who could help her; no other way than to ask him. Mama wouldn't help, and there was little money left in the canary envelope. Nothing remained in that doll. All she had now was Don Beto.

She gripped the back of the chair. "Por favor," she pleaded, "por favor, Don Beto. I already have two children, and it's hard. It's so hard. My husband wants to send them back to Peru. If it were up to him, we'd all go back. But I can't go back, and I can't let him take them from me. There's no way I can stay here if I have another. I can't leave. I won't. And I need my kids to stay here with me."

She faltered at every word. She loved her children. Her life had morphed into a mechanical, mundane existence since they arrived. She had resigned herself to the role of mother, of provider, of preparing and packing meals, of looking at the clock when she got home, urging it toward bedtime, of resisting the impulse to smack Victoria when she rolled her eyes or of yelling at Pedro when he refused to finish his dinner. She was a sleepless bundle of thinning hair, of fingernails stained a perpetual mustard, of patches of puckered skin, powered by a motor that constantly rammed at her chest. Her children and the circumstances of her life in another country had done this to her. Yet they were her children; she belonged here, with them. She loved Victoria's sass because it meant no one would ever shut her up. She loved Pedro's assuredness because he always knew what he wanted. Here, no one cared if she braided her daughter's hair. Here, no one told her to keep her boy out of the sun. They had no prejudices, made no judgments about her. She was only 'Mami' to them, and she hoped they could someday see her for that and more. She wanted to see, for herself, who and what she could be. She couldn't imagine doing that in a place where everyone had already made up their minds about who she was.

She needed to stay, but the only person she believed could help her now had already made up his mind. "I'm sorry," said Don Beto, "but I don't kill babies, Ana."

She wiped the tears from her face then gripped the edge of the chair. She struggled to keep her hands there. She wanted to wrap them around his neck, see him writhe like the animal he was as he struggled to breathe. "You don't get to judge me," she said. "I need the money, and you're going to give it to me."

His body shook as the room filled with his hyena-like laugh. "Goodbye, Ana." He rose from the couch, wiping his glassy eyes. "I've got a lot to do tonight. And shouldn't you be with those children you need so much?"

She grabbed his arm as he brushed past her. "You're going to give me the money," she gritted. "Mateo is dying. Mama doesn't have much time either. I know what those pills are for, the ones on her tray. They're not for her arthritis. They're for pain."

His lips became a thin line.

"You want to get everything, don't you?" she said. "The houses, the car, the money? Do you think she'll leave you with anything if she knows you've been sleeping with her clients?"

He gripped her face so quickly that her gasp got stuck in her mouth. He squeezed her cheeks until her face distorted. Her teeth seemed to swell beneath the pressure of his fingers.

"And what do you think your husband will do," he asked, "if he knows you're fucking around?"

She wrung her head and pushed her hands against his chest,

dislodging herself from his grip. She caught her breath, readjusted her jaw, and wiped his spit off her cheek. "He'll break your face for touching me," she said.

He smirked. "Not before he breaks yours. Now get out."

Her face was wet, though she couldn't pinpoint when the tears had started to come down again. She wiped her wet chin as she headed to the door. "Fuck you, Beto."

She wished she'd denied it, made up some lie. A small part of her suspected that Mama already knew about what had happened between her and Don Beto, or at least wouldn't be surprised by it. Still, it was a mistake to come to him, and she cursed herself for using all the money she'd put away. She hurried back to the station, the sleet coming down harder now. She needed to figure out what to do next.

A doctor, Lety had suggested. She could go to a clinic, but what if they asked for papers? She'd been told that hospitals and clinics don't in this part of the country, but what if they did? Even if they didn't, someone could be watching, listening, waiting for her to make a mistake and grab her.

And then how much would it cost her?

She was climbing the escalator to make her train transfer when she remembered one particular clinic. It was near the pawn shop where she'd handed over their wedding bands, her mother-in-law's earrings, and her mother's gold ring, just after Lucho lost his job. After she pawned her items, she fed her sadness a greasy buñuelo and a cup of sugary coffee from a Colombian bakery a few blocks away. She'd taken a seat at a counter, on a red swivel chair that faced the street. From behind the glass window, she'd seen a narrow blue awning with the words "Women's Medical Care" written on it in white letters. She thought it odd at the time. There was no shortage of women's clinics along Roosevelt Avenue. She'd passed by enough telephone booths and flipped through enough newspaper ads to know where to find one if she needed it. This clinic, however, was discreet. Its awning was on a second-floor window; one could walk by the building and miss it entirely.

And so, as the train now hauled itself east across the borough, Ana paid close attention to the shops that emerged at each station. It wasn't long before she saw the pawn shop's sign. When she got off, she walked along the street opposite the clinic, unnerved by the thought of someone seeing her near it and asking what it was she was doing on Roosevelt Avenue on a Thursday night. She passed a beauty salon with its murmuring blow-dryers, a Colombian karaoke bar ignited in black and fuchsia lettering, and a Chinese restaurant that looked out of place to her. She eventually stood across from the clinic, between the bakery and a travel agency, its window covered in flyers that touted deals on flights to Ecuador and Peru. From across two lanes of traffic, she could see the sign posted outside the clinic's first floor entrance. Open seven days a week. One could call twenty-four hours a day for information. They accepted all major credit cards. Not that she had any. A narrow staircase led to the clinic on the second floor, and even though the lights were on, the air conditioner and the sign and the blinds obstructed the view, which put her at ease.

Yet she couldn't move. Suddenly, the bustling of the passersby, the rumbling of the overhead train and the cars along the road fell away, and she was back on the bus that took her from Santa Clara to Lima. That night had been clear. The mountain air had invaded the bus's interior as it trekked along the incondite road. She tried to sleep, and leaned closer to Ofelia for warmth. Ofelia, whose eyes were wide and alert ever since she arrived in Santa Clara to retrieve her grandniece. In the days that followed her arrival, she had buried Ana's mother, helped Ana pack the few possessions left in the shack, including her mother's ring, then sold the property. They left on a Sunday morning, after a brief farewell to Betty, and with Ana sweating beneath the pair of jeans and the peach sweater her aunt had brought her for the cold ride and colder city that awaited them.

On that bus, Ana had huddled closer to Ofelia. She gazed outside the window, at the mountains that stroked the interminable sky with its luminescent eye. ¿Está ahí mi mamá? She had asked her aunt, hoping she'd lie.

But Ofelia was honest. "No sé," she had replied. And although Ofelia did not know where Ana's mother was, she made it clear to Ana why her mother wasn't here.

"No se cuidó," she had told her. Sara had only taken care of things when it was too late, she explained. It was too late, and that man found out. That's why Sara wasn't here.

As she stood on that street in Queens, she could hear Ofelia's voice, clear and crisp, even as the car horns blared behind her and the trains bulleted above her. She wasn't going to cry, no matter how angry or how scared she got. She kept telling herself that it didn't matter that she was alone; she had to focus only on the reasons why she was here in the first place. She had started something she had to finish, something that did not begin days or even months ago, but a shedding that had taken years. Do things for love, she could hear her mother saying, and for your own good, even if it hurts.

There was no turning back for her, yet in that moment, in the loudest and loneliest of January days she'd known, she couldn't move. She remembered the very first time she'd ever seen the inside of her body, when she lay flat on a bed and Lucho held her hand, gripping it tighter as a wand moved across her abdomen. The technician clicked on a gradient screen, describing what it was they were seeing, what it was she was hearing. It was so different from the distorted, bloodied pictures she'd seen on television and in newspaper ads; so different, she imagined, from what her mother had buried. It would become Victoria.

The noise that surrounded her grew louder, but she couldn't quiet the sound of her own thoughts. The noise only seemed to amplify the voices, all pouring in and seeping through her being, as if to cement her to the concrete.

But it was late, she realized. Her children were waiting for her, and whatever needed to be done couldn't be done at this moment anyway. Not right now. She had to move. And so she turned away, pulling her hood over her head, and hurried back toward the station, breathing fast, praying the voices might fade in the thudding of the rain.

15

ON THE TRAIN RIDE TO LEXAR TOWER, IT BECAME CLEAR WHAT IT WAS
she needed to do. She'd known all along, but simply couldn't bring
herself to think it, let alone say it. She'd go back to the clinic tomorrow, she told herself. She'd figure out exactly what the process
involved, how much money she needed, if she could really take care
of it without any papers.

It was late, however, and she was determined to set her mind
to more pressing matters. There were still clothes that needed to be
packed and labeled. There was homework that needed to be done.
Dinner needed to be plated, although she hoped Valeria would have
fed the children the leftovers by now. She stopped by the fruit
market on her way to Lexar Tower, picking up bananas and clementines and empty boxes the salvadoreño had set aside for her.
She'd forget about the day for now, focus on what needed to be
done tonight. She could think about tomorrow later, perhaps over a
cup of chamomile tea. She'd no doubt have another sleepless night.

By the time she got to Lexar Tower, the drizzle had turned to
snow. It dripped from the plastic bags in her hand, marking her
path along the mauve carpeting as she walked toward unit 4D. She

stopped short of the door as the shouts from inside the unit made her forget about the children's dinner, the packing, and everything else that had happened that day. She looked at her watch: it was just after seven o'clock. Valeria's muffled voice was incoherent. She never raised her voice at Michael; Ana concluded she must be yelling at Rubén. She jammed her hand inside her pocket, searching for her keys. She didn't want her own children in the middle of an argument between their aunt and uncle. Or worse yet, become a target for their aunt.

As she crept inside, Valeria's voice grew distant, and Ana realized the argument had made its way into their bedroom. She tiptoed into the hallway. The couple's bedroom door was shut, but she could still hear the muffled voices behind it.

She set her bags, shoes, and coat down in the kitchen, then headed to Michael's bedroom. The three children were huddled on the bed. Victoria and Michael were transfixed by a Mexican actress pacing in her soap opera living room on the television screen, while Pedro played with Michael's game console.

"Buenas noches," she whispered, shutting the door behind her.

"¡Mami!" Pedro jumped off the bed, hugging her and planting a wet kiss on her cheek.

"Pedro, you know I don't like it when you play with that," she said as he ran back to his spot on the bed. "Why don't we go out for a walk? It's snowing outside."

Victoria pecked her on the lips. "No, Mami, it's too cold," she said, holding one of her loose braids in her hand. "Can you fix my hair?"

Suddenly, the argument in the bedroom down the hall grew louder, then the floor reverberated as Rubén pounded against it. She waited until the couple passed the door, then opened it slightly and peeked outside. Rubén had his coat on; Valeria shouted at his back.

"De verdad que estás loca," he declared.

"I'm not crazy!" Valeria shouted. Her usually coiffed hair sprung loose from her head. Her black mascara was smeared and her red mouth hung open, trembling. "And I'm not stupid either. I see how you look at her. I know something's going on. I'm not an idiot!"

"I can't with you," he said. He turned around, but she stepped in front of him.

"Where are you going?" she asked, blocking him. "You're going to see that other one, aren't you?" She pummeled her fists into his coat. "That whore and your fucking bastard!"

He held her arms. "Stop it!" he shouted. "¡Basta ya con tus estupideces! If you want the body shop, then take it. I can't do this with you anymore."

"The body shop," she scoffed. "What body shop, Rubén? The one you've run into the ground? The one I'm trying to keep open? And for what? For you to give money to your whore and that kid? So you can have another woman—"

Ana heard a shuffling behind her, a reminder that she wasn't the only one taking refuge in the bedroom. Victoria inched closer to her as she tried to peer through the door.

"Mami, what's happening?" she whispered as Ana closed the door.

"Nothing, my love," she said. "Go back to the bed."

"They get like that sometimes," said Michael in English as he walked over to the television. "She yells a lot." He raised the volume, then hopped back onto the bed.

"Is she screaming at Tío?" asked Victoria, as she tried to reach for the door again. "I wanna see!"

"That's enough!" said Ana. "Stay here. I'm going to make sure your aunt is okay. Don't leave the room until I come get you."

When she stepped into the hallway, she heard Rubén's steady voice. "I'm tired, Valeria," he said. "I'm tired of all this." Keys fumbled and then, without another word, he let the door slam behind him, a *ding* ringing through the apartment.

Ana was about to go back inside Michael's room, then hesitated. Despite the loud cackling from the television, she could hear Valeria's low, muffled cry. She'd never heard Valeria cry. She couldn't remember ever seeing her shed a tear. The pain in her sob was so palpable that Ana's own throat clogged. She couldn't ignore it. She couldn't ignore *her*.

She inched her way down the hallway, past the living room, then peeked into the foyer. Valeria was on the floor, her back against the wall, facing the shoe tray. Her arms were folded over her knees, and her face was buried in them. For the first time in the eight years Ana had known her, she wanted to hold her. Perhaps it was because she needed to let out her own sadness and needed comfort herself that she wanted to sit beside her on the floor and cry with her.

She stepped closer, unsure whether to call out her name or just hold her. She remembered what it was that Lucho had said about dreams and nightmares: when you call out someone's name, you pull their soul back from wherever it wandered to. She couldn't leave Valeria alone, to linger wherever it was that she'd gone. It seemed too painful. So she whispered, "Valeria."

At the sound of her name, Valeria's head jerked. Her eyes were swollen from her crying, but her voice was even and sharp. "So you finally show up?"

Her tone made Ana stand still. "I picked up some groceries after work," she explained. "Can I bring you some—"

"Cállate," she said, moving off the floor almost cat-like. "After everything I've done for you, this is how you repay me."

Ana stepped slowly back into the living room, almost colliding with the recliner. She grabbed the back of it, her eyes never off Valeria, who looked ready to lunge. "What are you talking about?" she asked, ready to block her face if she needed to.

"You and Rubén," she said. Her black eyes were swollen, entangled in a web of thin red veins. "I know there's something going on between you two."

"Is this because we had tea the other night?" she asked. "Valeria, that's all it was. We were just having tea."

Her neck hollowed out, the vein on her temple beating as she tensed. "Be careful, Ana," she warned. "I see you. I see the lie that you are. You're nothing but an opportunist. You went from one brother to the next because you couldn't go back to whatever hole you crawled out of. It's too bad one of my cousins thought more with his dick than the other. And now you see Rubén and think, 'Mira a este gordo. With a nice home and money. He's looked at worse women than me, so why not me?'"

"I don't think that," said Ana.

"I think you do," she said. "Except Rubén will never look at you that way. Want to know why? Porque eres corriente. You're cheap. He has cheap tastes, I know. That Dominican is proof of that. But you've been passed around the family too many times. That's a special kind of cheap, and not even Rubén will go for that kind."

Ana clenched her jaw as she struggled to stay calm. "So you see," she managed, "I'm too . . . cheap . . . even for your husband. Then there's absolutely nothing for you to worry about."

"Nothing?" Valeria repeated, inching closer. "Absolutely nothing?" Vodka lingered on her breath. Her body rattled, then she went still before running into her bedroom.

Ana caught her own breath as she paced the living room. Valeria and Rubén had just had a fight, she told herself. She and Lucho were leaving soon. Perhaps these were things Valeria needed to say because she wouldn't have the power to say them once Ana was gone. But where was this coming from? The children didn't need to see this. She needed Valeria to calm down. Lucho was gone for the night, but she thought about calling him. He'd know how to handle Valeria. Maybe he could talk some sense into her.

Or maybe it was best to keep him out of this.

Then Valeria was back in the room. Ana's eyes darted to the box in her hand, the same white box with the fuchsia letters that Ana had hidden inside her closet. She clutched a ball of toilet paper in her other hand. Ana's stomach contorted, pulling blood from every corner of her body.

"Nothing going on, right? So you haven't slept with him, right?" She held up the box. "Then what the hell is this? Tell me. And what the fuck are these?" She threw the toilet paper at Ana, and two of the hexagonal pills Betty gave her rebounded off the floor. "You don't think I know what that is?" she said, pointing to the pills. "I've carried those in my suitcase before, Ana. I know exactly what they are!"

Ana fell to the floor. "You went through my stuff?"

"Why would you keep a pregnancy from Lucho?" she demanded. "Why, Ana, unless you didn't want him to know you were pregnant?" Her voice cracked as she wept. "Why don't you want him to know? Tell me."

Ana's heart hammered against her chest.

"You just want to get rid of it, that's why."

She picked the pills off the floor, shaking her head.

Valeria smacked the wall, and Ana's body jumped. "Don't pretend those aren't yours!" shouted Valeria. "I found them in the bathroom, and they're not mine. They're not mine."

Ana trembled in disbelief. "This is between me and Lucho, Valeria. I don't owe you any explanation."

"This is my house, you bitch! You live in *my* home. Who do you think pays for this place, Ana? Who pays for the food around here? For what your kids eat? I work like a mule to keep the shop open and for what? So you can sit with *my husband* at my table in my kitchen in the middle of the night and whisper shit in his ear."

"I was just giving him advice—"

"Is that all you were doing?" she asked, her voice cracking. "Or are you already sleeping with him?"

Ana held her hands in prayer by her lips. She took a deep breath as she looked into Valeria's eyes. "There's nothing going on between me and Rubén. There never was and there never will be. This," she said, holding up the pregnancy test, "is between me and Lucho."

Valeria's tear-filled eyes grew wide, fish-like. "So it's Lucho's?" she said. "It's Lucho's and you're doing this?" She swallowed hard, a look of disgust distorting her face. "You're worse than I thought, you know that?"

Ana let out a breath, knitting her brows as she tried to keep from crying. She wouldn't give Valeria the satisfaction. "I don't care what you think anymore," she said. "And now that you know this has nothing to do with you or your husband, you can leave it alone." She marched toward Michael's bedroom, and saw Victoria peer through the door and then quickly shut it.

"You could have hurt the kids, you know?" shouted Valeria. "Leaving that shit on the floor like that. What if one of them ate it, then what? But you don't care, do you? You only care about yourself. You've only ever cared about yourself. You dragged my cousin here, away from his family, his friends. For what? To cut meat off of dead animals and drive around títeres." She choked back her tears.

"And you come to my home and try to meddle in my marriage. You take over like this is yours when it'll never be yours."

The full weight of Ana's body was on the doorknob. She steadied herself, and took a few breaths as Valeria's words seeped through her skin. She'd never taken anything that wasn't already hers. She wished she had some of Valeria's things: her home, her education, her green card. She didn't want whatever she had with Rubén, but there was something about Valeria's relationship with Lucho that she *did* want. It was the one thing Ana truly envied about her, but she could never admit it, not to her.

And so she straightened, and said, "I don't want anything you have." She leaned her forehead against the door. "The truth is . . ." she paused, simultaneously saddened and empowered by what she said next. "Te tengo lástima."

Valeria froze. "You can't feel sorry for me," she whispered. "You have no right to feel sorry for me."

Ana ignored her and pushed open Michael's door. She shut it quickly behind her. Victoria and Pedro were on their feet, their eyes wide. "Mami, ¿qué pasó?" asked Pedro. "Why is Tía screaming?"

"She's fine, my love," she said, setting a knee on the ground so they were at eye-level. She rubbed his arms. "Don't worry. Go sit on the bed with Michael."

"But why is she screaming at you?" asked Victoria.

"Hijita, please don't ask me any questions right now." She had the box under her arm, the two pills in her maroon sweater's pocket. She was sure she'd taken them all. She swept the sweat off her forehead with the back of her hand. There was no doubt in her mind that Valeria would tell Lucho. One thing was clear: she couldn't stay at Lexar Tower any longer.

But where to go? There was only one place she could go. Brooklyn was a long, cold train ride away, but there was no other place she could think of running to. She needed to go to the Sandoval sisters. "You know what?" she said to her children, in the liveliest voice she could muster. "We're going to visit Tía Betty tonight."

The volume on the television was on full blast. Victoria turned toward it. "Can we go after *Amparo*?"

"No, I need you to get ready now."

"Is that why Tía Valeria is crying?" asked Pedro. "Because we're leaving?"

She didn't answer, and instead poked her head out the door once again. The hallway and living room were empty. Valeria's bedroom door was ajar. She whispered to her children, "Go quickly to our room. Come on, let's go."

They hurried across the hallway toward the mess Valeria had left in their room. The closet was pillaged. The boxes and suitcases Ana had packed were now empty. Clothes, papers, and bags were scattered throughout the floor. She darted to the bed and lifted the mattress as sweaters fell off it. The canary envelope, stuffed with the papers that documented their identities and the little money they had left, lay undisturbed between the mattress and the box spring. She scooped it up and tucked it beneath her armpit.

She then headed to the closet. The sweaters, once piled on a shelf, now littered the floor, along with the black plastic bag where she'd hidden the pregnancy test. She picked it up, put the box back inside, and then the canary envelope. She grabbed Liliana from the top bunk.

She took one of Pedro's sweaters from the floor, shook it, then tossed it to Victoria. "Here, help your brother get dressed. Get your schoolbags too. Hurry up." She put the plastic bag on the nightstand, forgetting the sacredness of the space she'd made for her saints and dead mother, then threw an old backpack onto the bed and began stuffing it with socks, several pairs of underwear, a few sweaters, whatever could fit. She did the same with her children's schoolbags, filling them with their uniforms.

She needed to call Lucho. At the very least, he had to know she was leaving and where she was going. She could explain the why of it later.

"I'll be right back," she said, before stepping out into the hall-way. "Avancen."

She could hear the muffled voices from the telenovela behind Michael's shut door. It was the only sound in the unit. Valeria's bedroom door was closed. Light reached out from its edges. She hurried toward the kitchen.

Her coat and the Key Food bags still hung on the chair. A puddle of water had formed beneath it. She threw on her coat, took a couple of clementines from one of the bags and stuffed them in her pockets. A magnet with the RapiCar address and phone number was on the fridge. She picked up the phone and dialed the number on it.

A man with a Puerto Rican accent picked up on the other line.

"It's Doce's wife," she said, referring to Lucho by his cab number. "Can you please get a message to him?" She was taking the children to Carla's. No, she didn't need to speak to him now. She didn't want him to stop her, and he'd get the message soon enough. "Tell him to call Carla's," she told the boricua, but she knew Lucho would nevertheless call Valeria.

She was in the middle of grabbing a few juice boxes from the fridge when the doorbell rang. She froze. She hadn't heard the buzzer from the lobby. It was a weekday; it was dinnertime. She thought it might be a neighbor. On any other night, she might have answered the door. On this night, she couldn't bring herself to budge from the safety of the kitchen.

When the bell rang a second time, she heard Valeria's footsteps as she made her way to the door. She passed by the kitchen. Her hair was now tied in her usual bun. Her face had been wiped clean of the streaks of mascara. Her eyes remained red and swollen. She didn't look at or utter a word to Ana as she passed by.

When she did, Ana snuck her head into the foyer for a second time that night. Her heart dropped as Valeria opened the door. She saw the shiny squares first, fitted on the left corner of the first officer's chest, then the uniforms, as black as San Martincito's scapular, before she processed who the men were at the door.

"Good evening, Ma'am," said the shorter officer. "Someone called about a burglary?"

"Yes, I called." Valeria spoke in English, her voice small and delicate, but it pounded in Ana's ear. "Do you speak Spanish? I only ask because the person who stole from me is here. She doesn't speak any English."

Ana scrambled back to her bedroom. Her sneakers squeaked as she ran down the hallway, its walls narrowing with her every step.

It's over.

She shut the bedroom door behind her.

"Mami, what's going on?" asked Victoria.

"Nada," she said quickly.

Don't panic, she told herself, over and over, as she searched the room for a way out, but there were only the windows and the door. She cursed herself for never finding another way out of the room. She whispered to her children, "I need you both to be very quiet, okay?" then walked to the windows. It was too dark to gauge the distance to the ground below.

There was a shuffling in the hallway. Valeria's voice grew louder, the officers' footsteps heavier, and before Ana could figure out how to climb out of the fourth-floor window with her two children, the cops were inside her room.

"Things have been disappearing from my room," she heard Valeria say. "She hit me when I confronted her." Her saccharine voice barely masked the hint of satisfaction in the words that followed. "Es ilegal."

The blood drained from Ana's face. The knot in her stomach once again began to twist.

"Her kids too."

She pulled her children closer. Victoria dug her face into Ana's abdomen. Pedro clung to her leg. Her own heart collided against the inside of her chest. The room spun silently around her as she struggled for air. *Breathe,* she reminded herself, but she was drowning.

She shut her eyes and grabbed at her heartbeats, hoping to stay afloat. She heard her children whimper. She thought of Lucho, alone, driving down a street somewhere in Brooklyn.

Then, as if he were rousing her from a nightmare, she heard Michael's voice. "Holy shit!" She opened her eyes, and watched as he ran inside the bedroom. "You're cops!" He bounced up and down, then reached out to touch one of the officer's uniform.

"Hey, buddy," said the man, gently setting Michael's arm down.

The other officer kept his eyes on Ana, then moved on to the children. He tilted his head, then rested his hands on his hips. "So what do you want us to do?" he asked Valeria. "Deport them?"

Her eyes widened, as if the answer should have been obvious to the man. "Yes, of course."

The officer cleared his throat. "Ma'am, we don't deal with immigration matters."

Valeria's eyes went from the officer to Ana, then back. "What do you mean you don't deal with immigration matters?" she stammered. "She doesn't have any papers. Just ask her. Ask her to show you her green card. She doesn't have one. At least arrest her. She stole my bracelet."

The other officer glanced around the room. "Whose room is this?"

"It's a guest room," said Valeria.

"Have you been staying here?" he asked Ana.

Before she could answer, Valeria interjected. "They've been staying here. And like I said, some things were missing from my bedroom, and I found them in here—"

"So who did this?" asked the officer, pointing to the clothes scattered on the floor.

"I came in here to look for my jewelry, which *she* stole."

"What exactly did she steal?"

"I told you, my bracelet. A gold bracelet that I got—"

"She didn't steal it." It was Michael who spoke. He was circling the officers, inspecting their uniforms, but he had the entire room's attention. The officers and his mother's, because he was contradicting her; Ana and her children's because it was one of the rare moments they'd ever heard him speak Spanish.

The officer bent down, and asked, "Why do you say that?"

Valeria interrupted. "Michael, amor, you're confused."

"No, I'm not. You gave it to Tía for New Year's, remember? When I was hungry and I went into your room. I saw you give it to her."

The shorter officer turned to Valeria, but didn't bother asking her if what Michael said was true. The answer was on her face and neck, where splotches of red had burst onto her skin. He turned back to the hallway, and his partner followed close behind. "Like I said, Señora, we don't deal with immigration matters."

Valeria chased after them, Michael behind her. "What do you

mean you don't deal with immigration matters? You're cops. She's undocumented. She's not even supposed to be here. She's in my house, and I want her out!"

"Señora, we have to deal with real crimes," he said. "Actual burglaries, robberies. You have an immigration problem, you call immigration. You don't call us."

Ana rushed to the door, shutting it behind them. She collapsed onto the floor, sitting against the door, making sure it stayed closed. Her heart was still audible. Moments later, the front door slammed, and its ding once again rang through unit 4D. She heard Valeria in the hallway, racing to her bedroom. "Get out!" she yelled as she stormed by.

The room grew still, and as Ana's heart steadied, she wept. Her children tiptoed to her. Victoria sat down beside her. Pedro crawled onto her lap. "Ya pasó, Mami," he whispered as he held her face between his hands and smiled. "Ya pasó."

Victoria interlaced her fingers with that of her mother's. She kissed her hand. "It's going to be okay," she said, with such certainty that it was enough to shake the fear out of Ana.

She kissed them both and stood. "Come on," she said. "We're leaving." She dressed them quickly and finished filling up the backpack and a carry-on suitcase. She grabbed the plastic bag on the altar. She placed her mother's prayer card in the inside of her coat pocket. She asked the Virgin for protection. *Don't abandon me,* she prayed, as she put her saints inside the plastic bag.

Snow hit the glass doors that opened to the balcony like bullets. She covered their bodies from head to toe, ready for whatever the winter night might throw at them. The children carried their bloated backpacks; hers was heavy on her shoulders. She pulled the carry-on suitcase onto the fourth-floor corridor. None of them looked back as they rushed toward the elevators.

"Hold the door open," she told Victoria when they reached the lobby. The snow crashed into the glass doors that made up Lexar Tower's main entrance. Her sneakers squeaked as she hurried to it. Her stomach was still in a knot as they exited the doors. The snow had piled on along the path that led to the sidewalk. Her coat was still unzipped. She reached into the pocket of her maroon sweater, and tossed the pills into the snow. She was still grabbing at her heartbeats as they made it out the last few steps and into the cutting January night.

16

CARLA'S APARTMENT WAS ANA'S ONLY REFUGE. SHE HAULED THE
carry-on suitcase up the subway stairs to the 7 train and, after two
transfers and what seemed like an eternal ride, made her way with
the children through Queens and into Brooklyn. She struggled
with every step, unable to shake the fear the frigid night had con-
gealed to her bones.

The threat of deportation had always been present, but never
quite so close. They were always surrounded by others who'd fled
home. That was the appeal of New York; they were merely four of
millions. It was only over the summer, when the slew of raids at the
meat-packing plants robbed Lucho of the job at his, that the threat
of deportation inched its way to the forefront of her mind. It was
always a possibility, one that tried to reach her but never could wrap
its fingers around her. The fear of it didn't feel real until tonight.

None of that fear had spread to Pedro. He was captivated by
the evening train ride under the pelleting snow. For most of the
ride, he stared out of the subway car window, mimicking the conductor's words at every station, watching the snow ricochet off the
glass.

But it had spread to Victoria, and as the last train headed to Carla's sat at the station, she asked her mother why it was that they had to leave their Tía Valeria's.

"We were always going to leave," Ana explained. "We just left a little early, that's all."

"But why did the police come?" she whispered. "Why was she yelling at you?"

"She was upset about something," said Ana. "It's not important. And the police just came to visit."

"No, Mami," she said, her eyes widening. She came closer, as if she was about to reveal a secret. "They take people away. Michael told me. All kinds of people, not just bad ones. People that aren't supposed to be here."

Ana wondered how long her daughter had known. She couldn't conceal the truth from her forever, yet it didn't seem quite right to admit that this was the reality in which they lived. "Sometimes they do," she conceded.

"Are we supposed to be here?" she asked.

Ana looked into her daughter's owl-like eyes. "We're supposed to be together," she replied. "Right? They didn't take us, did they?" Victoria shook her head no, pushing aside a lock of hair that fell around her eyes. The peach baubles that looped around the ends of her two braids had slid down to their tips, unable to keep them from becoming undone. Ana tucked the lock of hair underneath Victoria's hat. "And they won't," she assured her. "They'll never take me from you and Pedro. You understand?"

Victoria pressed her lips together. "But what if they do?" she asked. "Like they tried with Papi?"

Ana wrapped her arms around her daughter. She wasn't going to cry in front of her children, not again. "I promise you," she said,

"We'll find a way back to each other. No matter what happens. I'll find a way back."

She touched Valeria's forehead with her own. Victoria then rested her head on her mother's shoulder. "Sing me your song," she whispered. Ana knew which song her daughter wanted to hear, even though she hadn't sung it in more than a year. She held her closer, and as Pedro hummed along, she sang quietly of the chicks that cry when they are hungry and cold, and the mother who searches for corn and wheat, who brings them food and gives them shelter under her wings.

When she finished, she asked them not to mention the police when they got to Carla's. "I don't want you to scare the Lazartes," she said. The two nodded, then Ana tugged on Victoria's loose braid. "I'll fix these when we get there."

By the time they reached Brooklyn, the snow had slowed to a dance in the air. The clouds were low. She was back on familiar ground. It was the first neighborhood she and her family had lived in, before Carla told her they needed to find their own way. She rarely visited Carla since she left, returning only a handful of times in the years that followed. Nothing had changed. The bodega near the train station where she used to pick up coffee in the mornings was still open. The plastic chair beside its front door, where a Dominican man in his seventies sat in the mornings with his coffee, was still there. The boarded-up red building that once, she was told, was a bank, loomed like a mountain over the string of mostly shut stores and four-story walk-ups in the blocks ahead. Garbage bags lined the edges of the sidewalks, already punctured by burrowing vermin. It was all so familiar, and that familiarity drained her. She was back where she started. She allowed herself that moment, letting her body dip briefly into what felt like despair, then shook it off. She couldn't linger in sadness. She didn't have that luxury. "Vamos," she said to her children, as she hauled the suitcase beneath the fallen sky.

A fresh layer of snow coated the stoop in front of Carla's building. She hoisted the suitcase up the stairs as Pedro and Victoria shouted for Betty, then Hugo, Yrma, Jorge, and then Betty again. Ana knocked on the first-floor window before Carla finally came out to open the front door.

Once inside, they forgot the hello kisses and buenas noches, and immediately took off their wet coats and boots, piling them by the door. The late-night visit had reenergized the three Lazarte children, who were already in their pajamas. Victoria and Pedro scurried to the couch, blowing into their hands while Ana rubbed life back into their cold, wet feet. Carla disappeared into her bedroom, the last room in her wormy apartment, and returned with blankets and oversized socks that smelled like mothballs. Ana pulled the bauble elastics from Victoria's braids and shook the wetness out of her daughter's hair. Betty offered cups of warm milk, which the children finished quickly so that Yrma Lazarte could show them the musical keyboard she'd gotten for Christmas.

"Victoria, your braids!" Ana shouted, as her daughter ran behind Yrma into the bedroom she shared with Betty. She put the elastic bands in her pocket and realized her own body hadn't lost its shiver. She undressed in the bathroom, her fingers sore and tender from the cold and from gripping the suitcase. She threw on the oversized sweatshirt and pajama pants Carla had given her, but her jaw still trembled. She took several breaths and patted water on her cheeks to stay alert, stay calm. She was safe now, she told herself. They were safe. Yet as she looked at her own reflection in the mirror, she wondered when she'd ever stop running.

Her chest continued to thrum as she stepped into Carla's airless kitchen. Pots with mouths crusted in red and brown stains languished on the stove. Dishes bathed in the sink under a film of cloudy water. Boxes of cereal leaned against each other on the counter, their torn flaps inhaling the pungent air. A hint of onion and tomato seeped through the lid of the trash can, carried by the steam that whistled through the radiator. Even the refrigerator, at least a decade old, rattled every few minutes to protest the heat.

Despite the suffocating room, a cup of tea waited for Ana at the table. So did Betty and Carla, who stopped whispering to each other as soon as she entered the room. They'd want to know what happened, what it was that brought Ana and her children to their door. It was always hard for her to lie to the Sandoval sisters. They'd known her since she was a child, but aside from their long history together, they knew how to lie and how to spot it. Carla, in particular, had an ear so attuned to bullshit that hiding things from her had been particularly difficult for Betty. But Ana wasn't prepared to tell them everything that happened that night either. She just needed a plausible explanation for leaving Lexar Tower. She left out the police and the pills.

"I don't understand," said Carla as she fanned herself with a crinkled issue of *TV y Novelas* magazine. "Valeria thought you stole her bracelet? The one we all saw you wear on New Year's Eve? She'd never let you wear it without her permission. Why would she accuse you of stealing it?"

"I still had it," Ana explained. "I suppose she thought I wasn't going to give it back. But I never meant to keep it. With work and all the packing I was doing, it just got lost in all that mess. She asked for it back, and I guess I couldn't find it fast enough for her. So she lost it. She screamed at me, called me a thief and a freeloader."

Carla grunted. "Why, because she gave you a bed to sleep on? You're her family. Well, you by marriage, but Lucho and the children are her blood. He lost his job. You needed a place to stay. What, did she expect you to live on the street? She's supposed to help you."

"Everyone outstays their welcome at some point," she said, and as soon the words came out, Ana flushed. She didn't mean to sound ungrateful to Carla, but the look on her face meant she took it that way. "I mean," she tried to clarify, "Valeria never wanted me there in the first place. She loves Lucho. He's like a brother to her. She's always saying that at least, but she's never liked me. She keeps trying to convince Lucho to move back to Peru. She doesn't think we can make it here. Sometimes I think she just wants us to fail to prove a point."

"What, that it's hard here?" said Carla. "She doesn't need to prove that. It *is* hard here."

"Not that," said Ana. "That Lucho made a mistake by marrying me."

"She's going to think that," said Betty. "You were with his brother. Besides, every limeño thinks the same way she does. If you're not from the capital, you're just a savage. It's that Spanish blood. It's what makes them think they're better. She's got some Swiss in her, too, no? That only makes it worse. Anyone that looks like us or Ernesto just ruins the race. You can't let their ignorance get to you."

"That's easy for you to say, Betty. You don't even look like you're from Santa Clara."

Carla fanned herself more fervently. "She thinks we're savages, doesn't she? Ignorante. She tried to embarrass Ernesto on New Year's Eve, remember? When she said his mother was from la sierra. Her own husband is serrano, but she had to point out Ernesto's mother. Well, no one here cares about those things. Whether you're from Santa Clara or Lima doesn't matter. Peruvian, Puerto Rican,

Nicaraguan, Mexican. We're all the same to these gringos. She's been here long enough, she should know that."

"But she's white," said Betty, "and she's from la capital. That hasn't changed. And now she lives in a fancy building in New York and has a green card. I'm sure those things make her feel even more superior."

"But to treat your own family this way?" said Carla. "Accuse you, Ana, of stealing? Qué porquería. Y qué pena."

"It is sad," said Ana. "I feel it more for my kids. Michael's the only cousin they have here, but I don't want them anywhere near her. It's clear now the kind of person she is. I don't ever want to see her again."

They fell silent and, for what seemed like a long, long while, the only sound Ana heard was Pedro's laughter at what was on the television. The giggles came quicker, morphing into a refrain that made her pulse pound. Up until that night, she didn't believe Valeria was capable of any real harm. She was pretentious and selfish, but Ana was willing to bear the brunt of her flaws for the sake of Lucho and the kids. She could forgive the accusation of adultery, the name-calling, even the invasion of her privacy, if that was all that happened that night.

But she couldn't forgive the call to the cops. She couldn't erase the sight of Valeria pointing her finger at her, at Victoria and Pedro, calling them *illegal* as if their very existence were an absolute impossibility. What was illegal about them? Their presence? Ana's effort to make a life for them here? What was it that made her soulful son and her inquisitive daughter so criminal?

If there was one criminal that night, it was Valeria. She was the one who wanted to rob them: Victoria and Pedro of their mother; Ana, of her children; Lucho, of his family; the family of a life. Even if she hadn't succeeded at tearing them apart, she managed to take from them whatever sense of safety she and her children had left. Ana couldn't forgive her. Not this, not ever. If there was one completely true thing she said that night, it was that she never wanted to see Valeria again.

Then Betty asked, "When do you move into the new apartment?"

Ana snapped back into the room. "Next week, I hope. Sully said it's almost ready. I just can't go back to Valeria's." She paused, hoping Carla might pick up on what she wanted and offer help before Ana had to actually ask for it. When she said nothing, Ana turned to her and said, "Carla, I don't want to impose. I just didn't know where to go. We'd only be here for a few days—"

Carla immediately put her hand on Ana's forearm. "You don't have to ask," she said. "We don't have much space here now, but I'd never say no to you and the kids. And it won't be for long. Soon we'll be helping you move into that new apartment. Let me talk to Ernesto. I'm sure he'll understand."

"Thank you." Soon, thought Ana. Soon she'd move into a new apartment. If only soon could be tomorrow; if only it had been yesterday. If only Lucho could get Sully to finish faster, especially now that the lease was signed.

Then, suddenly realizing she hadn't heard from her husband, she asked, "Has Lucho called? I left a message with the base before I left Valeria's."

Carla and Betty exchanged glances, but neither had spoken to him that night. "I'm sure he'll call soon," said Carla. "He's probably got a busy night, what with this weather." She stood, ungluing her forearms from the plastic table cover. "I'll find some bedsheets for the living room, get you guys set up on the sofa bed. Vicki can sleep with you and Yrma," she told Betty. "There's enough room on that bed for the three of you."

Carla disappeared into the unlit hallway and, once she was out of earshot, Betty scooted her chair closer. Her eyes grew large, the skin beneath them thin and purple under the fluorescent light. "Now tell me the truth," she whispered. "What really happened with Valeria?"

Ana exhaled slowly. Her spine curved as she leaned over the table. Carla bought the pared down version of what happened that night at Lexar Tower. Valeria accused her of stealing that bracelet, and Ana left, unwilling to hear any more of Valeria's insults. That story was enough to get her and her children refuge in Carla's home. As far as she was concerned, that was the only story she needed to tell. If she spoke of the rest, it might feed gossip. Gossip that, without question, could make her situation worse than it already was.

But this was Betty, and the weight of the night was too much for Ana to bear alone. That her own carelessness could have gotten her and her children deported weighed on her with a heaviness that made it almost impossible to move.

"She found the pills," she admitted. "And the pregnancy test."

Betty's face went pale. "The pills? You said you finished them."

"I did!" she said, but she wasn't sure anymore. Her voice cracked as she whispered. "I swear I did." She replayed over and over the times she took those pills. In the bathroom, with the Malta. In the middle of the night. The shower was running once. She remembered her mother. Pedro came in. He woke up and she wasn't in bed. He was so scared. She was so, so tired. She wondered when it was that she'd made a mistake. "I don't know."

Betty's eyes sprinted back and forth. "But what do you mean she found them?" she asked.

"She found a couple," said Ana. "In the bathroom."

"Did she know what they were?" she asked, agitated. "Did you tell her?"

"She knew. Apparently, it's one of the things she takes in her suitcase. She asked about the pregnancy test. She thought I was sleeping with Rubén." She rolled her eyes at how ludicrous the idea seemed, but Betty still had a look of consternation on her face. "I told her I wasn't, which I'm not. Then she called the cops."

"¿La policía?" she repeated, as if she'd misheard.

Ana recounted what happened next. How the two police officers stood at her bedroom door while Valeria pointed at her and her children, told the cops they had no papers. She recalled more details in the retelling, as if it were another one of her dreams: the coolness of the bedroom wall as she pressed her back against it, how Pedro whimpered as she held him tighter, Victoria's hot breath on her stomach as she hid her face, her feet inching back against the wall even though there was nowhere to go. "If it wasn't for Michael," she said, "I don't know where we'd be right now."

Betty fell back in her chair. "Malvada. I knew she was a piece of shit, Ana, but to try to deport you? I never thought she'd go that far."

"I should've known," she said. A nagging in her gut prompted her to say what she said next. "Le gusta su trago," she whispered, as if she were betraying a secret. "She drinks every night. Every night. Sometimes its beer. Sometimes rum or vodka." She had never considered Valeria an alcoholic. That word was reserved only for men, those so drunk they stumbled in the streets or had to be brought home by a pair of equally inebriated friends. She'd never seen Valeria drunk, not to the extent that she slurred her words or needed to be carried to bed, but she did notice how quickly the bottles of alcohol and cans of beer disappeared from unit 4D. The alcohol that was there during Valeria's month in Peru was still there when she returned. Whenever there was a shortage of one bottle or another, it was quickly restocked. Even though she saw it,

Ana didn't want to acknowledge it. It seemed to her that neither did Lucho or Rubén.

"I don't think the shop is doing well," she continued. "It's why she's there all the time. It's why she's always taking stuff back and forth to Peru." It wasn't just her marriage that Valeria was worried about losing, but the body shop, the business that she'd poured her time and her parents' money into building. Ana suspected it was this that Valeria was most terrified of losing; that, and Michael. "I don't want your sister to know what happened," she said. "The last thing I want is to be de boca en boca, especially after tonight. I need to keep my family out of people's mouths." She didn't want Carla blabbing to the women at la factoría, but she was more concerned of what she might say to Mama.

"Don't worry, I'm not going to say anything," said Betty. "But my sister's not good at keeping things like this a secret. Neither is Ernesto."

"I know that," she replied. "By lunch tomorrow, I'm sure everyone will know what happened tonight. That's why I couldn't tell her everything. No one needs to know there's an alcoholic in my family, or that she tried to deport us. It's humiliating, all of it." There was no question in her mind that, however malicious Valeria was and whatever troubles she was going through, it was no one else's business. Not that she cared about protecting her reputation, but Ana couldn't shame Valeria without also hurting her own family by association. "I'd rather people wonder if I really did steal that bracelet. It's better than people thinking Lucho might also have a drinking problem. Valeria thought I took it, so I left. That's all your sister or Ernesto needs to know. We're moving into a new apartment soon, so we were going to leave anyway. That's all anyone else needs to know."

Betty threw her head back. "Are you sure she doesn't know I

gave you the pills? I don't want her starting any trouble for me, Ana." She insisted that in all that transpired that night, Betty's name was never mentioned. Her reassurance, however, did little to quell Betty's fear. "You should've known better," she continued. "It's horrible what she did. I can't imagine doing that to my worst enemy, let alone family. But Ana, come on. You know you should've taken better care of this."

"I did exactly what you told me to do—"

"I don't mean the pills," she said. "Well, that too. But you just said she likes to drink. She's losing her business. She's unhinged. And you know how jealous she can be, especially with her and Rubén's history. He's always been so different with you. Always thanking you for every little thing you do. It's like you're doing him this huge favor by just handing him a plate of food. He helps you clean up, he buys things you tell him you need for the apartment. He treats you better than his own wife, and it's very obvious. And you're young, you're pretty. You live with them. Wouldn't you be just a little jealous if you were her?"

She knew Betty was right. Ana had never flirted with Rubén. She was too reserved to flirt with anyone, and she didn't even find him particularly attractive. But it was the friendship, the advice, the secrets she and Rubén shared, however few they were, that were problematic. Even the appearance of intimacy was something both Valeria and Lucho had called out.

Yet nothing could justify Valeria's actions that night. "That doesn't make what she did right," she said.

"It doesn't," Betty agreed. "But she was in Peru for a month. An entire month! You were the only woman in that apartment, and you acted like the place was yours. Then she finds those pills and a pregnancy test in your room. I'm not saying she's right, but look at it from her perspective."

"I took care of the place while she was away," she said. "I treated it like it was my own, yes. That doesn't mean I was fucking her husband."

"No, it doesn't," she said. "But if you had nothing to hide, you could've told Lucho. You could've made the decision together and then you could have gone to Alfonso together and there'd be nothing to hide."

"Except it's not Lucho's decision to make," she said. "Besides, you know I can't tell him."

"But why can't you? If it's his child, then please tell me what the problem is. What is it that you're so afraid of?"

She opened her mouth to respond, then stopped herself. There was so much she was afraid of, but nothing she wanted to voice. A part of her believed that saying her fears aloud might make them real, but some were already tangible, alive and visible for all to see. She was afraid of being a mother again, of putting her body through the havoc of pregnancy once more. She feared losing the small sense of independence she had now that her children were a little older, no longer nursing or relying on her embrace as their sole source of comfort. The age that didn't show on her face showed elsewhere on her body. On the surface of her abdomen, with its torn and stretched skin, and in the breasts that hung unevenly on her chest. It showed in the lack of control she had over something as basic as urinating, and the constant need to line her underwear in case she carried something too heavy or sneezed. Lately, when she lay in bed unable to sleep, her heart palpitating and her breath short, she was reminded of being in her last month of pregnancy, when she could barely move without feeling like she had climbed four flights of stairs. She had become this señora, heavy with stress and scars, something, she convinced herself, that her friend— younger, childless, her body intact—couldn't possibly understand.

But it wasn't just reliving the physical and mental demands of pregnancy and mothering an infant that she feared. It was what she had now, even in the simultaneous chaos and simplicity of her life, or perhaps because of it, that she wanted desperately to preserve and nurture. She wanted her marriage. She wanted her children. She wanted her job and to keep working, to save, perhaps one day have that restaurant she dared to speak of over dinner with Lucho so many years ago. If she hadn't intervened, then what? She'd be sacrificing her future and that of the children she already had for something she did not know. Not that it was an easy decision to make. She tried to detach herself from it, thinking only of the reasons to do it. She kept going back to that day in la huerta, when she needed to pick up the blade and swing it, not because her mother told her to, but because, despite whatever she felt then, she needed to eat and a sacrifice had to be made.

She couldn't tell Betty this. "I told you," she said. "Lucho wants to go back. He just needs a reason. What better reason than another mouth to feed?"

Betty drew up her knee and rested her chin on it. Her voice was thick as she muttered, "Well, you can't have it now. You know that, right?"

She knew. There was no going back at this point. She had taken the pills; she'd bled. She'd know soon enough what effect, if any, they'd had on her. But there was no going back. She had started something and she needed to finish it.

Betty then whispered, "You should think about sending Vicki and Pedro back." She shot her hand up before Ana could protest. "Piénsalo. That's all I'm saying. Just think about it. What happened tonight could happen again. You could be snatched away just that fast. Those kids don't deserve that. They shouldn't live in constant fear of losing you or each other."

"But that's exactly what you're suggesting I do," she said. "You want me to break up my family. Send them away like they're one of Valeria's packages."

"Sending them to Peru is not the same as having them taken from you, Ana! And don't get mad at me for saying this, but you're not thinking about them. They need stability."

"They need their mother," she said, exhausted. Had this been any other night, Ana might have had the energy to continue arguing, to challenge Betty's authority on motherhood and marriage, on what Ana herself could or could not do with her own body. But she didn't want to argue anymore. What she wanted, more than anything, was for her friend to stop talking, to shut up and give her permission to cry.

But without missing a beat, Betty asked, "What about Lucho? You're going to tell him the same story you told Carla?"

The question made Ana shake away the silly need for a hug and a good cry. She cleared her throat. "No," she replied. "He needs to know the truth." She could get away with telling Carla and the rest of the world a redacted version of what happened that night, but not Lucho. "He's going to want answers from Valeria too. She'll tell her version. I have to make sure he hears mine."

Betty placed her hand on top of Ana's. "It might not be as bad as you think," she said.

Ana put her other hand on top of Betty's. She stroked it with her thumb, blinking to clear the tears that had made their way up. "You're wrong," she said. "It will be." She could hear Pedro's laugh, a sweet flitter, taking flight above the noise. "It'll change everything."

17

HOURS LATER, CARLA ONCE AGAIN OPENED HER FRONT DOOR. THIS time, it was Lucho who stood at her doormat. "Compadrito," she whispered, "come in, come in."

He entered the dark living room almost robotically. His seasons-old coat halted each step. His glasses fogged over from the heat in Carla's living room. His loafers were caked in snow, and although he'd beaten them against the mat, he didn't take them off when he entered the apartment. Like his wife and children earlier that night, he didn't greet anyone, not even Ana.

She sat beside Betty on the couch, covered in a blanket. The late-night talk show with Don Mario Villanueva flickered on the television screen. Betty stood, taking a few steps toward him, but Ana didn't budge from her seat.

"You should get out of those clothes," said Carla. She made a gesture with her hand, beckoning him to turn over his coat. "Vamos, you don't want to catch a cold."

But he kept it on, his eyes set on Ana. "Where are the children?" he asked.

"Sleeping," replied Carla. He continued to stand by the door, silent and unmovable. She looked over at Betty. "We'll go make you some tea. Peppermint, with a little honey?" she suggested. She didn't wait for a reply. She gave Betty a nod toward the kitchen, and the sisters hurried out of the room.

They were alone, but neither moved. No one bothered to turn on the light. Only the television screen illuminated the room, casting shadows that bounced off their faces and the walls. The windows rattled with the wind, louder than the television itself, but otherwise the apartment was hushed, so quiet they could have been the only two people in that building, on that block.

When he did move, it wasn't to occupy the space beside his wife that Betty had left empty. Instead, he sat on a chair to the left of her. In the adjacent room, one of the slumbering Lazarte boys shifted in his bed. "Lower the volume," he whispered to her, pointing to the remote control beside her on the couch. She did as he asked, and when the rustling had stopped, he said, "I just want to know one thing." She braced herself for whatever question he was about to ask. He looked at the floor and said, "Are you pregnant?"

It was a question she expected. He didn't call Carla's until nearly an hour after she arrived. Yes, Carla assured him, Ana and the kids were there. They were fine. But when she asked Lucho if she should hand the phone over to Ana, she didn't. Instead, she paused, hung up, then said he'd be there soon. That was all that Lucho had told her. It was then that Ana understood whom he'd called first. "I see you had time to talk to Valeria," she said, "but you couldn't even bother to talk to me."

"Don't try to change—"

"Did that drunk tell you that she called the cops on us? Did she tell you she tried to get us deported?"

He wrinkled his face. "What are you talking about?"

"I'm talking about the cops, Lucho." She pounded a fist into the couch, then lowered her voice. "She called the police. They came to the apartment. She told them I stole her goddamn bracelet. The one she gave me on New Year's Eve. She called me a thief, then she pointed at me, at Victoria, at Pedro." Her voice broke. "She told them we didn't have any papers. That we were illegals."

Saying the word aloud struck an unexpected blow. She'd heard it said so many times; she'd said it herself before without giving it much thought. She was undocumented, and isn't that what the word meant anyway? Illegally in the country because they didn't have permission to be there in the first place. They didn't have the paperwork; they didn't really belong. But it was different this time. This time, it was like a stick aimed not at her thigh or face, but straight at her gut. It was the realization that she couldn't protect her children, not even from a mere word. She couldn't shield them from either its implications or its consequences. They were deportable, discardable. Lucho couldn't shield the children from the word either, but she blamed herself for making them all susceptible to it. She was the reason they were in the country in the first place. She was the reason they were still at Lexar Tower. She said nothing, did nothing, even though she knew that Valeria was unstable. Worst of all, it was *she,* their mother, who had stood in that room, unable to move or speak, paralyzed by that single word as it infected the air.

A look of bewilderment settled on Lucho's face. "Right," she said. "She didn't tell you. Why would she? She just gave you her version of what happened."

"She didn't say anything about the police," he admitted.

"Well, she called them. And she wanted to get us deported. You would've known that if you'd called me first instead of calling her."

"I called her home because that's where I thought you were," he said. "I didn't think you'd put the kids on a train to Brooklyn at night and in this storm."

"What did you expect me to do?" she said. "I couldn't stay there after what she did. She was ready to put me in handcuffs, Lucho. And now our kids have to live with that memory. You should've seen how Pedrito was shaking. He was so scared. And Victoria's terrified they're going to separate us." Her voice quivered. She expected some reaction from him, but all she saw on his face was confusion. She tried to be still, but her hand once again hit the couch with the force of a whip. "Dammit, Lucho, don't you get it? She wanted to deport us. Your family. Your children!"

She couldn't hold it in. Neither her friend nor her husband had given her permission to cry, but she did it anyway. She shook with each muffled sob. She needed to accept the reality of what could've happened that evening. She needed to let go of the guilt.

He moved from the chair to the couch and sat beside her. He didn't console her, but his closeness was enough to give her comfort. When she finally grew still, he whispered, "She didn't tell me any of that. I'm sorry. I'm sorry I wasn't there. She wouldn't have done it if I was there."

She wiped her face with her sleeve. "I don't think that's true."

"I would've protected you, Ana," he said.

"No," she said, shaking her head, the tears still coming down. "You couldn't have, and that's what scared me. We got lucky. We got lucky that she called the police and not immigration. If she'd called them, there's nothing anyone could've done."

He rubbed his fingers across his eyes and then his temples. "Why would she do that?"

"Because she can."

He shifted on the couch. Then, as if he hadn't quite grasped the magnitude of what Valeria had done, he said, "But you didn't answer my question." Her stomach contracted again. "Tell me. Are you pregnant?"

She let out a long, tired breath. "It wasn't coming," she admitted. "That's what those pills were for. I'm sure she told you about the pills."

"What do you mean 'wasn't coming'? Since when?"

She looked up at the ceiling as if searching for the answer or some sort of relief from the heavens. "I didn't get it last month," she said, "or this month. So that's two."

He sunk into the sofa, befuddled. "I can't believe this. I thought you were taking care of this," he whispered.

"I was."

"That's what we agreed to, Ana," he said. "It's the one thing you have to take care of—"

"What do you mean 'the one thing?'" she demanded.

"And you're telling me you can't do it?" There was another rumble in the room next door. He threw his hands up. "We can't stay here. I'll call Sully tomorrow. I'll see how quickly we can move in. Maybe we can at least leave some of our things in the apartment."

She was stuck on what he'd said only seconds ago. He blamed her for getting pregnant, and this wasn't entirely unexpected—for all his progressiveness, sex was a domain she, as the woman, had to address. But it was his assertion that this is what they had agreed to that bothered her most. She knew that having another child was out of the question. But there was a bitterness in his tone that reminded her of the reaction he had when she told him she was pregnant with their first.

He kept mumbling, something about packing up whatever was still at Valeria's, getting the furniture into the new apartment, who would watch the children while they sorted it all out. She finally interrupted. "Lucho," she said, still in a daze. "Lucho," she repeated. "Do you really think that? That all I have to worry about is not having any more children?"

He held his hands and leaned onto his knees, still avoiding her gaze. "I know it's not," he said. "But after everything we've been through . . ." He let his voice trail off. "I don't know what you did or didn't do to try to fix it. And you know something? I don't want to know." He shut his eyes, his hands in prayer under his chin. "Just fix it," he said. "Just make sure it's fixed."

She blinked away her tears. "You mean how I didn't with Victoria?"

He didn't respond. She set the thought aside almost as quickly as the words slipped from her mouth. They said nothing for a long while, turning their attention to Don Mario, or to the sound of bedsheets rustling in the adjacent room. The tea eventually came, tepid and strong, and the sisters went to their rooms, unable and unwilling to linger. It wasn't until Ernesto came home, still dressed in his blue janitor's uniform and struck by the sight of the two on his couch, that they realized it was past midnight. "What are you doing here?" he asked as Lucho explained that there was a problem with Valeria, and that, if it wasn't too much trouble, he'd appreciate it if his family could stay there for a few nights. "Claro, claro, Compadrito," said Ernesto, the look of confusion still on his face. But there was no time to get into the details. There were several hours left before daybreak, and so Lucho zipped up his coat, threw on its hood, and left without making a sound to finish his shift.

■ ■ ■

THE NEXT MORNING, ANA HEADED BACK TO QUEENS. THE SNOW THAT had accumulated overnight had already turned into a gray-black mash at every corner. The trains ran slower than usual, even as she headed in the opposite direction as the rest of the world. She couldn't recall when she last rode the 7 train into Queens during the morning rush instead of out of it. It was always toward Manhattan, and she'd catch the city's skyline just before she made her transfer to the train that took her into Brooklyn. She didn't particularly like Manhattan; there was something almost menacing in the somber, metallic spikes that rose across the river. But the city slumbered like a child under the morning's veil, and there was an irrepressible sense of foreboding as the train moved farther and farther away from it that made her wish she was racing toward it instead of away from it. The shorter, stouter Queens buildings awoke reluctantly under the soft light of the still-dormant sun. Even the snow-topped warehouses and tombstones seemed to blister under the new day. She kept pressing the outside of her coat's chest pocket, tracing the curves of the bracelet that was tucked inside it. Un poquito más, she kept telling herself as the train snaked eastward.

At every subway stop, the faces that boarded the train became more familiar. They were dark-skinned and sleepless, like her, dressed in clothes she swore she'd seen in the shop windows along Steinway Street. Some slept or rested their eyes as they slumped in their seats, while others clutched the morning paper or a cup of coffee or the hands of small children with one hand while pushing a stroller with the other. It was a contrast to the riders she'd grown accustomed to seeing on her morning commute, the slow influx of the young and well-groomed, unloved by the sun, suited up or layering the finishing touches on their faces, with their backpacks and headsets filling the westbound trains the farther away they got from Valeria's.

The subway car itself was impeccably clean. A hint of lemon from whatever liquid was used to wipe the car's black-speckled floor lingered in the air. Across the car, an advertisement for a technical school was clearly visible. There were no flyers for psychics tucked

into its silver border, and so the man pictured on it, with a gradua-
tion cap and surrounded by his young family, smiled brightly at her
for a long time. She was sitting in the last car of the train, number
4257. She took out her address book and wrote it down. She'd play
Win 4 later with those numbers.

She listened closely whenever the conductor spoke, fearful she
might miss her stop. Fearful, even, of the stop itself. The conductor's voice, by turns sunny and harsh, kept Ana from dipping into
doubt. Not over what she had to do; there was no turning back at
this point. But doubt about whether she would have made the same
choices in the first place. She'd convinced herself that if she had
to do it all again, she'd do it exactly the same way. Ask Betty for
the pills, make the blood come. She reminded herself of the goal.
It was always to give herself and her family a fresh start. Change
was a natural part of the journey, but she wasn't going to lose her
marriage or her children to the heat of it. Whatever she'd done to
keep them together she'd done with them in mind. The hard times
would pass, just like their homelessness, just like Lucho's unem-
ployment had passed. The days to come, as difficult as they might
be, would also pass. That morning, as the black night turned amber, it became her mantra. Pasará, pasará.

Yet in those moments when neither the skyscrapers nor the
tombstones nor the faces could distract her from her thoughts,
there was a sense of doubt. Her choices might have indeed been
different if she knew that it didn't matter to Lucho how she fixed
it, as he put it, as long as she fixed it. Did that apply to everything?
she wondered. Did he not care what she did as long as it was just
fixed? As long as he didn't see or didn't know how she did it?

There was a bitterness there, at once familiar and foreign, that
lingered on her palate. So she clung to the conductor's voice, telling
the groggy commuters to stand clear of the closing doors, to help

her turn away from the realization that perhaps she could have done so many things differently. She focused not on where she was now, at this moment, but rather on where she needed to be.

In the end, she didn't need the conductor's voice to tell her the stop. The image of the diamond on the awning was unmissable. It appeared before the train even pulled into the station. When she got down to the shop, the owner was in the middle of lifting its metal roll-down gates. Guitars, drums, and other musical instruments occupied one window, while the other was filled with necklaces and rings on red velvet displays. The bracelets were kept inside, at the end of a long glass counter.

She dug into the inside of her coat pocket and pulled out Valeria's gold bracelet. Unlike the last time she was here, she didn't haggle with the owner. He offered her a sum that more than covered whatever she needed to pay at the clinic. She placed the money in her inside pocket and made her way a few blocks east. The scent of fresh-baked buñuelos swam through the morning air. She threw on her hood because she was cold, she told herself. This city was always so cold.

She wondered if this was it. If once it was done and over, she'd feel relief. If after this, she could really start again. If some wounds might finally start to heal, or even disappear, instead of marking her. Or would this be another one? Would she be punished for it? She asked God to forgive her, though at this point in her life, asking for forgiveness was almost a compulsion. What she was doing wasn't wrong, she told herself. It couldn't be. She had no choice but to believe that it was right.

Pasará, pasará, she kept telling herself, until she finally reached the dark blue awning, inhaled the thinning air, and took off her hood as she climbed the stairs to the second floor.

18

paperwork, paid upfront, then waited in a room filled with women, some alone, others with friends, less than a handful with their partners. Once inside the examination room, she was asked if she was sure. When it was time to confirm, her abdomen was covered in gel and the wand moved back and forth. To her relief, she wasn't allowed to hear or see anything. She needed someone to pick her up, and so she called Betty, gave her the address, and asked if she could come meet her. She'd be done in a couple of hours. She waited some more, until it was her turn to go under. She woke up groggy and in some pain, sitting in a wheelchair inside a crowded recovery room. She sipped a cup of chicken broth, sucked on a lollipop, and was told that, once she was better, she could leave. Her husband was waiting outside.

Half an hour later, she found Lucho sitting in the waiting room. He said nothing as he walked her outside, hailed a cab, and headed to Carla's.

Once they arrived, he left her with the sisters. He couldn't stay, he told her. He didn't want to be late picking up the car.

There was nothing either had to say to the Sandoval sisters. Carla understood—her face had drained of color the moment she saw Ana. Betty hurried to make tea and brought over blankets to keep Ana warm. "Ya pasó," was all Betty said to her. They never spoke of it again.

In the days that followed, Ana said little to anyone except the children. The palpable tension between her and Lucho made their reluctant hosts uncomfortable. Carla fidgeted, unable to meet Ana's gaze for days. She kept Victoria and Pedro entertained, distracting them with whatever task she needed help with in the kitchen or a television show whenever they clamored for their mother. The day after the procedure, Ana was well enough to offer her help with dinner and to clean up after the kids had gone to bed, but Carla never let her lift a finger. Sit down, lie down, take it easy, was all Carla said in those days, even after Ana had returned to work.

What made it worse for Ana was that Ernesto knew. It was impossible for Carla to keep it from him. In his own way, he showed his concern. "¿Todo bien?" he'd ask, nodding, as if he always expected her to say that, yes, everything was fine. He'd follow the question with another, "When's Lucho coming back? Soon, no?" He always seemed to want to talk to Lucho. Lucho, who said little to her in those days, except to ask if she needed anything, to which she always said no.

After a full day of mostly resting on the Lazartes' couch, her life continued as if that trip to the clinic had never happened. Not that there was any time to dwell on it. There was that familiar urgency to leave—this time, the Lazartes' apartment—and begin anew elsewhere.

On the day they moved in to the new apartment, more than a week after the procedure, there was little left to actually bring into it. Lucho had retrieved the undone suitcases and boxes from Lexar

Tower. On one of the few occasions he did speak to her, he told Ana he'd get the dresser and their beds on the day of the move, and that Rubén would help.

While Betty watched the children at Carla's, Ana spent that first morning in their new home cleaning it. She swept a new broom across it three times and sprinkled Florida water along the floors and walls. She bleached the powder-blue bathroom tiles and scrubbed whatever stubborn brown stains Sully's boots had left on the floor. She opened all the windows, then walked the length of the apartment with a lit incense stick, asking La Virgen to bless and protect the place and urging the spirits that lingered to leave.

When she was finished, she slumped on the empty living room floor with her back against its uneven wall. The incense stick was still in her hand, its smoke slinking toward the high ceiling. Her arms ached, her legs quivered, the nape of her neck perspired.

The cleaning and the incense and La Virgen—it had only been a halfhearted attempt to rid herself of the past, to protect herself from the unprotectable. She had moved almost mechanically in the days after the clinic. She had to keep moving, to keep each day going so as not to drift into the what-ifs. There was simply no room for that.

But it was then, in that empty, lopsided room, underneath its dim light, that she found herself alone, in silence, for the first time in a very long time. She was unprepared for it. The room contracted, compressing her body to the point where she could no longer take its pressure. She cried then, exhausted. If, in that moment, Lucho had again proposed returning to Peru or sending her children back, she would have said yes. For the first time, she wondered if Valeria had been right all along. If maybe they were not meant for this.

She wondered if Lucho had said anything to the woman, if he'd demanded an explanation for why she'd done what she did, if he'd cursed her out the way she wished she could have then; the way she still wished she could. She tapped the back of her head against the wall for even thinking about her.

She rubbed her wet cheeks with the bottom edge of her T-shirt. She didn't want anyone's pity, least of all her own. No regrets, she reminded herself. There *was* a point to it all, a reason for it. Her children were here; she was still here. She was not about to relent, not to this place or anyone, not to her own body. Certainly not to anyone named Falcón. She let herself finish her cry, then picked herself up, tossed the incense stick in the sink, and began to unpack.

The wind picked up as she sat on the empty bedroom floor, folding and sorting Victoria's sweaters and Pedro's jeans. It entered through the crevices along the window frames, and the entire building grumbled gently. She reached her hand out toward the window, sensing the cold air as it kissed her palm and encircled her feet. Winter, it seemed, had decided to stay after all. They'd need to cover the windows.

It was then that she heard Lucho and Rubén climbing the stairs. From the stairwell, Lucho shouted for her to open the door, and although she hesitated even getting up, there was no way to avoid either man.

It was the first time she'd seen Rubén since the night of Valeria's confrontation. As he set the mattress against the wall, she noticed his hair was freshly cut. Strands of gray sprouted from his mustache; he hadn't dyed it. His face looked thinner, and he had an almost boyish look to him now that didn't suit him. They brought up the box spring and frame next. The pair made several trips with the station wagon that morning, returning to Queens to pick up the television, the disassembled bunk bed, a few folding chairs, and finally the dresser. At the end of the first leg, Lucho asked for something to drink, and after that, she left Styrofoam cups filled with tap water on the table at the end of each run to avoid serving them. After the last trip, Lucho downed his water in a single gulp, then urged Rubén to sit down and rest as he ran back to the station wagon to fetch one last box. Just like that, after all those warnings and all that talk of impropriety, he left her alone with Rubén.

"This is nice," he said, giving the kitchen a once-over as he leaned against the wall. He poked his head into the living room. His voice was smaller, even with the echo in the room. "It's bigger than your last apartment."

She picked up Lucho's cup and rinsed it under her new faucet. It didn't matter if they were alone or not. She had no intention of saying anything to the man.

"May I sit?" he asked. She didn't reply, but like he always did, he sat down anyway, on one of the folding chairs he'd just carried up the stairs. She kept the water going as she wiped the counter, trying her best to keep him quiet while they waited for Lucho. But she realized Rubén had something to say.

"I'm sorry, Ana," he almost shouted. "I'm sorry for what Valeria did." He rubbed his hands against his thighs. "She can be a lot to handle when she drinks. Irrational at times. I never should've left you and the children there with her. Not in the state she was in." His voice was tinged with an almost childlike pleading. "I never thought she'd do what she did. Never. Not to you. Not to anybody. You've got to believe that. If I did I never would've left."

An unexpected wave of anger hit her. She turned around to face him. There was that look of his again, the one that she'd caught glimpses of during their talks, and she immediately resented that look of melancholy. He had no right to it.

"Come on, Rubén," she said. "You left Valeria a long time ago.

You've ignored her for years. It's why she is how she is. You can't sit there now with that stupid look on your face and try to apologize for it." It might have been Valeria who called the police, but Rubén was at least partly at fault for what she'd done. He let his wife navigate new motherhood alone. If he'd taken care of her then—if he'd paid more attention to her than whatever stupid impulse drove him to an affair, then maybe Valeria wouldn't have doubted him or her marriage. Maybe if he'd been faithful, or if he'd even stopped seeing the woman, or if he'd shown Valeria a hint of affection, some respect, perhaps she wouldn't have seen Ana as a threat. If he'd taken care of the business, then maybe that could have restored her faith in her husband. Maybe that would've been enough. Maybe then Valeria would've never called the police at all.

Ana held up her hand as if to stop herself from feeling any sympathy for the woman. "You know what? I don't care. I didn't marry her. I don't live with her anymore. She's your problem, not mine. I just thank God I got my children out of there."

He kept his eyes on the ground. There was nothing left for him to say, nothing she wanted to hear. Whatever apology he offered for himself or his wife couldn't change what happened that night. She couldn't fathom ever forgiving Valeria. The woman was as good as dead to her. Whatever affection Ana had for him, whatever friendship and love of a brother she might have felt, also died that night.

She turned toward the living room, set on getting the bedroom organized now that her furniture was there, when he said, "She's leaving me." His voice was once again small. His eyes were set now on the empty cup he kept turning in his hand. "She didn't actually leave," he clarified. "I left. She asked me to leave."

Suddenly, Ana understood the look of remorse on his face. It wasn't for the wrong his wife had done to her, but for the wrongs he'd done to his wife and their consequences.

"I'm renting a room for now," he continued. "Until we sort this out. She wasn't there just now, when we picked up the furniture. Lucho had to convince her to let me back in the place."

He stopped turning the cup and looked up at her. "You said she wouldn't leave me."

"She didn't leave you," she replied. "Like I said, you left a long time ago."

"I suppose you're right," he said. "I don't even know if I want to go back. I loved her once. She was so beautiful and smart. Smarter than I'll ever be. She still is. I just don't know if we can go back to how things used to be. Not after everything that's happened."

It never occurred to her that Valeria might actually end things with Rubén. There was Michael and the money tied up in the auto body shop, of course, but there were also the marriage vows. Once a Falcón made a promise, they kept it. To an outsider, it might appear as if they were loyal and devoted, but to an insider—to Ana, to Rubén—it was nothing more than hubris. A separation, a divorce, was a failure. There was something wrong with a person if they couldn't make a marriage work. For that reason alone, Ana always believed Valeria would stay, no matter how much Rubén betrayed her.

"Yes, you're different," she said. "You have Michael now. She's got this family that I know she's proud of. If there's one thing that never changes, it's that Falcón pride."

His gaze grew distant. "She won't stay with me for Michael's sake. I don't know if I want to either. I pushed her, Ana. I admit it. I pushed too far." He snapped his head up. "You know he's been asking about you. And Vicki and Pedro. Where'd you go, when you're coming back."

"Your son turned out to be my angel that night." She smiled weakly. "But I think some distance is good for everyone right now."

Her implication was not lost on him, and Rubén stood just as Lucho climbed back up the stairs. He declined Lucho's invitation to stay for lunch, and in the middle of their exchange, Ana disappeared into the bedroom, unwilling to put on a show of civility any longer than she needed to. When Lucho bellowed that Rubén was leaving, she ignored him. Did he expect her to run out and say goodbye? Good that he was leaving, and good that his wife had finally had enough. He deserved it for opening his mouth and telling Valeria who-knows-what about her. And good that Valeria's marriage was over. It had been over for a long time, but neither she nor Rubén was willing to admit it. *Qué pena,* she thought. Now all that remained of what they once had was that faltering business and Michael.

■ ■ ■

MOMENTS AFTER RUBÉN LEFT, LUCHO WALKED INTO THE BEDROOM.

"We need plastic," she said matter-of-factly, as she placed a pile of clothes on the bed. She pointed to the windows. "Look at those. They're uneven. The cold just keeps coming in."

"What did you say to him?" he asked.

Her head snapped. "That it's best for our families to avoid each other for now," she replied. "And that he's been ignoring his alcoholic wife for years."

He grunted. "You always like to point out other people's problems, don't you? You could've just accepted his apology."

"Why would I do that?"

"Because he's sorry for what happened, Ana. And now Valeria's thrown him out."

"You want me to show him compassion, is that it? You want me to feel sorry for that mujeriego? None of this would've happened if he'd just kept his pants on. Or bothered to pay her or that business of theirs some attention. I'd almost feel sorry for her if she wasn't the piece of garbage that she is."

His eyes narrowed. "Do you honestly think you're so much better, Ana?"

She hurled the sweater in her hand against the floor. "What are you saying?" she demanded. "That I'm garbage, Lucho? You're comparing me to her?"

"You're not perfect. And I'm not saying that what Valeria did was right. It wasn't. But you've got no right calling her or Rubén out on their mistakes when you can't even acknowledge yours."

"Don't do that," she said, standing up. "Don't start going down my list of defects when you won't even see your own."

A month ago, she wouldn't have dared to challenge him. She would've listened to that list. She would've accepted Rubén's apology, insisted that he stay for lunch, made lunch, even heeded Lucho's call to say goodbye, as if she were a child who needed a refresher on a lesson in manners. She might have prayed harder to La Virgen for things to work out. She would've forced the ghosts out of their new home, out of her, instead of only nudging them to leave. That's how much she feared losing him.

She realized that she didn't anymore, yet she felt deeply the sting of what he said next. "You lied to me. You lie so much. Do you even know what's true and what's not anymore?"

"I was late," she said. "And it's not like you even wanted to know. You never want to know anything. You just expect me to take care of things. Well, I did. I took care of it."

"Yes," he whispered, "you take care of things in ways I think I'd rather not know about."

The room held on to his words much longer than she thought possible. The walls yielded to the glacial wind as it poured through the crevices. Her face suddenly became hot. "Of course you'd rather not know," she said. Her pulse quickened, urging her to say what she had wanted to say for so very long. "You prefer not to see anything, don't you? The rent, the bills, how much we spend on food, when the kids need new clothes. It's so much easier to have someone else do it all for you." She wiped her brow with her sleeve. "But *I'm* the one who's had to make those decisions, Lucho. I'm the one who's had to make those sacrifices."

He slammed his hand against the door and her body jolted. "Don't act like you're a victim, Ana! I've had to make sacrifices too. I've had to wipe shit off toilets and pigs' blood from my mouth because *you* are set on staying here. If I were in Peru, do you think I'd be doing any of this? Driving around delinquents, trying to have conversations with people who barely have an education? You know I wouldn't even be here if—" He stopped himself and began to pace, letting out a long breath and grabbing the back of his neck.

"¡Dilo!" she shouted. She already knew what he was going to say. She never threatened to expose his own regret, not to spare him from the truth of his own feeling, but to spare herself from seeing just how deeply the crack in their marriage ran. "Say it, Lucho. I know you've been thinking it. You've been thinking it all these years. So won't you just say it? If I had never had Victoria. That's what you want to say, isn't it? If I'd only had an abortion then."

The word still felt blasphemous. She could hardly say it without a choke. She never regretted having Victoria. Her birth gave her a chance to grow and nurture a new family, her very own, the kind Ana had only imagined others had, the kind she tasted only in the moments when her father was home. She could be a good mother. She'd never yell or hit or blame her children for the circumstances of her life. But she had to let go of some things—her body, that restaurant. She had to try to make peace with the memory of her mother, of what she had to do to keep Ana safe. Her children had that at least. They were safe; they had her. They had their father. She'd had to let go of hers long ago; she didn't want to let go of theirs.

But soon after she had Pedro, she began to mourn the woman she had to bury under the soil of motherhood. Every birthday, every holiday, and soon every evening brought with it an impulse to create, to prepare a meal as if to serve her own dead parents, and this left an unexpected ache for what could have been. The dream to have a restaurant—what was once un sueño tonto—didn't seem so silly anymore. Not after being at Regina's; not in New York. She didn't know if the ache she felt was for that elusive dream, or if she merely longed for the father who never came back from the mountain and the mother she knew with certainty was gone. They were phantoms who never seemed to leave her side.

She thought she had buried away the what-ifs, but when the blood failed to come, the what-ifs rose up from the very pit of her being. What if, back when it was Victoria in her womb, she had chosen differently? What if she had chosen differently with Pedro? Would there be no ache for that dream of hers? Would that ghost of the person she thought she could be linger like it did now? Could she silence the voice that kept telling her that sacrifice was part of the journey?

She waited for him to say something. An admission, a confession that yes, he had wanted her to make that choice then, and he had wanted her to make it now. That it wasn't just she who cared about what was lost; about what could have been or what could be. That he might somehow lighten the weight she'd been carrying.

But when he said nothing, she pressed on. "You blame me for everything. But I never asked you to marry me."

He rested his head against the door frame. "We both know

things would've been different. If you hadn't had Victoria . . ." His voice broke, and he couldn't finish. "But she and Pedro are the reasons I keep going."

She swallowed the lump in her throat. "We would've been just fine without you."

"You would have," he said. "You've always managed to make your way through life. You've never needed any rescuing. I always admired that about you. You don't need me or anyone else."

"But you do," she said. "You need someone to save you, and I did. I saved you from the burden of another child."

He tightened his eyes. "You saved me from the burden of another child," he repeated. "I don't even know if that child was mine."

She glared at him. "It was yours, Lucho."

"I don't know that," he said. "I wanted to make things work, Ana. Everything was falling apart in Lima. I thought it was only a matter of time before it happened to you and me, too. I thought we had a shot here, I really did. But you're right. You've never needed me. You could have. You could've trusted me, Ana. You could've let me in. Really let me in. But you never have." He shifted, his face flushed with color. When he spoke next, his voice was steady. "If you'd been honest with me, then maybe. But you hid it all. The pregnancy, the abortion. And you lied. You lied about where you got the money."

Her heart picked up. He turned to face her, and his eyes held the unmistakable look of disappointment. "Did you get the money," he asked, "from Alberto Bustamante?"

She made no reply. She turned away, unable to look at his face.

"Ernesto said Mama's husband could always help," he said, "if we're ever tight on money. All Carla has to do is keep the man company." He shook his head in disbelief. "'If it doesn't bother her, it shouldn't bother you.' That's what he said to me. He said it was better than you having to make the choice you had to make."

Her eyes widened. *So stupid,* she thought. She should've known Carla might have been sleeping with Don Beto. If anyone felt the pressure to keep her family together, it was a mother of three who'd only just been reunited with her children. And of course, Don Beto would be all too willing to help. What did Ernesto care? As long as no one else knew, it didn't matter.

"It took every ounce of me not to hit him," Lucho continued. "But I knew. The moment he said it, I knew. Mama wasn't going to give you more money, not when you stopped paying her."

"I didn't stop paying her."

"Was it his?" he asked. "Did he pay for this apartment? The abortion? Tell me what he paid for. I want to know how little you value yourself."

"Shut up, Lucho! Whatever I did, I did for us and the children."

"That's a lie! You did it for yourself, Ana. Because if you thought of me or the kids, you never would've jeopardized *us.*"

"You're the one who's jeopardized us! You and Valeria with your constant talk about sending the children away. Do you think I was going to let you do that? I did everything I could to keep us together. I've only ever done what was best for us." She paused to rein in the supplication in her voice. She wasn't going to beg him, not for compassion or understanding, not for the marriage. "That's all I've done, and believe me, it hasn't been easy. But you don't see that, do you? All you see is a burden. We're nothing but a burden to you."

She had convinced herself that she was a reminder of the life that wasn't, of the life he had to forego. She was only a future of obligations. The child became the children, and the children erased who he was, who he had intended to be. How fortunate he was that everyone saw all that. To the world, he was a patient, hardworking man who'd sacrificed a respectable job in his country for a string of odd jobs in a place that relegated him to its shadows. No one questioned his dedication to his children; they simply underscored who he was at the very core.

But no one saw *her*. After all, what had she given up? A shack on a dirt road in the terrorized forest. A trabajito, an inconsequential post as a greeter in an office, the most she could ever aspire to have. She had little to lose because she had nothing to begin with. No one, it seemed, saw the effort it took to stitch her fabrics together or weave her meals or how much she'd given of her own body. No one saw the love and dedication that drove it all, not even her husband.

"I didn't manipulate you into this marriage," she said, "or into coming here. We decided to be together, and we both knew we needed to start over, or at least try to make this work. I'm not asking you to understand what I did. Just know that I did it for us."

He stood still against the door frame. His body hung there, as if dangling from a nail. He took a deep breath before he spoke again. "Ana, you only do things for you. No one else matters."

She bolted up. Her steps were succinct, silent, and in an instant she was in front of his hunched body. She searched his face for his eyes. She held up her hands, the calluses yellow and lined, the skin sagging in parts. "Look at my hands," she said to him. "Look at my face. Do you think I do this for me? Look at me!"

He did then, his eyes misted and almost full-mooned. She had not seen him cry since that night at the airport, the night their families had gathered to say goodbye. He held his mother and cried as if it were the last time they'd see each other; years later, when he finally returned to Peru and sat beside her on her couch in Jesús

María, he'd realize that the airport was, in fact, the last time she'd seen him. Dementia would erase Lucho Falcón from his mother's memory.

But as he stood there, pale-faced and on the verge of tears for the first time in years, Ana was struck by one simple truth, something she'd been reluctant to see or accept until that moment. She'd been wrong about him. All these years, she'd done her best to preserve a marriage that she believed was rooted in force and obligation, in a sense of duty to her and her unborn child. She had wanted to prove him wrong; show him that he had, in fact, not made a mistake by marrying her. For this, she had always believed she needed the children. If they were gone, how else would she prove it? How else would she keep the marriage from falling away?

Now, as she looked into his somber eyes, she finally saw what had been there all along. She'd seen it on that very first dinner, when she sat across from him in El Centro; when Victoria and Pedro were placed in his arms for the very first time; when he held her hand as they stepped off that plane at JFK. She'd seen it every afternoon, she realized, when she came home to him and the children, the same sense of longing, that wasn't for a past life he now mourned or the life he wished they had, but for her. He wanted her to need him. Had she been that absent all along?

She stepped back, unable to bear what it all meant. She retreated to the pile of clothes still on the floor, numbed by the realization that if she'd only trusted, if she'd had some faith in him, things might have been so different.

He disappeared from her periphery, and when the front door shut, her body sunk to the floor. After all their years together, she couldn't see what had been in front of her all this time. It wasn't a sense of duty that tied him to her. It wasn't the children. It was love, something she had never allowed herself to deserve.

The wind whistled again through the fractures along the wall. Narrow, threadlike cracks that withheld the cold, but yielded to its gusts. She blew into her hands, cupping her hot breath. They'd need plastic to cover the windows. Thick curtains, too, though she knew that nothing could keep the cold air out entirely, no matter how much she covered up the cracks. It took all this, all these years and distance, for her to understand that he could love her, that he did, and all she had to do was believe it.

19

TWO WEEKS AFTER THEY MOVED IN, ANA HEARD PEDRO'S SMALL, delicate voice whispering the words of her favorite lullaby as she lay beside him one early morning, her eyes still closed. He hummed between the parts of the song he did not know. *Pío, pío,* said the chicks, and sang her son, and the words floated in the dark air, bubbling in hues of blue toward the sibilant tarps that covered the windows. The plastic covers she taped up that first night fluttered as they had every night since they moved in. Their contractions and releases, their whooshes and flaps had soothed Ana, lulling her to sleep on nights she lay in bed staring into the semi-lit chandelier. Outside, the sky was silver, and between her son's hum and the quivering covers, she might have confused the moment for a dream. Except she knew dreams well, and this was not one. As ethereal as his voice was, as still as the moment seemed, she could not stay there. It was not a dream. She had to get up, and the sun, always searching for her, had already started to break up the room.

She indulged in another round of Pedro's humming, then, pretending to still be asleep, she filled it in with the lyrics. He giggled. "Keep singing," she whispered, but as she continued with the words, he only dug his face into the space between her and Lucho's pillows. Her husband, snoring gently, was sleeping on his side beside them. "Did you forget how the song goes?" she teased.

Pedro smiled, and whispered, "No."

"Then sing," she said, poking his belly. He laughed again, and she shushed him when Lucho stirred. Pedro held her face between his cool, sticky palms, and kissed her nose. "I don't like cockroach kisses," she joked. He kept kissing her and they both laughed, loud enough to wake Victoria in the bottom bunk of the bed beside them. When she saw her daughter's grimace, Ana picked Pedro up, and said, "Let's go outside before we wake your father."

And so their day began like the others before it. Since moving into the apartment, they took up a routine not unlike the one they had before they lived with Valeria. For breakfast, they sipped on honey-sweetened black tea and ate bowls of fruity cereal, leaving behind rainbows in their milk. They crunched on bread so toasted that it crumbled if Ana spread too much margarine along its edges.

"Do I have to wear my long johns?" asked Pedro as she slid the pants on. She'd set out their uniforms the night before, stacking the blue shirts and ties, Pedro's slacks and Victoria's jumper on the couch so they could change in the living room in the morning. As the children watched cartoons, she braided Victoria's two ponytails, then combed Pedro's hair sideways. She packed their lunch boxes with ham and cheese sandwiches, oranges, and fruit juice pouches, then packed a plastic bag with the same lunch for herself. They did not say goodbye to the still-sleeping Lucho. Instead, they shuffled out the front door as quietly as they could and set off for the ten-block walk to the school. Then Ana took off on a much longer walk down a deep street, the iron sky now layered in slabs of beryl, as she pounded toward la factoría.

Nothing with her husband, however, was like it once was. After being rootless for all those months, they finally had a place of their own. All along, she believed that was what they needed to rebuild as a family, as husband and wife. But ever since that very first night, it became clear to her that it wasn't enough. She couldn't bring herself to accept that she'd been wrong. He wanted to send the children away, she kept reminding herself. That's why she did what she did. Although now, she started to doubt how much of a threat that truly was to her family.

Still, she kept her distance, and he kept his, not that it was hard to do. They needed to make layaway payments on the new couch and table set they purchased, to buy new black leather shoes for the children's ever-growing feet, and of course, there was the rent and tuition they needed to stay on top of. And so Ana's days pedaling the sewing machine, and his nights behind the wheel, grew longer, with Betty caring for the children until Ana made it home from working overtime. He still gave her the money he earned, sliding cash inside her drawer so she could manage the ins and outs of their finances the way she always had. She was at least grateful to see he earned a little more each week. But they saw less of each other, and when their hours intersected, Lucho made sure one of the children was always with them. He left no room for conversation nor did he invite any. Nothing was asked of her that wasn't about Victoria or Pedro or a utility bill. He only greeted her with a curt "buenos días" and "buenas tardes," never kissing her.

Ana pretended to be indifferent. She didn't ask how his night on the job had gone, or about the article in the newspaper that he found so funny, or about the letter his mother sent that he tucked inside his wallet. She'd hear him climb the stairs as he returned from work, but she stayed in bed, praying for sleep. Their son became a physical barrier between them. Lucho would lie beside Pedro, gently pushing him closer to his mother to make room for himself in their bed. He no longer urged his son to sleep on his own.

On Sundays, the only day neither worked, they attended mass together, even though Ana's statues of San Martín and the Virgin Mary were tucked away in a dresser drawer with her socks and underwear. It was required, however, since Victoria had communion coming up later in the spring, and she had to bring proof that she'd attended mass on Sundays. Church was followed by their rounds at the supermarkets, then the laundromat, the silence between them, which was first grounded in anger and sadness, eventually taking root in the mundane. *Pasará* once again became Ana's refrain, but as the days went by, she understood that this was the new state of her marriage. He'd never understand how difficult it was to make the choices she made, or her reasons for making them in the first place. What room was there now for forgiveness, for trust? She wondered if the marriage itself would simply pass.

And so, in the quiet moments of those days, when her hopes of building a future as a couple faded, her focus shifted. It was no longer about preserving whatever was left of the marriage, but to unburden herself of the debt she still owed others, and to the once-silly dream that she still nurtured in her core.

She caught up on her payments to Mama. She didn't go inside anymore to make her payments. Instead, she waited by Mama's front door, handed over whatever groceries or prescriptions she picked up for her on the way there, then rushed out with the excuse that she needed to get home so Lucho could go to work or because the sitter could only stay for so long. She never saw Don Beto again. With the longer hours at the factory and the housekeeping gigs she picked up on the weekends, Ana anticipated paying off the woman by the summer.

Then, she could get back the deed to Lucho's house. The debt to her husband was the one she wanted to pay back the most. Whatever their relationship was now, they couldn't stay together because of the money or out of a sense of duty. If they were to be together, it had to be a choice. She needed to free herself of any obligation to him or to anyone. She owed herself at least that much. She owed herself the freedom to choose; so did he.

It was during those days too, that she once again filled her address book. Not with grocery lists or nightmares, but of that seemingly unattainable dream of having her own restaurant. On nights she could not sleep, she'd sit at their new table flipping through its worn and blackened pages. She'd go through its repository of imagery, menstrual start dates and grocery lists, and expand on the latter. Basil, spinach, and evaporated milk—ingredients she used to make Tallarín Verde, their first meal in the new apartment. She recalled how there was still dirt on the basil leaves, how the blender sent Pedro scurrying into the bedroom. She dipped saltine crackers in the leftover pesto sauce. She pulled a pen from the pocket of her maroon sweater, and beside the list, she wrote down "Korean market on Union, best basil."

Then came her Causa Rellena. How much ají amarillo she used, what Jerry Rivera song was on the radio as she beat the potatoes, if she'd had enough leftovers for lunch the next day. Soon, she was writing out the stories of meals from months and years past. She noted whatever dish she found soothing (oxtail soup), what had ended up sitting in the fridge too long (tripe), and what she indulged in alone and in secret (arroz con leche with raisins). She wrote down the first meal she made at Lexar Tower—cebiche, because Valeria had once told her it was her favorite—and the first meal she made for Lucho—escabeche, and the praise that followed was almost euphoric. She had no intention of sharing what she wrote, and so she went back further, all the way back to the chicken her mother had taught her to cook over an open flame all those years ago. There they were: the meals she'd make one day in that impeccable restaurant she'd envisioned for so long. Each nourishing ingredient and the songs and celebrations, the pain and the loss, the elements that made them what they were. Forget the saints and the prayer cards, she thought. The little address book would be her amulet, her protector. In it, was her.

But on that gusty early February morning, after she dropped the children off, and as she tried to pay a street cart vendor for a cup of coffee, Ana noticed that her address book was missing. She shuffled through the empty lip gloss bottles, receipts, and loose coins, but it wasn't in her handbag. A flicker in her chest made her catch her breath. Her recipes and musings weren't soul-baring, but her words were intimate. The thought of someone else's eyes over them, their fingers sifting through the pages, their hands on the black vinyl cover, was unsettling. She convinced herself it was home, and that if Lucho found it, he wouldn't read it; he was too proud to snoop. A part of her wanted him to read it. Maybe then, at least, he could see her.

As she approached la factoría, Betty, Carla, and a cluster of women from the fourth floor stood outside the door. Ana greeted them, but only Betty, shaking off the cold with a cigarette in her mouth, acknowledged her with a nod. The others clung to the words of another seamstress, the chisme simply too good to ignore. Ana squeezed into the crowd and heard her say, "Se salió con la suya."

"Who?" asked Ana. "Who got her way with what?"

"Pero que chismosa eres, Anita," the woman snickered, and the group giggled. "Your friend Nilda. I ran into her neighbor yesterday after church. She calls her to check in on the kid. Apparently,

Nilda spent a couple of weeks in Guayaquil with her mother, but was in Costa Rica just over a week ago, and now—" the woman made a sweeping gesture with her hand, "she's already in Texas."

"Texas?" said Ana, astonished.

"Texas," someone else repeated. "The woman practically flew across the border."

A mixture of shock and glee made its ways to Ana's mouth.

"Don't be too happy for her," said Carla. "I doubt very much that her husband will ever let her see that boy."

"Who cares what he wants," said Ana. "I'm sure her son wants to see her and that's what matters."

The bell rang. The women stomped out their cigarettes and tossed their coffee cups, hustling to the elevator bank. Ana climbed the four flights of stairs, as she did every morning, Betty following close behind. When she arrived on the sewing floor, the heaviness of the weekend had settled in with no rush to leave. The floor was mostly empty and stagnant. The fans, whirring in their corners, struggled to move the air through the room. Rolls of fabric, set against each other on the wall, succumbed to the heat of the sallow overhead lights. She could not recall when she last saw the large, elongated floor. Really saw it: how cramped the stations were, how the aisles had narrowed over the years, the room's palpable thirst for air and sunlight.

Ana settled into her station. The elevator doors opened, and the women poured into the room. "Thank God it's warm in here," said Carla as she sat down beside her and threw on her blue smock.

Soon, Ana forgot about her address book as the women shared stories about their weekend, hyped up the new Brazilian telenovela on Telemundo, and eventually returned to the topic of Nilda. Imagine Nilda, in her sparkly hoop earrings and lacy black top, crawling her way across the desert under that scalding Mexican sun. Nilda, back in New York, kissing her son and grinning that glossy grin of hers, right in her husband's face. The audacity of it all.

It was during their lunch break, as the women pulled out their plastic food containers in the cafeteria, that Ana asked no one in particular, "Do you really think Nilda's coming back?"

"Of course!" said one seamstress, "si es una descarada."

"She's ballsy, yes," agreed another, "but she's also a mother. She was going to come back for her son. You can't keep a mother from her child!"

"I doubt George would take her back here," said a third.

"No, she's definitely not coming back here," said Carla. "She's a troublemaker, and we all know how George feels about trouble-makers."

As the women debated, Betty gestured toward the flattened sandwich in Ana's hand. "What are you eating?"

"A ham and cheese sandwich," she replied, suddenly aware of the rectangular, white container Betty had in her hand, stuffed with white rice and beef stew.

"Why are you not eating, Ana?"

"I am," she said. "I'm just trying to save money."

Betty took the lid from her container and put some of her own food on top of it. "Take some," she said as she slid it over to her. "You look thin. You need your rice and your meat. And I know it's cold out, but you probably should've put that sandwich in the fridge."

■ ■ ■

AN HOUR LATER, ANA HURRIED TO THE BATHROOM WITH HER STOMACH cramping, cursing Betty under her breath. She checked the stalls to make sure she was alone, then went to the one at the far end. When she was finished, she splashed water on her face, and patted her skin dry with the brown paper towels she sometimes tucked inside her saddlebag and took home. She leaned onto the sink, her reflection dotted with the fingerprints that stained the cracked mirror.

She wanted him to find her address book. Maybe then he'd understand. The making and remaking of every meal; no dish was ever the same. A different seasoning, a new place to buy an ingredient, her own changing tastes. That is what kept her going: her ability to change, to evolve. To try again. That was the point of it all. She could keep trying, no matter her mistakes or the mistakes of others. There was always room for change. She could always start over.

Could they?

She loved him, with all his sullenness, his inability to make the hard choices, his nostalgic tendencies, his pride. She loved him. She accepted him for who he was, and all it implied. But she'd had enough of the silence between them. She'd wronged him, but he'd wronged her too. Could he accept her mistakes, forgive them? Could she do the same for him?

She went back to her station, determined to end the silence between them. She had to know where they stood, where they'd go from here.

Later, when she was asked about that February day, she'd recall how loudly her machine rattled beneath her fingers, how the breath of the ceiling fan, normally a whisper, seemed to bellow. She never heard the stomping that some say they remember hearing, nor the howls from the workers on the floor below. She only heard a single high-pitched scream from somewhere far, far back and then she saw the waves of black that swept the other side of the achromatic landscape.

She heard the word once, but it did not register. Then she heard it again and again, "inmigración, inmigración," falling on her, rolling between her feet, making her dart and stumble through a maze of blue. She pushed past some women who were crying, others frozen in panic and confusion. She ran to the gray door, the very door she had cleared when Nilda got caught weeks earlier. She slipped between one island and the next and the next. She glanced back, searching for Betty, but all Ana saw were white letters on black coats leaking into the room like ink. She was at the gray door when someone yelled, "Para," but she didn't stop. She shoved through the human clog squeezing through the door frame. She heard a shout from below. She had no choice but to run toward it.

Madre mía, she prayed, *déjame salir de aquí.*

She ran.

No pares.

Others ran with her. Faceless, pungent. The air tasted like salt.

No pares.

She collided against faceless, unknown bodies. She sought her own breath, and heard the familiar sound of her heart, this time, pounding against her ear. Her tongue stuck to her palate. Another wail echoed through the staircase. She scampered down each step as if it were on fire, but everywhere she turned was someone else in blue, another face she knew but couldn't recognize.

She hoped Carla could make it out. Carla with her green card. If she could get out, she'd tell Lucho before he'd come looking for her, before anyone could catch him. Before they could snatch the kids.

The kids. She could feel Pedro's morning kisses still fresh on her face, and Victoria's hair sliding through her fingers as she wove her braids. She could even smell Lucho, his constant, ever-present scent, the one that lingered on the pillow beside her own. She could hear Pedro's words, whenever the three held each other and she stayed back to watch, always afraid they'd disappear, that they weren't real. "Ven, Mami, ven." Why had she never gone to them?

If she were caught, what would they do? What would Lucho say to the children? Where would he say their mother had gone?

The staircase seemed to grow narrower, and as she sought to find her breath, she stopped herself from succumbing to the pressure of the bodies that tightened around her. She couldn't think of her family this way. She wasn't going to reduce them to memories. They wouldn't become her father; neither would she.

She charged through the crowd that blocked her from them, intent on crashing through any barricade of black that stood before her. No matter what she hit, she'd push through. She heard a voice call out again from behind, telling her to stop. But she could see daylight reaching in from the door only one flight below. All she had to do was get beyond it, make her way to the river. If she could make it there, she told herself, she could find a way home, and if she couldn't, she'd make it back somehow. After all, Nilda had made it back.

Voló, the women had said. She got back so fast, she practically flew across that border.

She clung to this even as a hand gripped her arm from behind and she stumbled to the ground. Wherever they took her, wherever she might end up, she'd find her way back. Back to Victoria and Pedro. Back to Lucho. She'd run across the dirt, swim against the river if she needed to. Fly above whatever she couldn't force her way through. There was her mother's voice. "You'll have to do things for love," she had said, all those years ago. It was the only way she'd ever learn to fly. No matter where they were or where she was, she'd make it back to them. She had to trust, finally. Trust that she could make it back to her flock. Back to los Falcón.

Acknowledgments

This book would not have been possible without the love and support of so many beautiful souls. A huge thank you to:

My agent, Julia Kardon, for your incredible insight, tenacity, and belief in my work.

My editor, Megan Lynch, who helped make this novel that much better, and the entire team at Ecco.

Lisa Ko and Sunita Dhurandhar, for all the writing dates and cassava cakes over the years. You taught me what it is to be a writer.

Ruchika Tomar, for holding my hand throughout the revision and publishing process. I'm so fortunate to have you as a friend.

Natalia Sylvester, Jenn Baker, Melissa Scholes Young, Stephanie Jimenez, and Kali Fajardo-Anstine, for all the advice and support.

Luis Alberto Urrea, Cristina Garcia, and M. Evelina Galang, for challenging me to go deeper with my work.

The Center for Fiction and my fellow Fellows, especially Nicola DeRobertis-Theye, Anu Jindal, Samantha Storey, t'ai freedom ford, Lisa Chen, and Sara Batkie.

Stacie Evans, Serena Lin, Christine H. Lee, Glendaliz Camacho, H'Rina DeTroy, Dennis Norris II, Vanessa Mártir, Grace Jahng Lee, and the entire VONA NYC community.

My daily sources of truth, strength, and inspiration: Ivonne Chaupis Phillips, Marilyn Ladewig, Lucia Travaglino, Regina Hardatt, Estefanía Vaz Ferreira, Lorena Llivichuzca, Stacy Almeyda, Jessica Baker, Irina Akulenko, Dalia Carella, Pooja Agarwal, Mary Anne Mendenhall, Emily Roberts, Megan Mann, and Bryn Haffey.

My support squad at the day job: Nitasha Mehta, Julia Blanter, Tijana Jovanovic, Ankit Patel, Betsy Brenner, Edward Fong, Marilyn Chew, Jessica Rotundi, Aaron Singer, Leah Aviram, and Jonathan J. Nasca.

The coffee shops that never kicked me out, especially Sweet Leaf Coffee Roasters in Greenpoint and Mountain Province in Williamsburg.

My family, especially those who helped inform the work: Johanna Moccetti, Judy Rocha, Ayda Luz Vasquez, Gladys Vasquez, Jimena Caballero, and my abuelita, Clotilde Isla.

My mother-in-law, Ewa Potocka, for your indomitable spirit and light.

My brothers, John J. Rivero and Sixto Elias Rivero, and my sisters-in-law, Teresa and Laura, for always cheering me on.

My incredible mother, Zadith Rivero, who taught me to never be afraid of hard work and to always love life. Es un orgullo ser tu hija.

My children, Sebastian and Gabriel, who teach and motivate me every day to be the best version of me that I can possibly be.

My husband, Bartosz Potocki, who always believed in me and understood why I had to write in the first place. Thank you for giving me the space and time I needed and for loving me just as I am.

My father, Juan G. Rivero, who was overcome with pride and emotion after reading the first poem I wrote when I was five years old. I hope that wherever you are, I'm still making you proud.